PLANTATION MURDERS

DR HAMISH HART MYSTERIES
BOOK TWO

KAREN THURECHT

Printed in Australia

First Printing: March 2022

Shawline Publishing Group Pty Ltd

www.shawlinepublishing.com.au

Paperback ISBN – 9781922594693

Ebook ISBN – 9781922701091

A catalogue record for this book is available from the National Library of Australia

PLANTATION MURDERS

DR HAMISH HART MYSTERIES
BOOK TWO

KAREN THURECHT

To my children Clinton, Tristan, Shannon, Minelle, and Ethan in gratitude for the way in which they have embraced my crazy.

ACKNOWLEDGMENTS

I would like to acknowledge the many Queensland citizens of South-Sea Island descent who have contributed to building the strong, diverse economy of our home.

CONTENTS

CHAPTER ONE

Morning Bulletin, Rockhampton. Queensland Tuesday 15 January 1884.

Can anyone who claims to belong to the civilisation of the nineteenth century defend this iniquitous kanaka traffic, in the prosecution of which the greatest atrocities are known to exist? Is it not known that of the Kanakas brought to Queensland, the greatest numbers are kidnapped or obtained by fraud or violence? In the face of these atrocities that have been made public from time to time, how is it possible Mr Griffith can uphold and propose to legislate for the continuance of kanaka labour on sugar plantations? Mr Griffith had it in his power to stop the iniquitous traffic without injury to the thriving industry it was meant to foster. Means had been provided ready to his hand by which he might have supplanted the kanaka and so rid the government and the country of the crime of conniving murder, kidnapping, fraud and slavery.

KAELO

Kaelo sniffed the salt air. Land was near; he could smell it as surely as if he could see the bump on the horizon. As he expected, an island began to take shape. It was purple in the early morning light, then blue as they drew closer, then green. The Pacific Ocean spread before him from the deck of the *Helena*, Ferguson Island, a bruise in the emerald sea.

He wondered how the Islanders would respond to the intrusion. They must have seen the great masts by now. The Captain was tacking first one way and then the other to catch the wind at the right angle. The *Helena* wouldn't sail too close to shore; there was a reef ahead. Kaelo took one more deep breath, both sorry and powerless. Then he noticed two tiny canoes closing the distance between the island and the schooner.

'Lower the boats,' cried the Captain. Two boats dropped to the sea, and six men scrambled down, three settling in each boat. Kaelo turned his eye back to the canoes. They were close enough to see one had eight Islanders aboard and the other six. The Islanders would be bringing fruit to trade for tobacco.

He knew this was how the negotiations for labour started. The government agents used sign language to lure the men aboard, offering guns, ammunition, tomahawks and tobacco as incitement. They made them agree to visit the white man's country for more of these things. They would hold up three fingers to indicate the duration of the journey. Home in three days, with guns and ammunition, the Islanders would think. But the Europeans mean three years of hard labour. Who would agree to that?

Kaelo was on the schooner because his father had been to Queensland before him. His father worked on the cotton plantations, learned some of the language and returned home with cash money. Educated by missionaries, Kaelo spoke more English than most. He expected it would be easy for him to work with these white men. Besides, he had his own reasons for joining the voyage to Queensland. At least he knew he was going for three years, and he knew about hard work.

At each Island they visited, he felt for the men coerced onto the ship. He felt their shock and fear when they realized they were trapped. Yet, there was nothing he could do. The Europeans would shoot him if he tried to stop them, or he tried to warn the Islanders before it was too late. Later, when he told them in their own language what was happening, he would listen to their cries.

Kaelo saw the two boats from the *Helena* closing the space between themselves and the canoes. He couldn't fathom why, but suddenly the canoes stopped and turned. The Islanders began to paddle furiously back toward the shore. Had they sensed danger? What had triggered their change of heart? Kaelo willed them on. The Government Agent, Dixon, called out an order, and one of the boats switched direction. It chased after the canoe carrying the six men. Dixon's own crew continued after the canoe with eight.

They were both gaining sea on their targets. Dixon called out to the Islanders to stop and wait. The Islanders quickened their pace. Without warning, Dixon stood up and aimed his rifle at the steersman of the closest canoe. A shot discharged, and the steersman lurched to one side and fell backward into the vessel. He had taken the shot in the neck. The remaining men leapt over the side into the sea.

As the men reached their quarry, Dixon hurled his axe into the hollow of the canoe. It pierced the hull and fell to one side, the bulk splitting in two, no longer a vessel but a pair of hollowed-out logs bobbing on the waves. The Europeans gathered four men from the sea and dragged them into the boat, where they kept them still at the end of a blade.

The other canoe had changed course and was heading for shallow water over the reef. The three Europeans in the second boat caught up with it before it reached the shallows. The Islanders dived into the water. As they resurfaced, the Europeans scooped three of them into the boat. The rest swam frantically for the shore.

'What is this?' Kaelo couldn't believe his eyes. A small child had been in the second canoe. The European men plucked him from the water and dropped him into the boat like a sack of yams. Both boats abandoned their pursuit of the remaining Islanders and headed back toward the schooner.

Kaelo could feel his pulse racing as the Islanders were herded up the ropes at knife point. They fell onto the deck, exhausted and terrified. One of the crew handed the boy to Kaelo while at the same time, they forced the Islanders into a hatch and locked them below to prevent escape. Once the Islanders were secure, Dixon grabbed the boy from Kaelo's arms. He had tied two coconuts to a rope which he placed under the boy's arms and lowered him onto the water. He floated there, bobbing up and down, kept afloat by the coconuts, as the cry went out to sail on.

Panic gripped Kaelo. He looked toward the boy and back to the men on deck. As if he had read his mind, one of the crew raised his rifle and pointed it at Kaelo's head. Kaelo didn't flinch. A vision swept through his mind of himself diving overboard to save the child. But he didn't follow the vision. He remained still as the *Helena* inched away from the tiny person bobbing on the waves. Even when he saw the ropes slip away from beneath the boy's arms, he didn't flinch. When he saw the little figure disappear beneath the waves, he took a deep breath of salty air. Another thing God would have to forgive.

Kaelo spent the rest of the voyage in the hold accompanied by the sixty-seven South Sea Islanders gathered on the schooner. Each of them had a piece of calico tied around their necks with a number registered in the ship's log. Kaelo didn't return to the deck to smell the air again, even though he was one of the few allowed to do so. His proficiency in the English language made him useful to the crew, and his understanding of the ways of the British earned their trust, to an extent. Nonetheless, he stayed close to the cries of shock and grief with the men below.

Twenty-four hours from their first port in Mackay, the Government Agent came below to speak with them.

'The Government Master will ask you if you want to work sugar,' he said, making a cutting motion in the air. 'Three yams. You tell him, yes, sir. He will tell you press finger in ink and touch paper. This is contract.'

Kaelo knew the men understood they were agreeing to something, but they had no idea what. It didn't matter. With European guns pointed at them the whole time, they would do as they were told.

Kaelo wondered where the white men got the notion that 'yams' signified 'years' in the Islander languages. It was not true. It never had been.

Some of the South Sea Islanders disembarked at Mackay. The remainder, Kaelo among them, stayed aboard until Brisbane. On arrival, they were herded into a fenced pen while white men called out from the fences. Some of the men were complaining the Islanders were too short or too thin. What did they expect after weeks at sea with only soup made from dried beef to sustain them?

Kaelo Rees stood firm, his eyes fixed on the spot he expected his new employer to appear. He'd been twenty-four hours on Australian soil, and the promise of money would soon be realised. The money would be good to have, but he had another reason for coming so far. After long weeks at sea, he could finally unburden himself of the promise he made to his father.

William Daniels had recruited him on arrival, with six others, to work on his sugar plantation at Cloverton, about twenty miles south of Brisbane. The labourers were to meet outside the Empire Hotel in Albert Street, ready to catch the Cobb & Co coach at eleven. As none of the Islanders knew how to read time, in the European sense, Kaelo expected they would gather in the morning and wait. Looking around, he saw only two of the men from the ship were with him. Where were the other four?

'I'll look for the others,' he said to the man standing next to him. The man's eyes flashed in acknowledgement. Though he didn't speak English as well as Kaelo, Kaelo knew he understood his meaning. He strode across the road, kicking up dirt with his bare feet, annoyed his countrymen had not turned up at the agreed spot. When he entered the Hotel at the corner, he blinked, taking a few moments to adjust to the low light. Scanning the room, he recognised a man sitting near the window. He was looking out onto the street, but Kaelo could see his face well enough to know he was the plantation manager, the man Daniels had introduced to him the day before. Four of the Islanders recruited with him were huddled in a corner at the end of the bar. Before he could make a move to join them, one of the men emerged from the huddle and slammed his ample fist on the bar.

'Gin,' he said. 'All of us,' he added, gesturing across to his mates.

The bartender watched him calmly. 'No gin for you lot today,' he said.

'Why not?'

'Not today,' the bartender repeated.

The Islander turned to his countrymen. 'Nothing for blackfellas,' he said.

'You fella give us drink,' he demanded of the barman.

Kaelo walked up to the Islander and took his arm. 'Come on now, we got work.' Kaelo held the man's eyes with his own steady gaze.

Kaelo couldn't tell if he was going to give up the fight and go with him or not.

Within an instant, Kaelo noticed a change in the bartender. He turned his head just in time to see Jock McDonald, the plantation manager from Cloverton, come up behind them.

'The law says no grog for you black bastards,' hissed McDonald, then he spat on the floor just missing the Islander's feet.

The group of South Sea Islanders at the end of the bar bristled. They were staring, fists clenched by their sides and muscles tensed.

'No worries, boss,' said Kaelo. 'Come on now. We wait outside.' He tugged at the Islander's arm. For a moment, he looked as though he was going to retreat with Kaelo, but he turned back.

'Fuckin' white cunt,' he shouted into the plantation manager's face. The manager lifted his fist and thrust it at the Islander's jaw. In the same instant, Kaelo raised his own fist and connected with the man's gut, sending his thrust wildly off course and dropping him to the floor. The other Islanders moved in, ready to take on any man who would further challenge them. The bartender jumped across the bar and leant over the fallen man. Everyone remained still for several seconds, trying to take in what had happened.

'What the devil is going on?' a voice roared from the doorway. Kaelo recognised William Daniels immediately.

'This man is dead,' cried the barman.

'What?' said Daniels, pushing his way through the South Sea Islanders so he could see the man on the floor.

'Good God!' cried Daniels. It's Jocko. Jocko McDonald. My plantation manager.'

The barman was removing a bar stool that had fallen across the man's body.

'Get the Police,' shouted Daniels, and the bartender rushed out into the street. Meanwhile, two men passing by had come into the Hotel to find out what the shouting was about.

'Hold him,' called Daniels.

They grabbed Kaelo and held tight; though it wasn't necessary, he wasn't struggling. The remaining Islanders, realising their predicament, scattered into the street.

A few minutes later, the police constable and the sergeant entered the bar.

'The black here killed 'im,' said the bartender. 'I saw it.'

Sergeant Bellamy walked across the room to inspect the body curled into a foetal position on the floor.

He took his time studying how the body lay from several different angles, then he checked the dead man's pockets. There was a leather pouch with a few coins he slipped into his own coat pocket and little else.

'It's my plantation manager,' said Daniels. 'Jocko McDonald.'

Sergeant Bellamy acknowledged Daniels for the first time.

'Did you see what happened?' asked Bellamy.

'I saw it,' said the bartender. The bastard killed 'im.'

'Not you,' said Bellamy without looking at the bartender. 'Did you see what happened?' he repeated to Daniels.

'No,' he said. 'I came in after he was on the floor.'

Bellamy turned to the bartender.

'What did you see then?' he said.

'I seen him bloody kill the man, the black cunt.'

'How did he kill him?'

'He punched him, hard, in the stomach. Then he fell down dead.'

'That's it?' asked Bellamy. 'He punched him once, and the man is dead?'

'That's all it takes from these big mongrels,' said the bartender.

Listening with his head on his chest, the enormity of what was happening was dawning on Kaelo. The men were pulling him one way and another, digging their fingers deep into his skin. But he made no attempt to move. The dead man lay at his feet. If he had killed the man, he would not try to avoid the consequences. He had never killed anyone before. It was a terrible thing, and God would punish him. Anything these men could do to him would be nothing compared to the punishment of his God.

'Is this true?' the sergeant asked him. 'Did you kill this man with a single punch?'

'I hit him,' said Kaelo. 'I hit him once.'

'Well then,' Bellamy turned to the constable. 'I suggest you put this fellow in handcuffs. We'll transport him to Petrie Terrace directly.' Looking at the two men holding Kaelo, he said, 'Would you two oblige me by carrying the body onto the cart outside. We'll take him to the hospital morgue.'

'The hospital?' cried the bartender. 'What the devil can they do for 'im at the hospital – he's dead, ain't he?'

'I have questions,' said Bellamy. 'I want to know how he died instantly from a single punch to the stomach. Were there any others who observed the event?'

'No,' said Daniels. 'There were a few Kanakas in here when I came in, but they scarpered before you arrived.'

The body was carried outside, the furniture was restored to its proper place, and the hotel began to look as though nothing had happened that morning. Except Kaelo was handcuffed to an iron rail stretching the length of the bar waiting for police transport.

Sergeant Bellamy stopped in the doorway.

'Why did he hit him?' he called out to the barman.

'Coz he's a black, ain't he?' he said.

CHAPTER TWO

The Brisbane Courier Queensland Tuesday 12 February 1884.

I was in town lately engaging men, South Sea Islanders for my plantation, and arranged for them to be ready to travel by Cobb's Coach next morning. Well, they were ready, and I had occasion to leave them for a few minutes to arrange for tickets, and when I returned, two only out of a dozen were to be seen. On inquiry, I found them in a hotel in Albert Street – getting served with grog!

HAMISH

Dr Hamish Hart and his friend Rita Cartwright were enjoying a pleasant morning in Hamish's new home in Wickham Terrace. The recently built terrace house was handsome with two floors and a pleasant view from the upper story across the hill where the old windmill stood and further to the mountains beyond. Hamish settled on the idea of general practice after returning from an exhausting visit to Stradbroke Island, where he and Rita survived two attempts on their lives to uncover a pattern of corruption and murder at the Benevolent Asylum. The adventure on the Island left him convinced it was a simple life he craved. He looked forward to establishing a regular clientele of middle-aged women who would bring their children to see him. He further expected they would bully their husbands into consulting him at least once a year. He purchased the property on the terrace with such a life in mind. He set up the downstairs area for his consulting rooms, equipped two rooms at the front of the house to provide the best of contemporary medical care and renovated a kitchen behind the rooms to the highest standards of cleanliness and efficiency. His own lodgings, a sitting room and a bedroom were upstairs.

Hamish convinced the asylum cook to accompany him to Brisbane to look after the day to day running of his household. Not that there was much to do, there was only Hamish and Wallace in the house. But Hamish enjoyed having the older man around. Hamish had no talent for ordinary tasks such as a household requires, and he hoped to be busy in his practice. Above all, he depended upon Wallace for intelligent conversation over a shot of whiskey in the evenings. Despite having been a ship's cook most of his working life, Wallace was remarkably well-read and certainly well-travelled. Wallace followed Hamish to Brisbane with Red, an equally intelligent wiry terrier, named for his political preference, which Wallace insisted leaned to the left.

'I like the duck egg blue,' said Rita as she sipped tea and glanced around at the walls. Hamish followed her gaze.

'It's calming,' she added. 'You must be pleased with yourself.'

Hamish smiled. 'How goes the work at Lady Bowen?' he said.

'The dispensary is busy, as always.' Rita placed her cup on its saucer. 'It's the house in Milton that worries me.'

'How so?' Hamish set his own cup down.

'The women are fearful. It's understandable, of course. But a couple of them are venturing out to the hotels at night and leaving the others responsible for their children. It's creating conflict. They know I don't approve of alcohol in the house, and none of them has flouted that rule, as far as I am aware.'

'Don't you have a caretaker at the house to look out for the women and children?'

'Yes, but she's not a policeman. The women are free to come and go as they please.'

'From what you have told me, these women have been through terrible torment from their husbands. I imagine they're seeking companionship, validation of some sort.'

'They place themselves and their children in danger when they frequent the taverns,' said Rita sternly. 'More worryingly, they place the other women in the house in danger. If they are followed home... if word went around town... The husbands of some of these women are ruthless, Hamish. I fear they would murder the women and children in their sleep if they knew where to find them.'

Hamish peered through his long fringe. It flopped over his face when he was at ease. It covered a scar he acquired as a child. He hadn't been comfortable when Rita purchased the house in Milton and set it up as a sanctuary for women abused by their husbands. He admired her compassion and her drive to act on her feelings in a practical way. But he feared the enterprise would prove more complex than she imagined. In his experience, people with tormented lives were often difficult to help, at least until they were ready for help. But Rita was a determined woman.

'It is your safety that concerns me,' said Hamish. Rita was glaring at him with one eyebrow raised when the doorbell rang.

They heard Wallace speak, followed by the voice of a stranger. A tangled red terrier burst onto the landing at the top of the staircase, trembling with excitement from nose to tail. Behind him came Wallace and a man in uniform.

'Constable Pennyweather,' said Wallace.

Hamish studied the newcomer. He was as tall and thin as Wallace was stocky, as young as Wallace was old. The constable's helmet had a large badge with a seven attached to the front of it. It seemed too big for his head. He removed the helmet, passing it from one hand to the other, not sure what to do with it.

Hamish realised he was being impolite and rose to his feet.

'How do you do?' he said, reaching out to shake the young constable's hand. 'Please take a seat.' Hamish gestured to a comfortable chair upholstered in royal blue velvet. He and Rita sat on the settee opposite.

Wallace turned to leave them, but the terrier perched himself on the settee beside Rita, showing no inclination to leave before finding out what the stranger wanted.

'Wallace, stay and hear what the constable has to say,' said Hamish.

Wallace stood by the fireplace where a philodendron grew happily, as a fire was barely needed in this sub-tropical climate.

'Tea?' offered Rita.

The constable sat on the edge of the seat. 'No. Thank-you. No.'

Rita smiled while stroking the scruffy head of the dog snuggled into her skirt. The young man seemed to relax a little, while Hamish thought how easily Rita relaxed people with her smile.

'What can we do for you, Constable Pennyweather?' he said.

'Sergeant Bellamy sent me to request your assistance, sir.'

Hamish straightened up. 'Really?' he said. 'How so?'

'There has been a death, sir. A man was killed at the Empire Hotel this morning. The sergeant would like you to examine the body.'

'Oh dear,' sighed Rita. The dog licked her hand.

Hamish and Rita exchanged puzzled glances.

'I am always at the disposal of the constabulary,' said Hamish, 'But I have no training in necropsy. Perhaps there is someone more qualified the sergeant could call on?'

'There is no one, sir. In any case, the sergeant has asked me to fetch you.'

Hamish looked at Rita again, then he glanced up at Wallace. The older man nodded, almost imperceptibly, but the nod buoyed the doctor's confidence.

Hamish sensed a knot in his stomach that suggested his peaceful existence was about to be upended.

'Well then,' he said. 'If Sergeant Bellamy has directed you to fetch me, I must comply. I won't cause you to fail in your duty.' Hamish followed the constable downstairs, grabbed his coat from the rack by the door and accompanied him outside, where a cab was waiting to transport them to the Petrie Terrace Police Depot.

Constable Pennyweather and Hamish found Sergeant Bellamy at his desk completing his report on the morning's events. He reached out to shake Hamish's hand as soon as they entered. Hamish thought the sergeant looked tired. He seemed to have aged since he saw him last. What had it been? Only six weeks since the trial of that villain Jim Grimes.

'Thank you for coming, Dr Hart,' he said. Then he turned to the constable. 'Thank you Pennyweather, you can get on with your paperwork before your shift ends.'

Hamish settled himself into the seat opposite Bellamy, where a large oak desk covered in loose paper separated them. An ink well held most of the paper in place, but there were some loose leaves that looked like they might spill off the sides. Hamish wanted to stack the papers into neat piles. Bellamy was of average height, but he seemed smaller behind his desk. His suit mirrored the disorder in front of him.

'I sent for you Hart because I hoped you might assist me with a case,' said the sergeant.

'I am willing to help,' began Hamish, 'but I assure you I have no qualifications in this field.'

'I'm aware of that. Nonetheless, you were valuable in unravelling the mysteries of the Dunwich Asylum recently. I would appreciate your professional opinion on this case.'

'I will do what I can, Sergeant.'

'Understood, Doctor. The thing is, this case has an element of social justice to it – something I believe is of great importance to you.'

'Indeed,' said Hamish leaning forward with more interest.

'Let me summarise the facts for you. This morning constable Pennyweather and I attended an incident at the Empire Hotel in Albert Street.'

'I know the place,' said Hamish.

'There was a scuffle when the barman refused to serve a group of Kanakas. Are you aware of the Kanakas?' asked Bellamy.

'Yes. The coloured labour brought from the South Sea Islands to work in agriculture.'

'That's right. I'm not clear on how the fight started, but what I do know is one of the Kanakas punched a man in the stomach, and he collapsed, dead. The deceased was the manager from the Cloverton Plantation. He and the owner recruited the workers the day before.'

'He hit him in the stomach, once only?' repeated Hamish.

'Yes.'

'And that killed him instantly?'

'Evidently so.'

'He must have hit him hard.'

'Indeed.'

They both stared at the papers piled on the desk for a few seconds.

'What would you have me do?' asked Hamish at last.

'I would like you to examine the body and provide me with a professional opinion as to the direct cause of death. You see, the Islander is going to be hanged for murder as the case stands, and it doesn't sit right with me. I'm sure there must be more to it. The public will be calling for a charge of murder as soon as word gets out. There's already ill-feeling towards the coloured labour. But there's something in the man's manner that doesn't say killer to me. The fellow's mates all scarpered when the police came. But the accused remained calm, stated he hit the man once, and now awaits the consequences of his actions without a word. There's no doubt he hit him, but is it murder? At the very least, the charge should be reduced to manslaughter. But there needs to be provocation, and the barman insists there was none. The only other witnesses are the South Sea Islanders who ran. I have men out looking for them now. They are the devil to find when they don't want to be found, so I hold little hope. Then there's Daniels to consider. He wasn't present at the time the incident happened, so he's no use as a witness. He's fuming about the loss of his manager, though, and perhaps more so about the loss of his new workforce. He claims he won't be able to make his harvest this year. I think that's overstating the case, but still....'

'A blow to the stomach wouldn't normally kill a man,' said Hamish ignoring all the superfluous detail. 'Was the man unwell before he arrived at the Hotel?'

'I don't know, but I can include the question in my interviews. I need to conduct a more in-depth interview with the barman as soon as possible.'

'What about others who travelled with him? When did the deceased and Daniels travel up from Cloverton?'

'Stayed in Brisbane overnight, I believe. Business to attend. They were planning to transport the coloured labour to Cloverton by coach today. I say, Hart, could you join me for the interview with Daniels and the bartender? You will know what to expect from them in relation to the man's condition.'

Hamish hesitated. He had agreed to examine the body, but he wasn't sure he wanted to be further embroiled in this investigation. How much assistance could he be during the interviews? There was his practice to consider as well. He needed to focus his energy on building a steady flow of returning patients. He already had several regular appointments to keep.

'The station will pay for your time and expertise,' said Bellamy.

'The money's not the point,' said Hamish. But he had to admit to himself, the story piqued his curiosity. He wanted to know what had killed the man in his prime, and he wanted to see justice done for the Islander.

'Very well,' he said. 'Let me examine the body first, and we'll see what that brings.'

'Thank you, Doctor. I am in your debt,' said Bellamy standing.

'Pennyweather!' he shouted.

The nervous constable appeared at the door.

'Arrange transport for Dr Hart to the hospital,' said Bellamy. 'The body is in the morgue,' he told Hamish, 'I have sent word to the hospital you will be examining the body this afternoon.'

Hamish sat upright. 'You must have been confident I would agree.'

'You were always going to agree,' the sergeant's eyes remained steady, but there was a small smirk at his lips. 'Another murder investigation? You were never going to miss that.'

Hamish sat in the cab as it rattled along the terrace to the hospital. He was surprised the sergeant found him so predictable. He would not have considered himself eager to take on a new disruption to his life so soon. He considered himself content in the mundaneness of his existence. Still, it would have been easy for the sergeant to conclude the death a murder and see the South Sea Islander charged for it. No one would have disputed the conclusion. Hamish thought he liked the sergeant very much. Perhaps he was more like himself than he felt comfortable admitting.

As the cab pulled up in front of the hospital in O'Connell Terrace, Hamish stared out at the modest, single-story building. There was nothing about it to reflect his growing sense of anticipation. He knew when he walked through the timber pedimented entrance into the open hall, he would be setting off on another adventure. Hamish thanked the driver and stepped away from the cab. He hesitated for a moment and called back.

'Driver,' he said, 'please go to my residence and collect Miss Rita Cartwright. Bring her here as quickly as you can.'

The driver tipped his cap and signalled to the horses.

CHAPTER THREE

Darling Downs Gazette Queensland Saturday 7 November 1885.

It has long been acknowledged by the best authorities that arsenic-eating is extensively practised in some parts of Europe. When arsenic eating was first brought before the notice of the world, it was treated as a great imposture would be, and the stories about it were classed with those of Welsh fasting girls and universal remedies. Indeed the profession confidently asserted that these people took of nothing more unwholesome than a piece of chalk because it was deemed impossible that a man could, unscathed, consume enough poison to affect a dozen people, and certainly enough to kill three. Fact, however, is stranger than fiction, and a fact so strange as this could not be unnoticed in the region of myths. It must not, however, be supposed that anyone takes to arsenic eating openly. On the contrary, it is generally begun in secret. A very small dose is at first taken once a week – bread and butter is the favourite medium – then twice a week and so on, until when the individual arrives at a daily dose, the dose is itself increased till as much may be taken as in ordinary circumstances would kill two or three individuals. When they first begin with their very small doses, they are seized with nausea and burning pains in the mouth, throat and stomach. But one peculiarity of arsenic eating is this, that when a man has begun to indulge in it, he must continue to indulge; for if he ceases the arsenic in his system poisons him; or as it can be said, the last dose kills him. It is impossible to stop the habit, for cessation causes death.

Hamish was less overwhelmed by the task now he knew Rita would be joining him. He believed Rita to be a more skilled doctor than he would ever be. She studied at the London School of Medicine for Women, where she graduated with Honours. She accepted the position as pharmacist at the Lady Bowen Lying-In Hospital only because, as a woman, she could not register to practice as a medical doctor in the colony.

Hamish had worked with Rita since arriving in Brisbane as a newly graduated medical officer, unsure of himself and far too eager. Rita protected him from the senior consultants. He had a habit of contradicting them if he thought they were wrong, and he often thought they were wrong. This made him unpopular among his colleagues, most of whom were turning themselves inside out to please those senior to them. Though he was known to be an exceptional diagnostician, Hamish didn't feel he belonged within the medical fraternity. Then again, he didn't feel like he belonged anywhere in society.

He'd grown up on the goldfields in Victoria where his father made his fortune, new money as others described it. Old money or valid money came from England or Europe. To make matters worse, his father maintained his wealth through bookmaking. Not only did Hamish come from new money, he came from money linked to shady activities. Most of those with old wealth were customers of his father, but that was not something they would publicly admit.

Hamish's father sent his only son to an expensive private school when he was twelve, expecting him to make the right connections. But Hamish spent his years at the school perfecting his ability to isolate himself, despite the number of people around him. Hamish moved to Queensland to escape his father's influence and to build himself a quiet life of science and service.

The corpse of Jock McDonald lay naked on a table in the middle of a dark room in the basement of the hospital. Hamish shivered, only partly from the cold. He dragged the table nearer to the window so he could make use of the natural light, put on an apron and scrubbed his hands. He stood before the corpse, ready to begin his examination, when he heard the sweep of a skirt lightly touching the floor and soft footsteps. Rita put on an apron and joined him.

'What are we looking for?' she asked.

'I'm not sure. He was hit once in the stomach and died.'

'Best begin with external observations,' suggested Rita. She retrieved a notepad and pencil from beneath her apron. 'You observe, and I'll take notes.'

Hamish's eyes lingered on her dark hair, short with a natural wave tucked behind her ears. She smiled with her eyes. 'Go on. This will be exciting.'

'It's not exciting,' said Hamish. 'It's frightening.'

'Tosh,' said Rita. 'What can be frightening about it?'

'I'm not trained in necropsy. Regardless of my efforts at Dunwich, I have no real experience in examining the deceased.'

'You're not going to kill him if you make a mistake, are you?'

'I might miss an important fragment of evidence, and my error could result in the accused being hanged.'

'My dear friend, you are the most thorough doctor in Australia. All your colleagues find your thoroughness irritating. You make them look negligent. It makes no difference that the patient is already dead. You'll find out what was wrong with him.'

Hamish began his observations of the body, looking for any signs of bruising that could provide clues about how the man spent his last days. He noted a patch of discolouration on his abdomen. Dipping a sponge into the washbasin by the table, he washed down the area to remove any superficial smudges that may confuse the nature of the mark. There was no mistaking the bruise. 'This discolouration is consistent with the impact of a single punch to the stomach,' he said out loud for Rita to note down. 'Still, it isn't enough to have caused his death.'

Hamish continued to examine the man's body. He leant over the man's face, peering into his mouth and around his lips. 'The lips are dry,' Hamish said slowly. He hovered over his mouth for a few moments, his head tilted to one side. 'There's an odour present around his mouth.' Rita recorded his words in her notepad. Hamish examined his neck, his torso and his limbs before moving onto his fingers. 'There's a blue pigmentation to his fingernails,' he said. Hamish checked his toenails and found the same pigmentation. He nodded to Rita to be sure she saw it too.

Rita assisted Hamish to turn the man over, allowing him to examine his back in the same way. When the external examination was complete, they rolled him over again and prepared themselves to open the body.

Hamish made an incision through the abdominal wall.

'Checking for signs of inflammation in the abdominal cavity,' he said. 'I can see no internal damage to suggest a blow significant enough to kill a man.'

He placed a ligature around the lower end of the oesophagus and another at the commencement of the duodenum, cut the tissue between the two and slipped the stomach into a dish. He opened the stomach along the lower curvature and poured the contents into a large glass jar. Hamish and Rita both took a step back and turned their faces from the corpse. An offensive odour emanated from the contents of the stomach.

Using a lens, Hamish examined the stomach contents. 'There are traces of indigo,' he said.

He stepped back and saw Rita standing with her pencil poised over the pad. She had stopped taking notes. He didn't need to voice his thoughts aloud to confirm the acknowledgement in her eyes. They both knew now what they were looking for. Hamish opened the oesophagus and said, 'there is evidence of corrosion from the mouth down the digestive tract.' Rita resumed her scratching across the pad.

Finally, Hamish sealed the glass specimen jars and began putting the man's body back together. He sewed the skin where he had made incisions, and he washed the man down. He reflected on how desperately he wished to restore the poor man's dignity, while he knew it was not possible.

'Is there anything more we can do to confirm our findings?' he asked Rita.

'We must analyse the body fluids,' she said. 'It seems clear this man was being poisoned, but we will need scientific evidence to define what the poison was and how much was in his system.'

'It's evident that while the punch may have precipitated the end to his life by a few hours at most, he was going to die anyway,' said Hamish.

'I agree. It will need verification, though, if we are to convince the authorities. Sergeant Bellamy may be onside, but others will not be as ready to agree. This man was not murdered by a coloured labourer but rather by someone he trusted. Someone was systematically poisoning him.'

'I'm not familiar with the testing process,' said Hamish.

'I am,' said Rita smiling. 'Is there an orderly about? He can go to the pharmacy to collect the items I need.'

Hamish was not surprised Rita knew exactly what to do. He had never met a more competent scientist, man or woman.

A young man carrying the scars of a childhood bout of smallpox returned with the items she needed.

'It's called a Marsh Test,' Rita said as she worked. 'After James Marsh.'

She added a sample of body fluid to a glass vessel containing zinc and acid, ignited the mixture and watched it begin to oxidise. She held a cold ceramic bowl in the jet of the flame, and the gas stained the bowl silvery–black.

'Arsenic,' she said. 'Someone has been giving him arsenic in smallish doses over a week or so, I would say.'

The blood rose in Hamish's neck and face. 'The South Sea Islander could so easily have been hanged for murder.'

Rita smiled at him. 'You won't let that happen. I know you. But the case will take some arguing.'

Her smile eradicated any doubts he had. He grinned down into her small face. Her presence was so much larger than her tiny frame suggested. 'My next step must be to inform the sergeant he was right in assuming there was more to the death,' he said. 'Then that's my involvement complete. It is up to the sergeant to investigate further.'

Rita's smile widened, and her right eyebrow arched. 'Yes, of course,' she said. 'That's you done.' She shook her head as she removed the apron and collected her purse.

Hamish sent Rita home in one cab while he took another to the Petrie Terrace Police Depot. He found Sergeant Bellamy sitting behind his mountain of paperwork.

'How goes it, Hart?' he said, not bothering to rise from his seat as Hamish walked in.

'You look worn out,' said Hamish.

'That I am,' said Bellamy.

'The news I have to convey won't make you feel any better.'

Bellamy leant forward over his desk.

'You were right in your thinking, the Islander did not kill Jock McDonald,' began Hamish.

'Go on.'

'There is evidence the deceased was being poisoned. Arsenic, to be precise. He had severe damage to his organs caused by the effects of ingesting arsenic. We know it was ingested because of the irritation in his oesophagus and down his digestive tract. The man would have been dead within the next twenty-four hours regardless of the punch perpetrated by the South Sea Islander.

Bellamy stretched back into his chair, lifted his arms, placed them behind his head and stared at the ceiling.

'How is this possible?' he asked at last.

'Small amounts of arsenic can be ingested over many days, and the effects will compound,' said Hamish. 'The man would have been ill certainly. Symptoms would include stomach cramps, diarrhea, possibly headaches and confusion. There's no doubt. We have conducted chemical analysis on the contents of the man's stomach.'

'We?'

'My colleague, Rita Cartwright, is a chemist. I asked her to assist in the examination.'

Bellamy nodded. 'How would it be done, Doctor? Wouldn't the fellow notice he was being fed arsenic?'

'Not necessarily. The powder is tasteless. It could be added to his food or drink, and he might not have been aware. There have been many cases of this type of poisoning. In my view, the substance is too widely available. You can purchase it at any pharmacy. The plantation would have a supply on hand for the extermination of pests.'

'The person slipping poison into McDonald's food would have to be trusted by him. Wouldn't he?'

'Yes. I would believe so.'

'I suppose the first thing to do is to confirm McDonald was unwell prior to the fight. That and your scientific evidence should be enough to release the Kanaka from blame.'

'What is the Islander's name, Bellamy?'

The sergeant checked his notes. 'His name is Kaelo. K.a.e.l.o. I'll need a strong case to let him go, Hart. The authorities won't want to hear it. A black man involved in the death of a white manager is going to raise the hackles of the population.'

'The accused was guilty of barely more than being in the wrong place at the wrong time,' said Hamish.

'We'll try to establish provocation in any case. It will be a back-up position, manslaughter rather than murder.'

'The man should be completely exonerated,' said Hamish. 'The stomach punch in no way caused the victim's death.'

'It may have been incidental, but the punch immediately precipitated death. You won't easily shift it from the consciousness of the populace.'

'What next then?'

'We'll send for Daniels. He stayed in Brisbane overnight rather than returning to Cloverton. And we'll get the bartender in as well. See how cocky he is here in the station, away from his own environment.'

Less than an hour later, Hamish and Sergeant Bellamy sat opposite William Daniels.

'I'm not sure how much help I can be,' Daniels was saying. 'I wasn't present when McDonald was hit.'

'We were hoping to gain a broader picture,' said Bellamy. 'How long did he work for you?'

'Eight years, close enough. What does that have to do with him being knocked down in the pub?'

'Bear with us,' said Bellamy. 'We're trying to establish a profile of the deceased. Was he a good manager, would you say?'

'Of course, he was a good manager. If he wasn't, I wouldn't have employed him.'

Bellamy continued. 'Was he a well man?'

Daniels looked taken aback. 'Well enough,' he said. 'He wasn't himself the last couple of days, but healthy for the most part.'

'What symptoms did he exhibit exactly these last few days?' Hamish asked.

Daniels looked at him suspiciously. 'He had an upset stomach.'

'How was he the day you left Cloverton? Was that the day before he died?'

'Yes,' said Daniels. 'He had a stomach upset. We had to stop the coach at one point.'

Hamish and Bellamy exchanged glances.

'What?' said Daniels.

Bellamy lowered the tone in his voice. 'Dr Hart found arsenic in his system,' he said.

'His organs were breaking down. He would have died anyway, regardless of the fight, according to the doctor.'

Daniels looked at Hamish as if he had given the man the poison himself.

'I don't believe it,' he said.

'There is no doubt,' replied Hamish.

'Can you think of anyone who would want to harm the deceased?' asked Bellamy.

Daniels put his head down. Hamish thought he was considering something. He shook his head and said, 'No.'

'No one?' repeated Bellamy.

'No one,' cried Daniels raising his voice and standing.

Bellamy considered telling him to sit back down, but he decided to release him instead. He was more interested in hearing initial responses from the witness present at the time of the fight.

'I must request you do not speak of this,' he said, 'until we complete our investigation.'

Daniels glared at him and strode out of the room. He didn't acknowledge Hamish in any way.

'That further validates the evidence you found,' said Bellamy when he was gone.

The constable entered, saying, 'The bartender from the Empire is here, sir.'

'Show him in constable.'

'Mr Thomas, the bartender from the Empire,' said the constable, showing him through the door.

'I'm Sergeant Bellamy, and this is Dr Hart,' said Bellamy as the man sat.

'I know who yer are,' said the bartender. 'Who's this codfish?'

'This is the doctor who examined the body, Mr Thomas,' said Bellamy.

'Call me Tommo, I can't be answerin' to Mr Thomas. What'd he examine him for? He's dead, and I saw who kill'd 'im. The black done it.'

'Could you explain exactly what you saw at the Empire this morning,' said Bellamy.

'I told yer. I saw the Kanaka kill that bloke – a manager, weren't he?'

'Take us through everything you saw,' repeated Bellamy calmly.

Tommo made an exaggerated sigh. With a show of summoning all the patience he could, he said slowly and deliberately, 'I saw the manager bloke sittin' near the window havin' a drink. I saw the black man demanding I serve him grog when the law says he can't have it. Another black came up, and the first one got nasty on account of I wouldn't give him the grog. He started creatin', and the manager came over. He said as I did, 'It's against the law to give you people grog.' Then the second black punched him, and he fell down dead. That's it, ain't it?'

'Did the manager appear well before the fight?' asked Hamish.

'Well enough, I s'pose.'

'He didn't appear to be in pain or ill?'

'I don't bloody know, do I? I had me work to do.'

'Was there any provocation before the punch?' asked Bellamy.

'None at all,' said Tommo confidently.

They thanked him for his assistance and let him go.

'We have the scientific evidence of the poison,' said Bellamy once they were alone. 'And we have the testimony from Daniels that McDonald was ill, consistent with the evidence. But I'm not convinced it will be enough to release Kaelo from blame. I'm going to have to keep him locked up until we find out who was poisoning Jock McDonald. I need someone to charge; otherwise, there is going to be mayhem.'

'Violence in the streets of Brisbane?' said Hamish shocked.

'You mark my words. A South Sea Islander punched a colonial, and he fell down dead in front of witnesses. An abstract story of chemicals and poisons in the body isn't going to change anyone's mind about what happened. No. The only chance Kaelo Rees has is if I'm able to make a credible arrest. I have to find the person who actually murdered McDonald.'

'I wish you well,' said Hamish. He was ready to go home. The nervous tension of conducting the necropsy and the frustration of yet another injustice had exhausted him.

'I'm going to visit Cloverton tomorrow,' said the sergeant. 'I'm convinced the answer is there. I wonder if you would join me?'

Hamish slumped back into the chair. 'What possible assistance could I provide?' he asked.

'You know what we are looking for,' said Bellamy. 'What symptoms the man would have shown, how the poison may have been provided....'

'Sergeant, I hate to appear unwilling to help, but I am reluctant to become involved in another murder inquiry. I'm hoping to establish my private practice....'

'Do you have patients tomorrow?'

'Well, no. But...'

'Meet you here at six then. We'll take the horses.'

Hamish dropped his head and brushed his sandy hair from his face. He held his head in both hands for a moment. When he finally looked up at the sergeant, he said, 'I'll see you at six.'

'Do you have a gun?' asked the sergeant.

'A gun?' cried Hamish.

'Do you have one?'

'Yes. I have a colt lightning somewhere. It belonged to my father, he gave it to me when I moved to Queensland. He thinks this is a wild frontier. I can't remember where I put it in the new house....'

'Find it and bring it with you,' said Bellamy.

'You think I need a gun to visit Cloverton?'

'We don't know what to expect at the plantation,' said the sergeant. 'Bring the gun.'

CHAPTER FOUR

The Week Brisbane Queensland Saturday 19 January 1884.

I urge the council under the Colonial Secretary to improve legislation as regards the expired Polynesians, as they are fast becoming a source of grave danger to life and property in this town. We are of the opinion that the police protection accorded is entirely inadequate to our needs. Time expired boys cannot be enforced to return to their Islands, and when they are asked to re-engage with the planters, they say, 'no, get better wages in town.' It is a fact, too, that they are supplied with grog. The citizens are greatly annoyed with the kanakas, but failure lies with those who pander to them – the storekeepers who take the kanakas into their shops and place them behind their counters, giving them the fat of the land, are far more to be blamed than the plantation owners.

AELO

Kaelo sat on the wooden bench that served as a bed in his cell. From this spot, he could see through the small square window to the trees beyond. A sharp rise behind the gaol was thick with foliage, wild, tangled, green-grey, like all the Australian bush he had seen. Not that he had seen much more than the coastline between Townsville and Brisbane from the ship's deck. He longed for the richness of the dense forests at home. For now, the smell of horse dung filled his nostrils, and the dust pricked at his eyes. He missed the smell of the sea.

Kaelo remembered the long days spent at the coral's edge fishing with his brothers, as comfortable in the sea as they were on land. He remembered the first time he saw a European ship appear on the horizon. It can't have been long after the death of his mother. Ships had come to the Island before, but he had been too young to notice them or too busy digging yams from the ground behind his hut. He watched this ship, this day, grow larger, huge sails moving its bulk forward. As novel as the image was, it captured his attention for a short time only. Kaelo and his brothers returned to their fishing, oblivious to the lives of the pale-skinned strangers who belonged to the ship. There was excitement among the adults when the ships came, but the lives of the strangers were too remote to have any relevance to the boys. As he picked the freshly caught fish from the nets, Kaelo caught glimpses of the officers' red coats slipping into row boats to come ashore. He hardly stopped to wonder what the men's motives were in coming so far across the sea.

But Kaelo recalled sensing a change as he made his way back to the family hut this particular day. He knew with absolute certainty nothing would ever be the same again, though he didn't know why. He cleaned the fish as he always did, and he folded them carefully within banana leaves ready to be baked on the fire. Kaelo's grandmother arrived as the sun was dropping into the horizon, and without saying a word, she sat by the fire and began shaving coconut into a metal pot. The pot had been Kaelo's mother's favourite possession. The boys had no idea where it came from, but they knew not to touch it. It was more precious than the gold coins they sometimes found when they went diving the shipwrecks on the reef. Kaelo saw his grandmother pick up the wrapped fish and place them on the coals beneath the boiling coconut milk.

He recalled wondering where his father was. He imagined him night fishing with the other men or drinking grog they had bargained from the Europeans on the other side of the Island. Kaelo wasn't concerned by his absence. He was used to falling asleep alone with his brothers. During the night, his father would often creep in, careful not to disturb them, even if he was full of grog. After they had eaten, the boys curled up together on the mats woven by their mother, the mats that still smelled of her and helped them to sleep. At some point through the night, Kaelo was troubled by a sense of trepidation, but it wasn't strong enough to keep him awake. He opened his eyes at sunrise to see their grandmother sleeping in the hut with them. Where was their father?

Kaelo watched himself in his mind's eye, leaving his brothers playing in the hills of crushed coral skirting their hut to wander through the village. He wasn't intentionally searching for his father. Still, he looked one way and the other as he went. At the edge of the village, a small wooden building glowed white in the morning sun. A cross stood out against the dark mountain beyond. Kaelo had known it all his life, but he had never entered. It was unlike any of the other structures in the village, crafted in the European style. It was solid, sturdy. It had a presence. It was God's house.

As Kaelo approached, a thin man with a shock of fiery red hair greeted him. He placed his hand on Kaelo's shoulder, and a flood of warmth spread through his chest.

'Out there,' the red-haired man said, pointing toward the ship. The schooner had set sail during the night and was already little more than a smudge on the horizon. Kaelo focused on the smudge.

'He's gone with them on the promise of work,' said the man. 'It's God's will that a man work to provide money for his family.'

Kaelo wasn't in the habit of questioning God; he was far too fearful. But he did wonder why God wanted his father to go away and earn money. What they needed from him was fish large enough to feed them all and palm branches strong enough to keep the rain from leaking through their roof. Kaelo was not yet ten years old. He felt an extraordinary burden settle on his shoulders. If his father was away, possibly for weeks, he would have to take responsibility for the family. His mother's mother would do what she could for them, but she was neither young nor strong. His mother's father sat with the other men of his age in the shade. He couldn't help them.

'You will be safe,' said Pastor John as though he could read Kaelo's thoughts. Kaelo often wondered how the missionary knew so much about what he was thinking. 'God will look after you and your brothers,' he said. 'And I will too. Come to Sunday School now and pray for God to watch over your father.'

Kaelo followed the missionary into God's House, where a few other children from the village were already singing Christian songs. This was his first real introduction to a relationship with the Christian God that would come to define his character.

Kaelo recalled the years spent when he was not hunting or gardening with Pastor John. He remembered sitting at his feet while he read stories from the Bible. Kaelo enjoyed stories of all kinds, and the Bible had good stories. One day, Pastor John said he could teach Kaelo to read if he would like it. Kaelo agreed and found himself rushing each day to finish his fishing to get back to Pastor John. He came to see that the shapes called a, and e, and o, were shapes he could make with his mouth. They could be joined together to form words. Pastor John pointed to words and made Kaelo say them aloud. When Kaelo called the words correctly, he gave him a coin. It made Kaelo feel good. He came to understand the way money could make a person feel important and how a little of it made a man desire more. He started to make lists in his mind of things he could buy if he had money. Some of the items on the list were things he didn't know he wanted, and some were items he had not even known existed before he read about them in the books Pastor John gave him as his skills grew.

Soon, Pastor John began teaching him directly from the Bible. It sounded like people talking in Kaelo's head. There were questions and answers. Kaelo read that it was God who created the world and everything in it. He read that there was not a single thing that God did not know or could not see. He'd heard the missionaries say these things, but to read them himself from the book, was to experience the words directly as if God were talking to him. Kaelo read that whoever believes in God and His dominion over life and death if he should die, he will live again hereafter. Kaelo wanted to live on in the hereafter. He would join his mother there.

'Kaelo, the sergeant is here to see you.'

Kaelo was still on the beach on Ferguson Island. He was absorbed in the light glistening on the water in front of his family hut. The sound of waves breaking against the coral filled his ears.

'Kaelo.'

All at once, the dark cell rushed into focus, and he was back on the cot in the watch house. It was cold. He looked up to see the Constable and Sergeant Bellamy standing over him. Kaelo blinked, his eyes taking a moment to adjust to the darkness.

'I've come to provide you with an update,' said the sergeant.

'An update?' Kaelo wondered what he needed to update him on. He had killed a man, and he would be punished. It was simple.

'The man who died,' began Bellamy, 'did not die because you hit him. He was poisoned.'

Kaelo thought about poison. His younger brother had eaten fish once, the kind their grandmother said they must never eat. He was sick for a day and a night. His brother vomited so much Kaelo was afraid he would wretch up his insides. But he improved.

'Kaelo,' Bellamy sat beside him, 'you did not kill that man. He was going to die anyway.'

A light came into Kaelo's eyes. Was this true?

'You will go free as soon as I can discover who killed Jocko McDonald. And gather enough evidence to prove it,' Bellamy added. 'I need to keep you here until then, for your own safety,' he said.

Sergeant Bellamy had questioned him carefully on the day of the incident. Kaelo traced his mind to recall his answers. He had been clear in every detail. He freely admitted hitting the man and seeing him fall. Kaelo believed himself at fault and deserving of punishment. He knew the Europeans would expect him to be punished. The new information that he may not have been responsible for the death would take some processing. In the meantime, he was prepared to stay put while the sergeant worked out what happened.

Hamish

Hamish stepped from his cab at ten minutes before six the next morning. He was surprised to find a group of newspaper men gathered outside the Police Station. 'Are you able to comment on the murder case, sir?' cried one of the men stepping in front of him, pencil and notebook at the ready. Hamish walked faster. 'When will the coloured labourer be charged?' shouted someone from behind the group.

Not a newspaper reporter, but a member of the public, thought Hamish. He kept moving forward, rattled but undeterred by the jostling going on around him, arriving in Bellamy's office to the roar of an official gentleman yelling at Sergeant Bellamy. The sergeant saw Hamish enter, but he waited for the man to take a breath before he spoke.

'This is Inspector Scratchley,' he said as soon as the opportunity arose. 'Dr Hamish Hart.'

The gentlemen immediately turned his fury toward Hamish. 'So, it is you I have to thank for this outrage,' he cried.

'Sir?' said Hamish, glancing at Bellamy for a clue about why he was being bellowed at.

'The Kanaka who murdered the plantation manager. I have been inundated with petitions from the community to have the man hanged immediately.'

'Good Lord,' said Hamish. 'The incident only happened yesterday. How has it become of importance to the community so quickly?'

'The newspapers reported on it,' said Bellamy. 'Apparently, it has caused quite a stir in the town.'

'Quite right,' cried the Inspector. 'The good people of Brisbane want to know when the man is to be hanged. The sooner, the better. These Polynesian labourers are getting out of hand. We need to show swift action to prove we have the situation under control.'

'But the Islander is not responsible for the death of the plantation manager,' said Hamish. He was confused about why the Inspector was being aggressive toward him.

'Of course, he killed him. There were witnesses, Hart. I don't give a damn about your scientific theories. The papers are full of stories about these coloureds wreaking havoc on our towns. And the public are demanding to know why the police are powerless to do anything about it.'

'Sit down, please,' said Bellamy to the Inspector. He closed the door to the office. 'Sit down, Doctor.'

The inspector and Hamish sat.

'I asked Dr Hart to complete an examination of the body,' said Bellamy, 'I was not convinced the Islander killed Jock McDonald. I instigated the investigation. After hearing the evidence supplied by Dr Hart, I am further convinced the Polynesian did not commit the murder. Dr Hart found evidence the man was being poisoned.'

Inspector Scratchley did not shift his attention from Hamish and appeared not to have heard his sergeant speak.

'Look, Hart, I understand you are some kind of bleeding-heart advocate for the lower classes, but this case represents the tip of the iceberg. You must understand. Up and down the colony of

Queensland, there is outrage over the behaviour of these darkies. I don't blame the men. I blame the drink. It's the supply of alcohol that has caused the problem. If all publicans were of the same ilk as the man who refused the Kanaka in this instance, we wouldn't have the situation we are in. This practice of supplying Kanakas with drink must be stopped.'

'Kaelo had not had a drink,' said Bellamy. 'He told me, and I'm certain the bartender will confirm as much when he is interviewed today.'

Hamish was still reeling from being called a bleeding heart.

'It's beside the point,' went on the Inspector. 'It's the expectation of drink that started the row. I hear the drunken orgies of Kanakas coming into town for alcohol have made Saturday nights loathsome further north. They return to their plantations, yelling, howling and making life hideous for everyone. Men who serve alcohol to these Polynesians should lose their licenses for good. That is the head of the reptile; you mark my words, doctor. Strike at that, and you kill the evils of the present system.'

Hamish's face was bright red. He felt he had walked into an ambush. He didn't know how to respond to this man who was blathering about issues that went far beyond the facts about the case against Kaelo.

Bellamy hastened to calm the situation.

'Getting back to the point, sir, of this particular incident,' he began....'

But the Inspector had more to add. 'On Sunday night last, eight or nine Islanders belonging to one of the recruiting vessels in port created a frightful scene while under the influence. They attacked a constable with a stone and threatened to kill him.'

'I know,' said Bellamy. 'Five of them have been sent to Brisbane Gaol. We have them here. The point is that this incident is not connected to....'

'The public are wondering what the police are about allowing bands of armed Kanakas prowl around town to the danger of life and property. As it is, there seems to be nothing to prevent the town from being sacked and its citizens murdered. A band of the devils were quarrelling in Ann Street last week, armed with axes, tomahawks and rifles. They turned on a white man who was simply curious and came at him. Seemed determined to brain him, by all accounts. Fortunately, the fellow ran into the house of one of my men. When the Kanaka followed him, my man got out his gun and pointed it at the devil. The black coward turned tail and left the house muttering.'

'I've also heard of the incident you describe, sir. It has no bearing on this case,' said Bellamy. 'If we could turn our attention to the case at hand, Sir. The man in custody was not drinking alcohol, and while he admits hitting the deceased, the evidence is clear, he was not responsible for his death. I need to investigate this case and identify the actual killer. That will take time.'

'We don't have time, Bellamy. You're missing my argument. The public wants an end to this. They already think we have been instrumental in letting this situation with the Polynesian labour get out of hand. We need to show a severe and immediate response to this incident. I suggest you dismiss Hart and get on with charging the savage.'

The Inspector stormed from the room and presumably made his way through the waiting reporters outside.

Hamish was lost for words. The tirade had caught him completely off guard. He was never his best first thing in the morning, but this barrage of racist slurs and insults left him depleted.

There was a tentative knock on the door, and it opened a crack to show Constable Pennyweather's anxious face. A rolled-up newspaper was poked through the crack. Bellamy took the paper and sat back at his desk, where he leaned back against the wall, the front two legs of his chair off the ground. Bellamy rocked on the back legs for a moment while he read the page Pennyweather had marked for him.

'This is the article that alerted the whole of Brisbane,' he said.

'A South Sea Island Labourer has been arrested for murdering a plantation manager only hours after arriving on our shores. The man became violent when he was refused alcohol at the Empire Hotel yesterday. The publican informed the Kanaka he could not supply him with alcohol under the law. When the Polynesian became angry, a plantation manager, Mr Jock McDonald, stepped in to clarify the situation. He repeated that the

Hotel was not allowed to serve alcohol to his race. The Islander then hit the plantation manager with such force he was immediately knocked down dead. The Polynesian's countrymen escaped into the streets of Brisbane and were lost to the authorities. The plantation manager was at the Hotel to collect the labourers contracted to work for him and escort them to his plantation in the Logan area.

Our sympathies go out to the plantation owner who has now lost both his manager and his new contingent of labour.'

'That is scandalous,' protested Hamish. 'The article misrepresents the facts entirely!'

'I'm afraid it has inflamed the situation. It will certainly influence public opinion,' said Bellamy. 'But regardless of what the Inspector says, I'm going to investigate this case. We can't afford to waste any time.'

Hamish remembered he didn't have to continue supporting the investigation. He could go back to his practice and leave Bellamy to it. Yet, if the insults from the Inspector were intended to intimidate him, they'd had the opposite effect. He was more determined than ever to see justice done.

CHAPTER FIVE

The Brisbane Courier Thursday 29 October 1885.

Just where the main Southern Road crosses the Albert River is a nest of plantations which can be counted as the oldest in the country. The owners of them have jogged along in a quiet, steady way quite heedless of the excitement which caused untried localities in the North to be rapidly converted into sugar-growing centres, an excitement which created mills of such a size that the capabilities of one would equal almost the whole of the original manufactories of the Logan. At the Logan Mills, all the cutting and loading is carried out by kanakas. Usually, the mills purchase cane from neighbouring farmers, but this year they have more of their own than they will be able to work. On the opposite side of the Albert is a stretch of fine level land all under cane. This belongs to farmers who have no mills and, in all probability, will remain unsold. The southern end of the railway beyond Beenleigh will run right through this estate. Thus, these pioneer planters, as likewise those on the Brisbane end, by the circumstances of the Colony's progress, find an increased value upon their land, such an increment indeed that the owners need not trouble themselves much whether the sugar cane growing pays or not.

KAELO

Kaelo's father returned when he was fifteen. During his years of absence, Kaelo had come to believe he was never coming home. He was so committed to the idea that when his father turned up at the hut at dawn one morning, Kaelo feigned indifference. His sudden appearance would not entice a response. Kaelo's younger brothers didn't know who the man was at first. The morning of his return, Kaelo rose from the floor where he slept and pushed past the shadow in the doorway out into the light. He left his father standing there while he gathered his spears and nets for the day's fishing. Kaelo could hear the younger boys coming to life inside the hut, and he listened to their slow realisation that this man was their father, returned from the great land across the sea. There were squeals of delight. That will be gifts, Kaelo thought. He wasn't interested in the trinkets from Queensland. He headed to the water to begin his day's hunting. Without the daily supply of fresh fish, the family would not survive. He had been responsible for feeding the younger boys and his grandparents for much of his life, and he would continue to do so.

Later in the morning, Kaelo was aware of his father's presence alongside him, but he didn't acknowledge him. He laid the long net onto the sand and began rolling it up in the way he did every morning. He checked the tips of his spears he'd only finished making the night before. They were good and sharp; he was pleased. Kaelo's father took up one of the spears from the ground and examined it.

'This is well made,' he said.

Kaelo ignored him, piling his equipment into a canoe resting against the crushed coral. He went to the bow of the canoe and began pulling it into the water. There was a shift in the weight of the canoe as his father began pushing from the back. But still, Kaelo didn't speak to him. They were well beyond the reef, and Kaelo and his father had caught two large coral trout before either of them broke the silence.

'You have grown into a man in my time away,' said Kaelo's father.

'Why is he speaking to me like this?' thought Kaelo.

'I have brought money home with me. We can build a strong house, send the boys to school.'

Kaelo didn't want a strong house, and he was pretty sure the boys didn't want to leave the village to go to school. He wasn't sure what he wanted, except for his father to stop talking to him.

'You can spend more time with the other young men now,' his father said. 'Soon, you will choose a wife.'

Was this man mad? What use was a wife when he already had so many to worry about?

The distance between Kaelo and his father was not reduced by the following three months. They worked together on the tasks that needed doing. They hunted for fish, fixed the roof of the hut after each big wind, and ensured there was a fire in the evenings for grandmother to cook and keep the mosquitoes at bay.

Kaelo attended services at God's House while his father was in Queensland, and he continued to do when he came home. He was grateful for the friendship of the missionary who recited the sermon. Kaelo didn't understand a lot of what was being said in the first months, however over the years, a kind of acceptance had settled in. He had faith that God knew his mind, monitored his actions, and was there to serve punishment if he did wrong. God had not abandoned him to look after three younger children and elderly grandparents. His father had done that. God had ensured he had a decent catch each day, and a harvest from the gardens, even during the wet season. God had cured his youngest brother's fever when he slept for two full days, and Kaelo expected him to die rather than wake. Where had his father been when God did these things?

One day, Kaelo returned from fishing to find his father curled up on the floor of their hut where he had been that morning. Kaelo pushed him with his foot, but his father didn't move; he only groaned a little. Kaelo lent over him. 'Are you sick?' he said.

His father lifted himself into a sitting position, his head falling between his knees.

'What is it?' Kaelo said. Kaelo saw his father's face was grey, and his skin shone from sweat. 'I am ill,' said his father. 'Make the fire and sit with me. There is something I need to tell you.'

Kaelo did as his father directed. When the fire was burning hot in readiness for preparation of the evening meal, Kaelo returned to sit by his father, curious about what he had to say.

'When I left you, I knew nothing,' he began. 'I thought I would be away for three weeks and come back with fishhooks and axes and tools for planting. I thought a man could sail to Australia and back in two days.'

Kaelo listened. Even if his father did believe this, he couldn't forgive him for leaving them.

'You know, son, when I got on that ship, I saw a figure at the stern, a man standing by the wheel. I thought to myself, this is not a man.

This is a spirit who guides the ship across the sea. The figure was steady on his legs, while others brought onto the ship were falling about. He never turned his eyes but stared forward, his eyes always on the sea. His beard was so long it covered his breast. I thought for sure he was a spirit standing guard over the ship. It was much later when I saw him walking about and talking to others, when I saw him eating food, I realised he was a man like any other. He was the Captain, and to be obeyed, but a man, not a spirit as I thought.'

Kaelo wondered at his father's ignorance. Many ships had visited the Island in the six years he had been away. Many Islanders had taken the journey to Australia. It was impossible to imagine any grown man could doubt the white men on the ships were human. Even if they were unsure why they were being coaxed to join them or how far they were going. Still, Kaelo thought, it was a different time when his father left.

'I have a wife,' his father went on. 'In Queensland.'

Whatever Kaelo expected to hear next, it was not this.

'She is an Aboriginal woman. Her name is Araluen. She worked on the same plantation in Mackay. I loved her, and I married her in the chapel on the plantation.'

Kaelo's face did not change. He had become used to keeping his emotions to himself. There wasn't anyone to talk to about the things that bothered him besides the missionary. He wondered what Pastor John would make of this.

'I wanted her to come home with me. It was the end of my second contract, and I wasn't allowed to stay any longer. The government said I had to come back. There was passage for Araluen because we were married, but she wouldn't come. She said my people would never accept her. But her mob in Australia didn't want her either.'

Kaelo's face creased into a frown.

'It's not only her,' his father said. 'We had a son.'

A knot formed in Kaelo's stomach. He became dizzy.

'It broke my heart to leave them, Kaelo. I gave her some money, but there was nothing I could do. The government was sending us back, those with expired contracts. And she refused to come with me. I heard she travelled to Brisbane with the baby. She wanted to get work and make a new start, and no one would know them in Brisbane.'

Kaelo lent back on the wall of the hut and closed his eyes. Somewhere in the strange land across the sea, he had another brother. Someone else who needed him.

'Find them, Kaelo. Go on the next schooner. Take this money I have saved and give it to them. It is not possible to live without money in that place.' Kaelo's father curled up on the floor and went to sleep. He stayed there for three days and nights. When Kaelo woke one morning at dawn, as he had done since he was nine, he noticed the rasping noises his father made in his sleep had stopped. His father was dead.

Kaelo spent the next seven days dwelling on his father's words and on his life on the Island. He noticed a tightness had crept up on him in the past months. He felt it in his chest. He imagined a great burden holding him down, as though he were caught beneath the hull of his canoe with only his nose above the sea. He watched his younger brother bringing in the fish each day and failed to find any shame in his not accompanying him. His brother was a competent fisherman, after all. He watched his grandmother silently prepare the evening meal for his brothers, and it troubled him that she never spoke. The boys tumbled and wrestled and laughed with one another, but their companionship was no longer enough for him. He thought about the words in the Bible and the comfort he found in them while his father was away. He thought about the way Pastor John taught the villagers and how they listened to his ideas about what was right and wrong. Kaelo wanted to learn more about the Christian world beyond his village. He thought about his father's instruction to take money to his wife in Australia, and he thought about the brother he didn't yet know. One morning he woke up to find the pressure in his chest had been released, and he could breathe easily again. He knew what he would do.

HAMISH

Hamish and Bellamy set off toward Logan an hour later than they had intended. The ride south was a pleasant one. The greatest part of the ride took place during the cooler hours of the morning, despite their late start. Hamish drank in the olive blue-grey tones of the landscape as gums and acacias moved past him. He could almost believe he was standing still while the endless forest of twisted gums marched toward Brisbane. A ragged army they were, crooked and unruly, but tall and determined, nonetheless. Every now and then, a wallaby stopped by the side of the road to watch them pass, its grey nose twitching curiously.

They frequently passed others on the road. Farmers and commercial travellers moved daily between the southern villages of Beenleigh and the Brisbane markets, delivering their wares to buyers.

Hamish had to admit to himself he was enjoying the ride. He wasn't sure of the value he could add to the interviews at Cloverton, but he was happy to be out of Brisbane. It surprised him to realise he had become bored in the confines of his consulting rooms. Being at home when he had no patients only served to remind him of how far he yet had to go to establish his practice. Any opportunity to meet new people was an opportunity to extend his connections, he thought. In any event, Hamish didn't intend to sit by and allow Kaelo to be charged with a crime he didn't commit to appease a political agenda he didn't believe in.

They rode past two or three settlers' huts to either side of the road, and Hamish marvelled at the ingenuity of the pioneering families. The huts were built from local timbers and sheets of recycled tin. There was no glass in the windows to shut out the cold or the squalling rain. Yet the children he could see in the surrounding gardens looked strong and healthy. Their limbs were dark, and their hair bleached by the sun. These children didn't need houses with glass windows to protect them from the outdoors. They spent their lives revelling in the harsh light of the Queensland sun.

They crossed Bulimba Creek on a rattling wooden bridge, and as they rode into Runcorn, they met up with the new Logan railway line. There was a platform already constructed for passengers but no buildings. The line followed the road for one and three-quarters of a mile, passing Mr Olley's nursery, which now overlooked the railway. The line continued through thickly timbered country toward Kingston. Hamish and Bellamy veered east toward the plantations flanking the Logan River.

Hamish wondered how this land would change once the railway opened. Presumably, there would be settlers eager to take advantage of the improved transport moving into the area. Following the settlers would be businesses, churches and schools. The bushland would be cleared for small plots that could be worked by a man and his children. The rambling plantations of the earliest pioneers were already becoming a relic of the past.

By mid-morning, they had reached Cedarwood, a smaller plantation settled between the Logan and Albert Rivers. They would need to pass through Cedarwood to reach Cloverton. As they turned away from the road onto a side-track, Hamish noticed a pleasant looking house on a hill in the distance. Drawing nearer, an appealing garden caught his eye. There was a slip beyond the house linking the property to the river and providing access to the steamer that travelled up the river daily. There were also wooden and iron tracks running alongside the river's edge toward Cloverton.

A large man, sunburned and swarthy, moved toward them, taking the longest strides Hamish had ever seen. Hamish thought he must be seven feet tall. Teeth shone white from a face that was withered from the sun, but there was a glint that took on the light spectacularly. It was a single gold tooth in the front of his mouth. Familiar with the way the light bounces off gold from his childhood living around the mines in Ballarat, Hamish was intrigued. It was difficult to tell the man's age, but Hamish guessed him to be in his fifties. The energy in his stride belied the aged exterior. This is a man who had worked hard all his life.

'Hello,' he said.

'Good day to you,' called Bellamy. Both horses came to a halt in front of the man.

'Name's Vincent. I'm the manager here at Cedarwood. What can I do for you, gentlemen?' The hand that stretched upward toward Bellamy was enormous. Hamish watched the sergeant grip the man's hand and shake it enthusiastically.

'I'm Sergeant Bellamy, and this is Doctor Hart,' Bellamy said. 'We are passing through on our way to Cloverton if you have no objection.'

'You are welcome here,' said Vincent in a voice as large as the man. 'Would you care to rest for a while before you ride on? I'll have the boys look after the horses, and you can enjoy a drink.'

Hamish was parched. He desperately hoped the sergeant would agree to the proposal.

'Thank you, good man. That is uncommonly kind of you. We would be most grateful,' he said.

Hamish breathed a sigh of relief, dismounted and handed a black man, who had appeared from nowhere, the reigns. Bellamy did the same, and they followed Vincent through the garden to a pretty veranda at the front of the house. They sat on a wooden bench while Vincent called to a woman inside the house to bring them tea.

'Two hundred and fifty acres we have here,' said Vincent. 'Down to the river and as far in that direction as you can see. Along the river that way is Cloverton.' Vincent pointed to the east.

'A large estate?' said Hamish.

'Much larger than this one,' said Vincent. 'They have about seven hundred and ninety acres. And more to come now Daniels' girl has married Pete Tennyson.'

'What do you mean?' said Bellamy.

'The Tennyson's own the land behind us, toward Beenleigh. Now the two families are linked by marriage, they'll merge the land and businesses. That will make the largest plantation in southern Queensland.'

'How will that affect you here?' asked Bellamy.

'Not sure,' said Vincent. 'Small holdings are struggling. We send our cane to the mill at Cloverton. They have the modern machinery. My bosses, the owners of this place, have plantations at Gympie and Maryborough as well. They are far more profitable than this place. I expect Daniels will buy this lot out at some stage. It sits like a pig-in-a-poke within the boundaries of his land now.'

'Won't that put you out of a job?' asked Hamish.

'Aye. I'm not bothered. The boss'll see me right on one of the properties. Or Daniels might even take me on,' he said, grinning. 'Someone's got to work the land don't matter who owns it.'

A woman with a pleasant round face and a bright smile brought the tea trolley onto the veranda. There was a pile of warm damper, a large pat of cold butter and a jug of golden syrup on the trolley alongside the teapot.

'This is my wife, Ruby,' said Vincent. He placed his arm proudly around her waist.

'Gerroff,' she said in a playful voice and nodded to the strangers.

Ruby had the darkest brown eyes Hamish had ever seen. He found himself staring.

'Ruby is Aboriginal,' said Vincent, as though an explanation were necessary. 'She's not from around here. We met down south. Sydney, in fact. I was on my way back from the goldfields. We been married, what ten years now, is it Ruby?'

Ruby smiled and nodded. Hamish thought it the most honest smile he had ever seen. He would have guessed Ruby's age to have been at least twenty years less than that of her husband, but the affection between them was obvious.

'It gets a bit lonely here, though, doesn't it, love? Ruby's entire family were killed by white settlers. She wandered into Parramatta, nothing more than a girl. We're happy here at Cedarwood, but as I said, it gets a bit lonely for Ruby.'

Ruby kept her eyes down as her husband spoke. Her hands moved quickly, pouring tea into enamelled metal mugs and dripping great globules of fragrant golden syrup onto the bread.

'This damper is delicious,' said Hamish.

'Ruby's specialty. You should try her kangaroo stew,' said Vincent. 'Call around one night for tea. Are you in Cloverton long?'

'We shouldn't be there more than one night,' said Bellamy. 'But I trust we'll be back.'

'I'd love to have tea with you both,' said Hamish. 'We'll look forward to it on our next visit.'

Another half-hour was spent pleasantly chatting about the comfortable temperature for the time of year and the recent cane harvest. Hamish could have stayed in this big man's company for hours. But they had work to do, and Bellamy was eager to get moving.

They said their good buys, retrieved the horses and started the final leg of their journey.

Encouraged by the knowledge that Cloverton was over the next hill, Hamish wondered if the new information that the two plantations were consolidating had any bearing on the murder of Jock McDonald.

CHAPTER SIX

The Maitland Mercury Saturday 18 July 1885.

Wearing coloured hosiery develops some peculiar facts. It would seem that cheap coloured stockings would be more liable to have poison in them than the higher priced ones, but the fact is just the reverse. You never hear of poor people being poisoned by wearing cheap hosiery. It is only those who wear the best material. It would scarcely pay to put arsenic in the cheap article.

When the weather is warm, the cheap coloured hosiery runs, and the colour gets all over the feet. At night the colour is washed off, and no harmful effects are felt. When the weather is warm fine coloured hosiery also runs, but very little. So little, in fact, the effect is deleterious and frequently results in blood poisoning. The poor people have a wonderful immunity, it seems, from poisoning produced in this manner. If arsenic were used in cheap hosiery as much as in fine, the hospital might be full of patients now, suffering from poisoning of the feet and limbs.

HAMISH

They rode for twenty minutes through paddocks with horses, cattle and pigs and passed fields of chicory, coffee and tobacco. Riding up toward Cloverton, it was the grandness of the property that impressed Hamish. A large weatherboard homestead with wide verandas wrapped around all sides was perched at the highest point overlooking the Logan River. Built on stumps, so the air circulated below, the verandas took on the breeze from whatever angle it came. Closer to the house was a European style garden with beans, peas, carrots and onions. Passionfruit and grapes dripped from long wire supports, and coconut palms towered over the lot. From the hill where the house was situated, and as far as the eye could see toward the Bay, there was sugar cane. Great carpets of silver-green swayed in the breeze, interposed between acres of brown where the cane had already been cut. There were outbuildings scattered across the plantation, and a rail snaked through the sugar cane a good mile down the river and back to the mill.

Hamish and the sergeant pulled their horses to a stop in front of the house. A man strode up from the stables and took the reigns as they dismounted.

'Thank you,' said Hamish as the man led his and the sergeant's horses away. He didn't respond. Hamish wondered if their welcome would be as cool inside the house.

'What, precisely, is the aim for this visit?' asked Hamish.

The sergeant was silent for a moment, presumably deciding how to articulate their aim to himself, as well as to Hamish. 'We are aiming to establish an assessment of the members of the family and of the key employees as individuals and come to some understanding of their relationships with one another,' said Bellamy. 'More precisely than that, we need to know if anyone had any reason to want Jock McDonald out of the way and had access to the means of poisoning him.'

They climbed the wide steps and stood on the veranda, the front door was open, and they could hear movement within. Sergeant Bellamy leant in through the door and called out, 'Hellooo.'

A young woman, heavily pregnant, came to the door dressed in a simple skirt which sat high over her increased middle. She wore a blouse of pale blue crepe with a long sash tied in a bow at the neck. Both skirt and blouse were of the highest quality, and she had an air of sophistication that indicated she was not a domestic servant. She stared at the two men, who stared back. Sergeant Bellamy broke the silence first.

'Sergeant Bellamy and Dr Hart,' he said, holding his hat in his hand.

The young woman continued to stare.

'We would like to speak with William Daniels,' said the sergeant.

'My father is not at home,' said the woman. 'He has not returned from Brisbane.'

'We have preceded him then,' said Bellamy. 'I believe he's on the coach due this way this morning. Is that not so?'

'I'm afraid you know more about my father's movements than do I,' said the woman. 'We were expecting him yesterday, along with the new labour.'

'I apologise, Miss Daniels...er....' Bellamy glanced down at the swollen belly and lost his voice.

'Mrs Tennyson,' the woman corrected him.

'I'm sorry, Mrs Tennyson. Unforgivable of me. Perhaps we can wait for your father inside?'

The woman turned around and disappeared into the house. Hamish and Bellamy stood in the doorway at a loss. It would be ill-mannered to follow the woman inside, but it didn't seem appropriate to stand in the doorway either. Hamish glanced in the direction of two cane chairs on the veranda. It looked like a good place to wait. What time does the coach come in anyway? he thought.

As Hamish was about to settle himself among the cushions on the wicker chair, another woman appeared at the door. She had similar features to the younger woman, but they seemed softer on her. A mass of dark hair piled high on her crown created a complex pattern of curls and puffs, and her blue eyes were accentuated by the darkness of her hair. Her fashionable dress was high at the throat, with slim sleeves to the elbow. A huge bustle drew the fabric tight across the hips and bundled it into a waterfall effect over a cushion at her posterior. While the bustle would not have been unusual in Queen Street, it was surprising in this rural backwater. The fabric had an intriguing weave of silver and gold thread throughout. This woman would have seemed at home in a fashionable salon in Paris. Not that Hamish had ever been in a fashionable salon in Paris himself, but he had seen illustrations of the fashionable ladies. The woman reminded Hamish of such an illustration. What was she doing here?

The woman smiled. 'Sergeant Bellamy,' she said, 'and Doctor Hart is it? I apologise for leaving you standing here like this. Please come in. We are all at sixes and sevens with my husband and the manager away. They were due back yesterday. I can't think what has happened to delay them.'

Bellamy glanced at Hamish.

'No problem at all,' he said. 'We happen to know your husband will arrive on the coach this morning.'

'You can wait in here,' said the woman leading them into a well-furnished sitting room. 'I am Charlotte Daniels. William's wife and Alice's mother.' She gestured toward Alice, who was hovering near a large open fireplace. Hamish noticed that, unlike his own, this fireplace had recently been in use.

'Thank you,' the men said in unison.

'The maid is on her day off,' said Charlotte, and I'm afraid we've lost the cook. I mean to say, we have no cook at present. I have nothing to offer you other than tea.'

'Tea would be most refreshing,' said Bellamy. He glanced at Hamish.

'Yes. Yes, thank you,' said Hamish.

Charlotte left the room to see to the tea, leaving Alice where she was standing. She was frighteningly still.

'I can only assume since we have a police sergeant and a doctor who have come so far to visit us, there is something unfortunate to report,' said Alice.

Hamish coughed.

'Perhaps we should wait for your father,' began Bellamy.

Alice cut in, 'Will the news conveyed be any less unpleasant, or any less a statement of fact when my father is present?'

'Er...no,' said Bellamy. At that point, Mrs Daniels returned with the tea tray. She paused and looked from her daughter to Bellamy before placing the tray on a low table. She set out pretty china teacups ready for pouring. Motioning the men to sit, she arranged her bustle and lowered herself onto a settee opposite them. Although Alice was more suitably dressed for sitting than her mother, she remained standing.

'Uncommonly pleasant weather for this time of year,' Charlotte said, 'I trust your ride from Brisbane was enjoyable.'

Hamish and Bellamy smiled awkwardly. Hamish felt his eyes drawn to Charlotte's ephemeral beauty. He hoped she didn't detect him staring, but something in her confidence assured him she was well-aware of her effect on men.

A loud bang from the direction of the door caused them all to turn. William Daniels was dragging a suitcase through the door, banging it against the architraves on either side as he went. He stopped when he saw Hamish and Bellamy in his sitting room.

'What the devil are you doing here?' he said.

Sergeant Bellamy stood up. 'We are here to carry out further investigations,' he said, 'in light of...' he glanced toward Charlotte, 'the incident,' he said finally.

Charlotte glided across the room to her husband and kissed him on the cheek. Daniels ignored her.

He said to Hamish and Bellamy, 'Wait will you until I get my things into the other room.'

He was back within seconds and seated next to his wife.

'Have you told them anything?' he asked.

'No,' said Bellamy.

'You better get on with it then,' he said.

Charlotte stared wide-eyed at the sergeant, and Alice moved a few steps closer.

'There was a scuffle at lunchtime yesterday, and your manager, Jock McDonald, was killed,' he said.

Hamish watched the women's expressions. Charlotte's face paled visibly, while Alice showed no sign of emotion at all.

A man has been arrested. He was in a fight with McDonald before he died, though we have reason to believe the man is not responsible for his death.'

'How so, Sergeant?' Charlotte asked.

Bellamy took a deep breath. 'Dr Hart found arsenic in McDonald's system,' he said. 'He was being poisoned, and according to Dr Hart would have died within hours regardless of the fight.'

Charlotte let out an audible cry. She covered her mouth with a handkerchief and turned away from them. Alice stared, without showing any sign she had heard them speak.

Daniels went to his wife and put a protective arm around her shoulder. She stiffened rather than settling into his body. 'My wife has had a shock,' said Daniels, 'I'll assist her to her room.'

Charlotte allowed herself to be led by her husband. She looked so frightened that it took Hamish all his discipline not to jump up and assist her himself.

Out of genuine concern, he asked Alice, 'Do you need to go with your mother? She has clearly had a shock.'

Alice ignored him and continued to stare at Bellamy.

'Was Mr McDonald close to the family?' Bellamy asked Alice.

'No, he was an employee,' she said sternly, as though the question were absurd. She added, 'I believe my mother's anxiety is not because the man has died, but because you appear to be implying someone here at Cloverton poisoned him.'

'You have a preference for plain speaking,' said Bellamy.

Alice again ignored the statement. 'Have you word on the coloured labour my father organised?' she said.

'They all scattered when the incident occurred,' said Hamish. 'Except the accused, of course. He is in gaol.'

'This will slow production,' said Alice to no one in particular. 'We are now without a plantation manager as well as six labourers. The inconvenience is intolerable.'

'I beg your pardon,' said Bellamy, 'but the inconvenience is rather more for Jock McDonald than yourself, Madam. And the murder of a man is more than an inconvenience to the police. It is our duty to find the assailant.'

'I assure you, sir, the murder of this particular man is no more than an inconvenience. There will be few who will genuinely mourn his loss, though some may pretend to do so.'

Daniels returned from settling his wife. 'She has taken one of her powders,' he said. 'She will sleep now. What can I do to assist you in your enquiries?'

Hamish noted he did not speak to his daughter, and she did not acknowledge him.

'Perhaps you would be kind enough to show us around the plantation,' said Bellamy. 'We could get a sense for how the place runs and meet some of the people who work here.'

'How will that help in the investigation of McDonald's death?' asked Daniels.

Bellamy waved his hand casually. 'It may not help at all,' he said. 'I do find, however, that it is useful to have as much context as possible.'

'I'd love to see how the mill works,' cut in Hamish.

Daniels hesitated.

'You have created something quite extraordinary here,' said Hamish. 'I've heard you have the most advanced machinery in the colony.'

Hamish saw that this was enough to convince him.

'Certainly, let me wash up and change clothes,' said Daniels. 'Please make yourself at home, gentlemen.'

Uncomfortable with Alice staring at them, Hamish got up from his seat and moved onto the veranda. He looked out over the plantation and beyond. The landscape was like a painting. The cane floated in a wash of green against the muted grey hills, and the river twisted and turned like a silver ribbon between land and sky. The tropical sunlight threw glints of gold onto the hills here and there for effect. Gazing across the sea toward the horizon was Stradbroke Island, a long blue form nestled on the bay. Hamish remembered his recent stay on the Island, with all its beauty and all its mystery. His mind tried to make comparisons, but there were none. The beauty of this place was different from that of the Island in every way. This place Daniels had built in the shadow of Brisbane was an Eden on Earth.

Closer to where he was standing, he admired a garden that would have made any landowner in England proud. Citrus trees were in fruit. Colourful flowers adorned ornamental shrubs. And there were shady trees under which a family might picnic. Still, there was something startling about the garden. Amidst the calm, orange flowers burst from within clusters of leaves so tall they might have come from the Jurassic period. The absurdity of trying to create a scene evocative of England within a landscape that refused taming was revealed in those flowers.

When Daniels joined them, they walked from the house toward the mill. Hamish could see South Sea Islanders loading slashed cane into punts. A steam winch hauled them to the mill when they were full.

'The land along the river was reclaimed before we took over the lease,' said Daniels. The government granted us a freehold to the land seven years ago. Now they have the deeds against a loan to pay for the new mill and the machinery.'

They reached the mill, a cavernous timber building packed with machinery.

'All the latest,' said Daniels. 'Highly efficient. We process the cane from all around here. Not viable for small holdings to mill their own.'

Hamish and Bellamy stared up at the massive machines before them, great metal pumps slipping up and down, pulling back and forth. The sound was enough to swallow them. Hamish wondered at the cost of such machinery. Either William Daniels was very wealthy or very much in debt.

'When the cane arrives at the mill, we weigh it on this Fairbanks platform weighing machine,' shouted Daniels over the noise. 'We pay ten shillings per ton for the cane from the small holdings. The cane then goes under these rollers.'

Hamish saw several rollers about three feet long.

'They're driven by a twelve-horsepower engine and fly wheel,' yelled Daniels.

'The sugar substance goes into these three, five hundred-gallon drums. The juice is clarified using lime, then it passes into the flat open pans you see there for evaporation. Next, it goes through this centrifugal system and on to the copper vacuum pans. Finally, the liquid's pumped up into the boilers.'

That's Mr Stratton. He's the sugar boiler attendant. He takes his work very seriously. It takes considerable attention and skill to properly boil the juice.'

Hamish's gaze followed the direction Daniels was pointing into the boiler house, where he saw two large boilers, but no man he could attach to the name.

'Cornish,' said Daniels. 'The engines pump the water from the river and into the nine thousand-gallon tank over there. The final boilings go to the still for making rum.'

They still hadn't caught a glimpse of Mr Stratton, the boiler attendant. Was it Mr Stratton who was Cornish? Or was Daniels referring to the origin of the boiling tank?

Another man approached them as they were leaving the mill.

'This is Eddie Hotham, our engineer,' said Daniels. 'Sergeant Bellamy and Dr Hart.'

Hotham held out a greasy hand, and both Bellamy and Hamish shook it.

'When are we expecting McDonald back?' asked Hotham.

'We're not,' said Daniels. 'I'm afraid he's met with an accident.'
Hotham took a step back and breathed out, 'What?'

'We'll talk later,' said Daniels.

Hotham looked from the sergeant to the doctor and back to his boss. Hamish detected a small change in the engineer's face. Was it a tightening of the jaw?

'Right,' he said and disappeared into the dark depths of the mill.

Daniels, Bellamy and Hamish walked on. It was a relief to be out in the fresh air again. The noise had left his head thumping to the rhythm of the machines. Apart from the engineer and the boiler attendant, the only men Hamish saw working on the plantation were South Sea Islanders. Even then, he hadn't seen the boiler attendant, only assumed he was there because Daniels said as much.

'How many people do you employ here?' he asked.

'Six Europeans and thirty-two Kanakas,' said Daniels. 'I suppose there are only five Europeans now that Jock is dead. He'll have to be replaced.' Daniels tilted his head upward and seemed to change his mind. 'Then again, we are consolidating the holdings of my daughter's new family with our own. We'll only need one manager across the whole business. It would have been beyond the capacity of McDonald to manage such a large venture.'

'What would have happened to him?' asked Hamish.

'I would've sent him to one of our smaller farms,' said Daniels.

They walked across a track and into an area of marshy scrub dotted with tall, scruffy paper bark gums. There were several slab huts about a quarter of an acre apart. Each had its own vegetable garden, growing root vegetables, taro and sweet potato. It was difficult to see how the huts were ventilated. The only opening was a narrow entrance at the front.

'This is where the Islanders would have stayed. Four of them together.'

Hamish stuck his head in the front entrance and became overwhelmed by the smell of smoke. It was dark inside, but he could make out an earthen floor with the remains of a fire in the centre. The walls were coated in soot. There were small sleeping places arranged against the walls with the same government-issue blankets he had seen at the asylum at Dunwich. Hamish tried to imagine how it would feel to sleep in one of these huts in the scorching heat of summer. The fire was necessary, he knew, even in summer to protect the inhabitants from mosquitoes. He couldn't think of a less healthy environment.

'Well, gentlemen, that's the extent of our holding. You'll have seen the other crops we grow and the livestock as you rode through our paddocks on your way from Cedarwood.

'Who are the remaining Europeans working here?' asked Bellamy.

Daniels stroked his chin as he thought about it.

'Let's see, there's Gerard; he looks after the stables and the horses. Stratton works the boiler. Simpson is handy with machines, so he assists Hotham. And then there's Ginny, my wife's maidservant. The coloureds' do the rest of the work. They clear land, dig drains, build and repair fences, look after the livestock and slash and haul cane. I don't know how I'll get the harvest in, having lost the new recruits. I suppose I'll have to go to Brisbane and recruit again. No doubt the same fellows will come forward,' he laughed, 'I wouldn't know any of them from Adam.'

Tall trees with skin peeling from the limbs in shabby sheets towered over them as they walked toward the house. Kookaburras screeched in the tops of the trees, and a maniacal laughter pierced the growing tension in Hamish's head.

'The women have been preparing lunch for you,' said Daniels. 'I hope you'll join us.'

'Delighted,' said Bellamy.

An idea occurred to Hamish, and he spoke before he'd thought the idea through.

'Did your wife say you are without a cook?' he asked.

'Yes. Unfortunately, our cook left us without notice last week. My wife is distraught about it.'

'I know a cook,' said Hamish. 'He was a ship's cook for most of his life, then he cooked at Dunwich for years. I would strongly recommend him.'

Bellamy stared at Hamish as though he had gone mad.

William Daniels stopped walking.

'Do you?' he said. 'My wife is extremely anxious about the situation. With Alice now married, she has little help. I fear she's run ragged.'

'I'll speak with my man,' said Hamish. 'Wesley Wallace is his name.'

'Have you lost your mind?' whispered Bellamy. 'Who will cook for you if you send Wallace here?'

Hamish turned his back and pretended to examine movement high in a towering blue gum. Bellamy followed his lead while Daniels continued walking.

'I may well regret it,' Hamish whispered to the sky, 'but Wallace could find out who tried to poison McDonald.'

Bellamy spoke into the air as well. 'It's a genius idea, I have to admit. But what if Wallace doesn't want to come?'

'He'll come. I'm going to ask him as soon as we return.'

Daniels stopped and looked back to find Hamish and the sergeant staring into a tree.

'What is it?' he called.

'Not sure,' said Hamish, 'I thought I saw a koala.'

CHAPTER SEVEN

The Brisbane Courier Saturday 24 October 1885.

I had expected to see the industry in a state of strangulation, the mills lying idle, and cane fields everywhere being converted into cornfields. What I did see, in the Beenleigh-Logan district was, almost every mill busily at work, the crops good, except where the frosts were severe, and a good quality and large quantity of sugar being produced. One new mill has been opened this season; it is fitted with modern machinery, and at three mills, there have been lately erected vacuum pans which are now working successfully. The mill proprietors, although grumbling at the low prices now ruling for their product, have no intention of ceasing crushing operations; indeed, they even say they do not know how they can get through their work before the wet season commences. The cane growers who are co-proprietors of various mill companies are fairly satisfied and do not talk of ceasing cane-growing though they hope for better times, but the cane-growing farmers who have no mill nor any interest in mills are complaining loudly and earnestly. It is on this class the pinch is being put. The reason is that as little as 6 shillings per ton is being paid for cane, cut, carted and delivered to the mill. When it is remembered that 10 shillings per ton standing in the field was the previous price offered to growers, it is no wonder they are dissatisfied and talk of rooting out the cane. One reason for the excessively low prices is the mill owners have so much of their own cane they don't really want to buy. In the cane fields of the small farmer who has to sell his cane at the lowest figure, I saw no kanakas, but I did see women and boys and girls. It is evident that only by the employment of family labour, for which no cash is paid, a living can be made by cane growing.

AMISH

They entered Cloverton House to the welcome smell of roasting chicken. Bellamy was still in shock that Hamish had given away his manservant.

They took their seats, and Charlotte served a delicious meal of chicken and roast vegetables. The meal was put together from the produce of the Cloverton garden.

'Dr Hart has recommended an experienced cook, my dear,' said Daniels.

Charlotte's face lit up. 'Oh, Dr Hart, that is wonderful. I am most obliged to you. I didn't know how I would cope. When can this person start work?'

'Dr Hart has yet to speak with him, dear. Don't be too eager. He may not want the position,' cautioned Daniels.

Charlotte looked at Hamish with large eyes.

'Oh, Doctor,' she said. 'Do you think it is so? Do you think there is a chance he will turn the position down?'

'I am certain he won't,' replied Hamish. 'He'll be delighted.' A warm glow was triggered at being able to please Charlotte, even though he had his own motives for placing Wallace at Cloverton.

Bellamy stopped chewing to stare at him again. Hamish was aware Bellamy was staring, but he chose to ignore him.

'Now, if I could only replace Ginny,' said Charlotte. 'She is hopelessly unreliable. If it is not one aunt ill and requiring her attention, it is another. Almost every week, there is something.'

'Could you not hire one of the coloured women in the house?' asked Bellamy. 'Don't some of the labourers have their women with them?'

'Oh yes, Sergeant. They bring their wives sometimes. But we're no longer able to employ them indoors under the new laws. I'm surprised you're not aware of the changes to the legislation. We may no longer employ Pacific Islanders in the working of machinery or in domestic duties.'

'I'm afraid I pay little heed to the changes in immigration laws. There are government inspectors to track compliance in that regard. I struggle to have enough time to police the laws against theft and violence in the colony at present.'

Hamish poured more gravy on his chicken. 'The meal is superb,' he said to Charlotte. 'You have done an excellent job of it in the absence of a cook.'

Charlotte blushed. 'Thank you for saying so,' she said. 'Alice helped. She is a fine cook. Although she is much more fortunate than I, in that the cook at Tennyson House has been there for two decades and has no designs on another life elsewhere.'

'Our compliments to you too, Mrs Tennyson,' said Bellamy.

Alice rolled her eyes. 'Please don't compliment me on preparing a meal,' she said. 'I willingly do what is needed, and if a family needs to eat, I will cook. But I take no pride in it.'

Charlotte shifted uncomfortably in her chair. Alice's ungracious response may have embarrassed her, or it might have been that she needed to adjust her bustle. Either way, Hamish found it amusing and had to restrain a laugh.

'How are the labourers paid?' asked Bellamy.

Everyone at the table stopped eating to look at him.

'Sorry to change the subject,' he said. 'But I'm curious. They never seem to have much cash when they're in town.'

Daniels put his knife and fork down and lent back in his chair. He watched Hamish and Bellamy closely before answering.

'The sugar plantations pay the South Sea Islanders in the presence of the Polynesian Protector of the district,' he said. 'That way, there are no complaints about the amounts that are handed over, and it gives the men a chance to pass their earnings to the Protector for safekeeping.'

'What happens if they die before they collect their earnings?'

'The money is released to the curator of estates,' said Daniels. 'Often it is not known how or when an Islander has died, then the funds go to what is called the Missing Kanakas Fund. That way, if the fellow turns up, he can claim it.'

'What if he doesn't turn up?' Hamish pushed the point.

'I can only assume the government has a great deal of money accumulated in that fund.'

Hamish held his fork a few inches from his mouth while he pondered the implications of the government holding the Kanakas wages. He tried to imagine the enormous sum that would have accumulated, given the high death rates of the Pacific

Island labourers.

'I have the impression from the papers the coloured labour system is on its way out,' said Bellamy, interrupting Hamish's calculations.

'I hope not,' said Daniels. 'I attended a meeting at the beginning of the year in Brisbane. The people were vocal about the problem of the Islanders hanging about in town, causing trouble at the end of their contracts. The majority at the meeting held the view the Kanakas should be compelled by law to return to their islands at the expiration of their time in service. It was also put forward that plantation owners should be made to keep their Kanakas on the plantations after seven o-clock in the evenings. The public are anxious about the behaviour of the Kanakas in town after dark. They're of the opinion the police have failed in their duty to control them.' Daniels avoided looking at Bellamy as he spoke.

'Yes, I am aware of the growing anxiety,' said Bellamy. 'Although the incidents you refer to have been greatly exaggerated by the newspapers. People are far more excited by the risk to their health and safety than is warranted.'

'Isn't there some protest from the unemployed that the Kanakas are taking jobs that white men could have?' asked Hamish.

'Yes,' said Daniels. 'There has been a debate about the need for coloured labour when white men are seeking work. This fellow, Samuel Griffiths, who pushed the Immigration Bill through Parliament, would have an end to the import of Kanakas if he could. As it stands, the Bill provides for indentured white labour, as opposed to the coloured trade. They're still bringing men from overseas.'

'How does that suit you?' asked Bellamy.

'From a planter's point of view, it might work. The European labour would have to be suited to the work. And they'd have to be content to work at a rate lower than the wages being paid to other white men. They would also need to recognise the legality of their contracts when they arrive. Planters have told me the new European arrivals can't stand the heavy fieldwork in the heat. They don't prove fit enough to work out engagements of longer than a few months. And as soon as the work is difficult, they enter into combinations against their employers, making demands.

They refuse to work unless their demands are satisfied. It is not yet clear contracts made in a European country can be enforced here if indented labourers refuse to acknowledge their legality.'

'I can see the difficulty,' said Bellamy.

Warming to his topic, Daniels added, 'the newspapers are saying Queensland is to be overrun by hordes of low-class whites, or whitey-browns, from Italy and Germany, to replace the Polynesians. But as I said, I can't see how it can work to the planter's advantage.'

'Whitey-browns?' The levels of racism at play sent Hamish's mind reeling. He was about to protest when Alice cut in.

Appearing relieved the conversation had moved forward from meal preparation, she said, 'There is always the argument there is no work on a sugar plantation that a white man could not do, and do willingly. However, white men will resent the level of payment on offer. There is little enough profit in sugar as it is.'

'Low-class Whites?' enquired Hamish, unable to keep the sarcasm from his voice.

'Would you go out of business without the coloured labour?' Bellamy asked.

Daniels placed his knife and fork neatly across his plate. He breathed deeply and nodded his head.

'I fear so, Sergeant,' he said. 'Sugar growing will not pay at fifteen pounds per ton while Kanakas cost twenty-eight pound per head to import. This will be the cost when they enforce the new regulations.'

'Are any of the plantations using European labour?' asked Bellamy.

'A few plantations are experimenting,' said Daniels. 'There is one in this region, at which labour is contracted to Europeans at half a crown per ton for cutting and topping. At that rate of pay, I hear the men can earn as much as three pounds a week.'

'That's excellent wages,' said Hamish, surprised. He thought it an admirable solution.

'Indeed, however, comparing this price with the price paid for cane, we face the fact that half a crown a ton is exactly one half the cane's value. If this price is to be paid for the simple act of cutting it, the owner is left with the responsibility for ploughing, planting, hoeing and cultivating, all for half a crown. On the face of things, it is obvious cane growing cannot continue under such circumstances.'

Hamish thought about the slab huts coated in soot and wondered how many European men would tolerate the conditions. He also couldn't help wondering, if sugar wasn't profitable, why were so many farms growing it?

'I've heard the government is offering between forty and fifty pound per annum and free passage to Queensland for Germans who wish to come here and work the plantations,' said Bellamy.

Alice scoffed. 'Any man under forty years can obtain a passage to Queensland for one pound and buy their own land in the colony without being tied to any previously arranged contract. I doubt any man would swallow that bait.'

'Still, the regulations imposed by the Government on the labour trade have put significant pressure on the sugar industry. I fear you may be right, Sergeant,' said Daniels. 'The colour labour market may indeed be on its last legs. Several Captains of labour ships have been prosecuted. One vessel, the Forest King, was captured by a man-of-war vessel and brought here to Brisbane. Other vessels are returning without recruits. If no more Polynesians are to be had, I fear to think what will become of the sugar industry.'

Charlotte had been quiet throughout lunch. It seemed to Hamish she was satisfied knowing the group were enjoying the meal. She didn't seem interested in the conversation. Consequently, when she spoke, it came as a surprise.

'My word, gentlemen,' she said in a mildly scolding tone. 'This talk of business is depressing at the dinner table. We will all have indigestion, I'm certain of it.' She turned to her daughter, 'Alice will you help me clear the table? We'll have to make do without Ginny this afternoon.' Charlotte shifted her attention to her husband. 'Take the guests to the sitting room William, if you insist on discussing business, you can continue your conversation there.'

Hamish watched her elegant back as she glided from the room.

CHAPTER EIGHT

Bathurst Free Press Tuesday 17 March 1885.

On Thursday morning, a member of the family and household of Mr Riley had a narrow escape from being fatally poisoned. Mr Riley, two daughters, Mr Walsh and two servant girls ate some porridge for breakfast, the other members of the family not doing so. Immediately afterwards, those who had eaten the porridge were seized with vomiting and showed other symptoms of arsenic poisoning. The family of Constable Cobane, who had purchased oatmeal from the same store as Mrs Riley, were similarly affected the previous day. It seems that at the store, poison to get rid of mice had been put into some oatmeal six weeks previously, and though it was supposed to have been afterwards thrown away, there was reason to suspect that some had inadvertently been returned to the oatmeal bin.

*H*AMISH

The men did as they were instructed and moved to the sitting room, where Sergeant Bellamy changed the topic of conversation entirely. 'We'll need to conduct formal interviews this afternoon,' he said to Daniels. 'Could you arrange times for us to interview Simpson, Stratton, Gerard and Hotham? We'll also need to carry out formal interviews with your wife and daughter. Is there somewhere private we can use?'

'Yes,' said Daniels. 'You can use the library. Daniels started to walk away. 'Also, we'll need to interview you again, Mr Daniels.'

Daniels' face was set, unreadable. He bowed and left to carry out the sergeant's requests. Alice appeared a moment later to lead them to the library, where she left them without saying a word.

'What do you think?' asked Bellamy when they were alone.

'We need to find out more about the relationships between these people at Cloverton, as you said,' replied Hamish. 'Someone wanted to be rid of McDonald.'

'We have Daniels and his wife Charlotte, who own the plantation, though I believe it is under lease to the government to pay for the machinery,' says Bellamy.

'Yes,' agrees Hamish, holding back the hair from his eyes. 'They have one daughter, Alice, who has married into the Tennyson family. According to Vincent at Cedarwood, this is the first step toward a merger of the two plantations.'

'Yes,' said Bellamy, 'and Daniels referred to the merger himself.'

'Then there is a scattering of employees, all managed by Jock McDonald until his demise. We need to know how they felt about him as their manager,' said Hamish.

'I'm going to share the information about the poisoning,' Bellamy said. 'I want you to watch them as I do.'

The first person to appear at the library was the stableman, Gerard. Bellamy asked him his full name and wrote it down carefully in his notebook. 'Tell us about your work here,' he said.

'I look after the stable and the horses, nuthin' else to tell,' said the man, his face barely visible behind a substantial shaggy moustache and beard.

'What was your relationship with Jock McDonald?' said Bellamy.

'He was me boss.'

'Was he a good boss, would you say?'

Gerard hesitated. 'He was a hard boss, but he got the job done for sure.'

'Was he hard on you?'

'He were hard on everyone.'

Gerard stared hard at Hamish and Bellamy, his tiny eyes looking out over the tumultuous facial hair. He seemed unsure what they wanted from him.

'In what way?' asked Hamish.

'He made yer work hard, like. There were no sitting around. He wanted things done quick, and he wanted 'em done right. If yer was caught sitting around, you'd feel the lash of his tongue... or worse.'

'What do you mean by worse?' said Hamish, his eyebrows raised.

Gerard opened his mouth to speak and closed it. He seemed to rethink his answer before starting again.

'There is some that got a floggin' from his horse whip,' he said.

'Did you ever receive a flogging from Mr McDonald?' asked Bellamy.

'No. I ain't ever been caught sittin' on the job.'

'Who then?' Bellamy demanded.

Gerard looked at his hands.

'The coloureds mostly. He was quick to take the whip to them if they wasn't meeting his standards.'

Bellamy changed tack. 'In the last few days, before he went to Brisbane, did you see much of McDonald?'

Gerard stopped to think about it. 'Can't say as I did,' he replied. 'I saw him once briefly. He said not to bother getting the horses ready for the boss's trip. Mr Daniels had decided they would take the coach.'

'Did Mr McDonald seem well the last time you saw him?' cut in Hamish.

'What d'yer mean, well?'

'Did he seem, himself? Or did he seem unwell?'

Gerard slumped in the chair and ran his fingers across the bottom of his whickers.

'He looked a bit piqued if yer askin' me to comment. Grey, like,' he said.

Bellamy nodded toward Hamish, prompting him to ask further questions.

'Did you have cause to see Mr McDonald every day?' Hamish went on.

'No. I would see or speak to him no more 'an twice a week. I might see him around, in the distance, like. But not close.'

'Did anyone have any reason to wish Mr McDonald harm?'

Gerard suddenly became twitchy. He lent forward in the chair and placed a gnarled hand on the desk.

'What's this about then?' he said. 'The boss said he was killed in a bar fight in Brisbane. What you asking questions of us for?'

Bellamy didn't respond immediately. He and Hamish watched Gerard closely.

'Jock McDonald did die in a bar fight,' Bellamy said. 'But it wasn't the fight that killed him. He was being poisoned.'

The blood drained from Gerard's face. He squeezed his hat tightly and went mute, his little eyes wide and face pale behind the hair.

'Is there anything you can tell us about anyone who might wish Mr McDonald harm?' repeated the Sergeant.

Gerard continued to stare at him.

'This is a murder enquiry,' cautioned Bellamy. 'If you have any relevant information, you must tell us.' Gerard's lips remained sealed as though he had lost the power of speech.

'Thank you then,' Bellamy said. 'You can return to work.'

As Gerard left the room, Simpson entered. He appeared a more educated man than Gerard. He wore a working man's shirt and vest, but he was tidy and cleanly shaved. Bellamy wrote down his name and began with the same questions. Simpson told him he didn't have much to do with McDonald because he answered to Hotham. He said he found Hotham to be a fair man to work with, but he did not like McDonald at all.

'Why is that?' asked Sergeant Bellamy.

'He was an arrogant man,' said Simpson. 'He was a bully. He liked wielding power over others.'

'How did he treat the Kanakas?' asked Bellamy.

'Let me put it this way, no white man would tolerate the treatment he handed them. I'm not surprised he died in a fight with one of them.' Simpson lent back in the chair and crossed his legs.

'The problem is,' said Bellamy, 'McDonald did not die from injuries sustained in the fight. He was poisoned.'

Simpson looked confused. 'He was poisoned at the Pub?' he said.

'No. He was being poisoned daily. The toxin was building up slowly in his body. The doctor believes he would not have lived another 24 hours.'

Simpson looked at Hamish. 'Could he have been exposed to the poison accidentally?' he asked.

'No,' replied Hamish. The amount in his system is not consistent with incidental contact. I believe someone was deliberately poisoning him.'

'Do you know anyone who would want to harm Mr McDonald?' asked Bellamy.

Simpson thought for a moment. 'I don't know of anyone who liked him. But I don't know of anyone who would bother poisoning him. The men would have happily punched him in the face, but poison?' He looked both Bellamy and Hamish in the eye. The confusion looked genuine to Hamish.

'How did he get along with Hotham?' asked Bellamy.

'They had to work together. But they didn't like one another. I believe McDonald felt threatened by Hotham. Eddie is smart. What he doesn't know about machines isn't worth knowing. They had a run-in once because McDonald knocked one of the Kanakas off his horse with a whip. He was about to get stuck into him on the ground. Mr Hotham jumped in and took the whip away from him. McDonald confronted him but backed off. He stalked away, swearing that Mr Hotham would keep.'

Hamish and Bellamy exchanged glances, then Bellamy told Simpson he could go. He opened the door for him and saw that Eddie Hotham was waiting on the other side, ready to come in. Bellamy gestured for Hotham to enter and sit.

Eddie Hotham was a slight man, handsome in his way, but he looked more like a poet than a working man. Long, dark curls framed his face, and he had unnaturally long eyelashes for a man. He appeared flushed and nervous when he entered the library.

'Gerard says the manager was poisoned,' he said as he placed himself at the edge of the seat.

'Yes,' said Bellamy, a little annoyed that word had already got around, and he could not measure the reaction of his suspects as he revealed the news to them.

'Did you have contact with Mr Bellamy every day?' he asked.

'He checked in every day to make sure production was going well.'

'Did you get along with Mr McDonald?'

'I got along with him to the extent that we could work together. But I couldn't stand him personally. He was full of his own importance.'

'Is it true you had an altercation with him recently?'

Yes, it's true.' Hotham said, indicating he offered no apology.

'He enjoyed humiliating people. He was a cruel man. I stepped in to prevent an injustice when I saw the need.'

'That would have humiliated Mr McDonald if he was as proud as you suggest.'

'I'm sure it did,' said Hotham. 'I hope it did him some good. Although it hardly seems relevant now.'

Hotham took a pipe from his coat pocket, stood and walked across to the fire- place. There were embers simmering there, despite the warmth of the day. He plucked a wick from the vase on the mantle, lit it and sucked in deeply. Then he returned to his seat and settled himself before his interrogators.

'Indeed,' said the Sergeant, staring pointedly at Eddie Hotham.

Hamish had trouble reconciling the neatly dressed, mannered gentleman before him with the vision of a man taking a whip from Jock McDonald and running him off with it.

Hotham calmly puffed smoke circles from his pipe while Hamish and Bellamy continued to stare at him.

'I had no need to poison him,' Hotham said at last. 'Daniels needs me far more than he needed McDonald. If it came down to a choice between us, it would have been McDonald dismissed. He did work hard, I'll give him his due, but he didn't know anything about the new agricultural methods we're employing here. He was out of his depth and rapidly becoming obsolete. He knew it. That's why he was so stroppy.'

Hamish thought Hotham was probably right. Jocko McDonald may well have been full of bluster because he knew he was inadequate in the context of the modernisation at Cloverton.

'Did he seem ill in the days prior to the Brisbane trip?' asked Hamish.

'He did. He had to interrupt a discussion about the boiler maintenance to vomit. I told him to see a doctor.'

'Where does everyone eat?' asked Hamish.

Both Bellamy and Hotham looked surprised by the question.

'In the evenings, we eat in the mess over there.' He pointed through the window to a structure with a roof, no walls and a long wooden table in the middle of a lawned area beyond the garden. The coloured labour look after themselves. But we have a meal supplied by the kitchen. I believe poor Mrs Daniels is preparing it by herself lately.'

'Everyone eats the same meal?'

'Yes. It usually comes out in large trays, and we serve ourselves. The same with the tea. We scoop tea leaves from a bulk tin and pour boiled water from the kettle. We stop for tea and a bite at lunchtime. They leave bread and cheese on the table in the mess. We all break at different times, so we don't eat together at lunch.'

Hamish couldn't see any obvious opportunity for someone to poison one individual when food and beverages were served communally.

'Is there any arsenic trioxide kept at the plantation?' asked Hamish.

'Yes. It is used for exterminating pests. I can show you where it is if you like. I use it myself in the mill. The place is steamy, moist, smells of molasses, perfect place for rats.'

'We'll take you up on the offer later,' said Bellamy, 'thank you.'

Stratton came in next. He was small and bald and smelled of molasses. He looked every bit of seventy years of age, reminding Hamish of some of the inmates he met at the asylum during his time at Dunwich. He looked like a man who would disappear in the shadows, and Hamish understood now why he had not seen him when Daniels pointed him out in the boiler shed.

'Did you know Jock McDonald well?' asked the Sergeant.

Stratton fidgeted with his hands and appeared to be trying to work out the question.

'Jock McDonald,' the sergeant repeated. 'The Manager here at Cloverton. Did you get along with him?'

'The boss?' said Stratton.

'Yes, the boss. Did you spend much time with him?'

'He was just the boss,' said Stratton. His eyes had a way of darting about when he spoke. Hamish couldn't work out whether he was looking at Bellamy or himself.

Bellamy persisted. 'So, you had naught to do with him beyond the fact that he was your supervisor?'

Stratton's lips quivered as he seemed to weigh up possible responses. Hamish thought he was not considering stories to tell, so much as trying to figure out what he was being asked and what answer would be taken as acceptable.

'No,' he said.

Bellamy sighed and leaned back in his chair. 'Go on, then,' he said. 'That'll do. Get back to your work.'

Stratton stood up and ran from the room, bumping into Alice in his relief to be out of the library.

Daniels shook his head and took a deep breath in readiness for the next interview.

Alice brushed down her skirt after bumping into Stratton and sat opposite Sergeant Bellamy with her back straight and her head held high.

'We're sorry to trouble you,' began Bellamy gently.

'Good Lord,' burst out Alice. 'I am with child. I'm not ill. Please don't trouble yourself you have to be careful around me for fear I should break. I assure you I am neither fragile nor faint of heart.'

'I can see you are neither,' said Bellamy. 'Could you tell us about your relationship with Jock McDonald?'

'I had no relationship with that man at all.'

'You had no occasion to speak with him?'

'None. I avoided him at all costs. He was insufferable. I told father more than once to get rid of him. But he rarely listens to me in affairs of business. If I had been a son, it would have been different. As I am a woman, I must stand idle while men make mistakes that define my future.'

Hamish smiled. Bellamy was struggling to gain the upper hand in this interview, and he didn't feel inclined to assist him.

'Mrs Tennyson,' Bellamy began again, 'Can I conclude that while you had very little to do with Mr McDonald directly, you disliked him?'

'That is correct.'

'May I ask specifically what caused this dislike?'

'There are many causes. He was a stupid man and a cruel one. While I may have forgiven the former, I cannot forgive the latter.' She was picking at her lace cuffs.

'Do you know of anyone who would profit from Jock McDonald's death?'

Alice Tennyson looked up from her cuff to meet the Sergeant's eye. 'I do not,' she said.

Bellamy released her, and she strode from the room with

complete confidence.

'She has exhausted me,' he said to Hamish.

'If she's telling the truth about having very little to do with McDonald, she could not have been systematically poisoning him.'

'True. But I wouldn't put anything past that woman.'

Hamish smiled. He thought Alice Tennyson's bark was probably worse than her bite.

Charlotte Daniels came into the library as her daughter left.

After the initial acknowledgements, Bellamy got straight to the point.

'Could you describe your relationship with Mr McDonald?' he said.

Charlotte sat with her hands in her lap. Her eyes were wide and attentive. She seemed childlike to Hamish.

'Mr McDonald was an employee of my husband,' she said. 'My husband had daily contact with him and relied on him a great deal. I myself spoke to him only occasionally and then only to greet him in passing.'

'What sort of man did you think him?' asked Bellamy.

'I thought him a valuable asset to my husband. He was a hard worker, according to William.'

'Do you know of anyone who would want to harm him?'

Charlotte looked up from beneath long lashes. 'I'm sure I do not,' she said.

Hamish felt a twinge as he blushed. Recovering himself quickly, he said, 'When you take the evening meal out to the mess, Mrs Daniels, do the men serve themselves from trays?'

'That's right.'

'Could anyone put a chemical into the food aiming to poison any one person?'

'I don't see how,' said Mrs Daniels.

'Do the men drink alcohol together? In the evenings perhaps?'

'My husband frequently had a drink after dinner with Mr McDonald. They would discuss the business, I imagine. I never joined them. As I told the Sergeant, my husband relied heavily on his manager. He had no reason to wish him harm. Indeed, he has no idea what he will do without him.'

'Alice seemed to think he was of limited value to the plantation,' suggested Hamish.

'My daughter has strong opinions.'

'Your husband does not agree with her view?'

'He does not.'

'We have heard Mr McDonald was hard on the labourers,' prompted Bellamy.

'He may have been. My husband expected him to ensure the work was done.'

'Have you been advised of how Mr McDonald died?' asked Bellamy.

'He was poisoned,' she said flatly.

'And you have no idea who might have wanted to harm him?'

'No.'

Bellamy thanked her and opened the door for her to pass. As she went, she managed to brush past Hamish leaving a giddying scent of lavender in the air around him.

When Bellamy and Hamish were alone again, he said, 'Someone is lying.'

'We know none of the workers liked Jock McDonald, black or white presumably. But I tend to agree if any of them wanted to kill him, they wouldn't have poisoned him slowly,' began Hamish. 'We know Alice hated him. It seems to me her feelings are unnecessarily strong. She didn't have to work with him. Why would she develop such a strong emotion against him?'

'I agree there is more to it,' said Bellamy.

'The answer lies in the relationships between these people,' said Hamish. 'That's why I offered up Wallace as a cook. These people are not going to tell us anything useful. We need someone here to gain their trust, observe them.'

'You mean spy on them?' said Bellamy.

'Exactly that,' said Hamish.

'I think you're right, Hart. Questioning Daniels again at this point is not going to gain us anything.'

When William Daniels returned to the library, the sergeant stood up.

'Can you show us where the arsenic trioxide is kept?' he said.

Daniels led them to a shed near the mill and the boiler house. Inside there was a wooden barrel with a metal lid. Hamish removed the lid and saw the white powder. Anyone on the plantation could easily access it.

The three men left the mill silently and walked back to the house. Hamish assumed the other two were deep in their own thoughts. He was also going over in his mind the information they had learned that afternoon. All he could gather at this point was that no one at Cloverton liked Jock McDonald, except for Daniels, who needed him to work. In theory, anyone could have been poisoning him, although Hamish was unsure how it was being done.

'We should be heading back at once if we are to reach Brisbane before dark,' said Bellamy, startling Hamish from his thoughts. 'Thank you for your co-operation,' he said to Daniels.

Hamish wasn't sure why the sergeant had decided not to interview Daniels. He supposed he didn't expect Daniels to tell them anything they didn't already know. It was difficult to see why Daniels would want to kill off a valued worker.

'I will send Wallace to you tomorrow,' Hamish said. 'I'm sure he'll take the position. He can work for you for a few days as a trial. I'll return to you in three days and see if you are satisfied.'

'That is uncommonly kind of you,' said Daniels.

CHAPTER NINE

Williamstown Chronicle Saturday 23 August 1884.

As a vent for the surplus energy of ladies who are engaged at present agitating for women's suffrage, we would suggest that a large field of labour has been opened up for them by the operations in the old country of some very sensible women, who are endeavouring to bring about a reform in the prevailing system of women's dress. The necessity for reform is even more urgent in this country than in the United Kingdom, as there can be no doubt that modifications of the existing system, to suit the peculiarities of the Australian climate, would tend largely to the comfort and health of our fair colonists. Women of the dress reform movement in England advocate the adoption of Turkish trousers and a short skirt in place of the absurd jumble of inconvenient and incommodious garments with which women are at present hampered, and a large number of English women of all ranks of life are prepared to support the reformers by putting their ideas into practice.

Naturally enough, however, the great majority of women, though admitting the disadvantages of their present attire and greatly desiring the physical freedom afforded in such costumes as the reformers suggest, are diffident about making any great and noticeable changes in their mode of dress, as their modesty recoils from the idea of presenting themselves in a costume which would excite special attention, and perhaps subject them to the rude comments of the street lout.

HAMISH

The ride back to Brisbane was sombre. The sun was low over the hills to their left and cast a yellow glow across the land. The bush had lost its definition, it was no longer an army of marching trees but more a sleeping animal stretched comfortably along the roadside. It was dark by the time Hamish and the sergeant passed the new railway station house in Stanley Street.

The sergeant pulled up his horse, and Hamish halted alongside him.

'This is where I leave you,' said Bellamy. 'My home is down the rise there, in Roma Street.'

Hamish leant forward and placed his hand on his horse's neck. He felt the tension there. 'Not much further,' he said. 'It looks like we ride on alone.' He smiled farewell to Bellamy and urged his ride gently forward. Every muscle in his body ached, and he looked forward to falling into his bed. The remainder of the journey was marked by the silence of Brisbane's streets. Only the odd shadow of a man stumbling from the yellow light of the tavern's egress broke the monotony.

Dismounting to the side of his home, at last, Hamish was intent on making to his bed immediately to welcome sleep. But when Wallace greeted him at the door and announced that dinner was being kept warm for him, and he had only now removed fresh rolls from the oven, Hamish was suddenly more hungry than tired. Red bounded about his feet as he hung his coat and hat. He fished a piece of dried liver from the pocket of one of Wallace's coats hanging on the next hook. 'Here you go, mate. Lucky, I know where the boss keeps the goodies.' Red stood on his hind legs to accept the treat. His small body trembling with excitement.

Hamish's life had been pleasant since Wallace returned with him from Stradbroke. He'd never had a manservant before. On political grounds, he didn't approve of domestic labour. He considered himself well and truly able to dress and feed himself and did not need another adult to assist him. He didn't like the power imbalance embedded in the relationship, assuming one person to be inherently better than the other. The notion that a class of humans could be born to serve was abhorrent to him. But his relationship with Wallace was a more personal one. Wallace was a friend, a confidant. And the fact that he could cook was a bonus.

Hamish drew renewed energy from the anticipation of a

delectable meal, confidant he needed to deal with his hunger before he could settle to sleep.

He relayed the details of his day to Wallace while he served dinner, after which, as was their usual practice, Wallace sat at the table to eat with Hamish.

'It's a beautiful place,' Hamish said in summing up. 'The garden is one of the most beautiful I've seen. A plentiful kitchen garden as well, full of vegetables and herbs. A cook's paradise, really.'

Wallace scooped a spoonful of soup into his mouth. He kept one eye on Hamish as he dipped his spoon in for another.

'Right on the river,' Hamish went on. 'The fishing would be superb, I would wager.'

Wallace continued with his meal, taking a roll and breaking it into his soup. 'Why do I feel like you're trying to sell me a plot at Cloverton?' he asked.

'The family members are quite distant toward one another,' Hamish said as if it were an after-thought, ignoring Wallace's question.

'There's a coldness between them. But I can't see any of them poisoning Jock McDonald. Why would they? No one seems to have liked him particularly, but what would the family have to gain by getting rid of him? The same is true for the employees as far as I can see.'

Wallace listened to Hamish's account of each family member and each European employee at Cloverton. 'You don't think one of the coloured labourers could have killed him?' he asked.

'I've no doubt they thought about it, but surely they would not poison him slowly if they decided to act. They would act on the spur of the moment in response to some humiliation or other. Anyway, I don't think they would have access to the means of poisoning a man slowly without his suspecting it.'

'Then there is a need for deeper insight into the relationships between the white employees and the family,' Wallace said. 'People rarely divulge their deepest secrets in a police interview.'

'I agree,' said Hamish. He hesitated. 'I'm afraid I've volunteered your services to Cloverton as Cook, temporarily,' he said, spooning fruity pudding into his mouth and holding his breath.

Wallace smiled behind his moustache. 'I thought you may have,' he said.

'Grand idea,' he added after a moment, 'I can listen to the talk behind the scenes. It's the servants and the workers who will know what's going on.'

Hamish released the breath and swallowed his pudding.

'Are you sure you don't mind?' he asked sheepishly.

Hamish was aware of the irony in the question, given he had already told William and Charlotte Daniels that Wallace would come.

Wallace assured Hamish he was happy to accept the challenge. 'As much as I enjoy this pampered life,' he said, 'I'm afraid I might die from boredom.'

'I thought as much,' said Hamish.

'I am convinced the solution to this murder lies in the relationships within the household at Cloverton,' Hamish said. 'Daniels seems a decent man on the surface, but his relationships with both his wife and his daughter appear strained to me. And I'm sure there is tension between mother and daughter. There's something that keeps them at a distance from one another.'

'They'll close ranks against an outsider,' commented Wallace. 'But servants hear everything that goes on in the house.'

The red terrier lifted its front paws onto Wallace's lap. Its lower half again trembling with anticipation of a tasty morsel from the table.

'A week or so on the plantation,' Wallace said to his wiry terrier, 'will do us good.' He popped a scrap of fat from his plate into the dog's mouth, and the terrier swallowed it in one gulp.

'Are you taking Red?' said Hamish.

'Of course, I am. He'll enjoy putting the toffs in their place,' said Wallace.

Red earned his name through his politics. Wallace assured everyone the dog was a committed socialist.

'Charlotte Daniels, the mother, is a beautiful woman,' said Hamish.

Wallace stopped patting his dog to give Hamish his full attention.

'O aye,' he said.

'She has come from money,' said Hamish. 'She dresses like a fashion plate. Far too splendid for Logan. I can't help feeling she's lost in a place like that and married to a down-to-Earth farmer like Daniels.'

'Better suited to a doctor's wife?' asked Wallace.

Hamish blushed. 'Don't be absurd. I'm only trying to give you some background. I'm saying she is out of place, that's all.'

'Don't worry,' Wallace said with a chuckle, 'There's no shame in admiring a woman for her beauty. I look forward to meeting Charlotte Daniels.'

'Her daughter Alice has a formidable character,' said Hamish. 'It's odd. She bears a strong resemblance to her mother, but she is more angular, and she has a pointy personality.'

'I'm anticipating an interesting stay with this family,' said Wallace.

Wallace left for Cloverton early the following morning.

Hamish sat in his favourite chair, enjoying the sunlight filtering through the window. His house was still new to him, and he was full of wonder at having his own home and practice. This day had a sense of returned normalcy to it, with patient appointments scheduled throughout the morning. As he gazed out of the window, he felt himself looking forward to a time when there would be nothing more to worry him than his well-to-do Brisbane society clients. He wondered why he'd let himself become involved in another mystery so soon after returning from Dunwich and setting up his practice. As he stared through the window, focusing on nothing, his mind registered the fleeting image of navy and white stripes billowing past. He checked himself and took a closer look. The bundle of stripes turned in a circle in front of his house and steered toward his front door. 'What the devil?' He said out loud. He jumped up and ran to the door to see what was going on.

'Rita!'

Rita had dismounted the contraption she was riding and was leaning it against the outer wall of his house. She untied a parcel in the shape of a tennis racquet.

'I purchased a bicycle,' she cried in delight, her straw boater sitting askew on her head. She straightened it and smoothed down the billowing navy and white striped skirt. A long jacket in the same stripe flowed onto the skirt, forming an overlay pulled up on both sides and tucked into a purple velvet belt at her waist.

The skirt was short, only slightly touching the instep of her white leather boots.

'I can see that,' said Hamish stepping aside to let her in. 'Is this an outfit designed for bicycle riding?'

'No, it's for tennis,' she said. 'I have also taken up lawn tennis.' She handed him the racquet shaped parcel.

'A surprising and sudden interest in sports has overcome you,' said Hamish.

Rita swept past him and into the kitchen. 'Since you sent Wallace away, I suppose I have to make my own tea.'

'How do you know Wallace is away?' he asked, following her. Hamish watched while she lifted the boiling kettle and poured water into the teapot. She set up a tray with cups and saucers. 'I ran into him,' she said, 'rather he ran into me, or his cab did. I was cycling round the bend, and the cab almost tipped me into the street. They stopped to check I was not injured. He said you were sending him to Cloverton.'

Still carrying the tennis racquet, Hamish led the way upstairs to the sitting room.

Rita set the tray on the occasional table and perched herself on the settee, grinning. Hamish placed the racquet on the sideboard and joined her.

'What are you up to?' he said.

'I'm not up to anything,' she responded, feigning offence.

'You look far too pleased with yourself. What is this sudden expression of athleticism about?'

'Collette,' said Rita throwing her slender arms in the air.

'Oh dear,' said Hamish. 'Who is Collette?'

'Collette has been employed at Lady Bowen. You'll love her, Hamish. She's intelligent and cheerful. She's studying to work in illnesses of the mind. She's a member of the Society for Psychical Research in London.'

'A spiritualist, then.'

'No, Hamish! She's a scientist. The Society uses scientific methods to illuminate phenomena we don't yet understand.'

'I see. 'Presumably, such phenomena include the iron horse.'

'Don't be silly. Bicycles are well understood. It's a simple and efficient way of getting about. I'm thinking of joining the Brisbane

Amateur Cycling Club. There was a wonderful event at Toowong on Saturday. Although the track was a bit soft and there was loose gravel, several riders fell. Still, it was invigorating competition....'

'I shudder at the thought of riders coming off those contraptions at high speed,' Hamish interrupted her.

'And how does your scientist come to entice an interest in lawn tennis?' he asked.

'She plays. She's very good. She won matches against every one of the men she played on Sunday. One after the other, they fell. She has offered to teach me. We're going to play this afternoon. But I wondered if you and I might do something first?'

'I have patients until noon.'

'After that, then. I play tennis with Collette at two.'

'What is it you want to do?' asked Hamish tentatively. 'I'm not participating in a séance.'

'Don't be ridiculous, Hamish. I've had an idea,' she said as she poured their tea.

'Oh yes.'

'I think we should visit Kaelo this afternoon.'

Hamish set his cup down.

'Why?'

'Because he's alone,' said Rita, as if it were obvious. 'He's travelled from the South Sea Islands, no doubt under horrible conditions. He's been sold for labour, abused and charged with murder.'

'He hasn't been charged,' said Hamish. 'He's being held for his own protection. Still, I take your point.'

'Regardless, he's locked in a cell and alone in this country. It must seem as though he's been forgotten in all this.'

'I'm sure Sergeant Bellamy is keeping him informed about the progress of the investigation,' said Hamish.

'I think we should visit him.'

Hamish hesitated for a moment. 'Of course, you are right,' he said. 'As always. It would be a kindness to check on him.'

'Then after that, you can watch me play tennis.'

'Lawn tennis?' cried Hamish.

'Yes. Come and watch me play. You can meet Collette. Oh, do come Hamish. You never do anything but work.'

Hamish thought about that. He didn't consider travelling to and from Cloverton to be work. It was true Sergeant Bellamy was paying him for his assistance in the murder enquiry. And it was also true the money would prove useful as he didn't have many clients in his private practice. Nonetheless, it didn't feel like work. If you included the investigation in the category of employment, he couldn't argue with Rita's statement.

'But lawn tennis?' he said.

'You'll enjoy it, I promise.'

Hamish doubted he would enjoy watching women exerting themselves chasing a ball back and forth across a net, but he agreed to attend. The idea of being with Rita, whatever she was doing, was irresistible

When they arrived at the watch house, Constable Pennyweather was taking the remains of Kaelo's lunch away. The chunks of bread and cheese looked like they hadn't been touched.

'Good morning, Sir, Ma'am...Miss,' Pennyweather said when he saw them.

'Good morning, Constable,' said Hamish.

Rita smiled.

'The Sergeant is not in his office at present,' said Pennyweather.

'That's quite alright,' said Hamish, 'We've come to see Kaelo.'

The young Constable raised his eyebrows, and Rita raised hers back.

'Oh,' he said, 'Right.'

He moved away awkwardly, neither giving them permission to enter nor disallowing it. Hamish imagined this would serve the constable as a defence if Sergeant Bellamy were to question why Hamish and Rita were allowed access to the cells.

The door to Kaelo's cell was open; he was not going anywhere.

Kaelo jumped up from his bunk to greet them, looking around for somewhere the lady could sit.

'Please don't worry yourself on my behalf,' Rita said. 'I am perfectly comfortable standing.'

Just as she spoke, the constable dragged a chair in from the office. He placed it before Rita.

'I'll fetch another for you, Doctor,' he said.

'No, don't bother, I'll sit here,' said Hamish lowering himself onto Kaelo's bunk. Kaelo sat beside him.

'I'm Doctor Hamish Hart,' he said. 'This is my colleague, Doctor Rita Cartwright.'

Kaelo's eyes widened.

'I know,' laughed Rita. 'A lady, Doctor. Most people are surprised.'

Kaelo smiled.

'I'm so sorry you have been confined in this way,' said Rita, glancing momentarily at the open door.

'Yes,' said Hamish. 'I hope the sergeant has assured you we are doing everything we can to bring this mystery to a speedy conclusion.'

'Thank you,' Kaelo said hesitantly.

They all sat for a moment in uncomfortable silence.

'Is there anything we can bring you?' asked Rita. 'I noticed you hadn't eaten much. Is there something more to your taste we can bring?'

Kaelo shook his head slowly.

'You won't keep up your strength if you don't eat,' she added.

Kaelo sat quietly, avoiding eye contact with either of them.

Hamish noticed a weathered bible open on the bunk. He picked it up without losing the open page. 'Do you read?' he asked, unable to hide the surprise in his voice.

Kaelo took the bible from him and lay it gently, face down, on the bunk. He nodded very slightly.

'Well, if there is nothing we can do for you...' said Hamish, about to stand up.

Kaelo lent forward, so his head was close to Hamish.

'I need to find someone,' he said quietly.

Hamish and Rita exchanged glances. 'Who do you need to find?' asked Rita.

'My father's wife,' he said.

'Your father's wife is in Queensland?' cried Hamish.

Kaelo nodded.

'Do you know her name?' asked Rita.

Kaelo handed her a crumpled note.

Araluen.

Rita passed the note to Hamish.

'This looks like an Aboriginal name,' said Hamish.

Kaelo nodded again. 'My father worked in Mackay. He married this woman, but she would not return to the Islands with him.'

'If your father married her in Mackay, you won't find her here,' said Hamish.

'He told me his wife travelled to Brisbane for work after he left,' Kaelo said.

'Why do you want to find her?' Rita asked gently.

Kaelo looked into her eyes. 'I want to give her money from my father. And I want to meet my brother.'

'She has a son?' asked Hamish.

'We understand,' said Rita placing her hand on Kaelo's arm.

Hamish was not sure that was true. His brain was processing the information. Kaelo's father had married an Aboriginal woman while working in Mackay, and they had a child together. Now Kaelo says he wants to find the woman and child and give them money. Why?

'Is your father waiting to hear about them?' asked Rita, still resting her hand over Kaelo's forearm.

'My father is with God,' he said.

'Good grief,' said Hamish.

'We will help you find your father's wife and son,' said Rita as she released his arm from her touch.

Some of the tension fell from Kaelo's shoulders.

Hamish took a deep breath. 'I'm not sure where to start,' he said. Rita is always a step ahead of him, he thought. Why does he always feel compelled to follow?

Kaelo looked earnest.

'We'll put an advertisement in the paper,' said Rita.

'What? In the newspaper?' Hamish looked at her as though she had taken leave of her senses.

Kaelo looked hopeful, 'Yes,' he said eagerly.

'I doubt your father's wife can read,' said Hamish.

'Someone might know something about her whereabouts, though,' said Rita. 'It's an excellent idea.'

Hamish knew if Rita was in favour of the idea, they would be acting on it, so he didn't waste any energy on resistance.

'I suppose it would be best to place the advertisement in both the Brisbane Courier and the Mackay Advertiser then,' said Hamish.

'Surely Araluen is working for someone who'll read the papers.'

'It is a start anyway,' said Rita, flashing Kaelo an engaging smile.

'What would you like the advertisement to say?' asked Hamish, notepad and pencil at the ready.

Kaelo opened his mouth to speak but closed it again.

Rita put together the words while Hamish wrote them down:

> *Seeking contact with Aboriginal woman named Araluen. Previously from Mackay, may now be residing in Brisbane area. Please contact Dr Hamish Hart, Wickham Terrace, Brisbane.*

Kaelo nodded.

◇◇◇◇◇

Having stopped at the Post Office to send telegrams to the Brisbane and Mackay papers, Hamish arrived at the address Rita had given him in time for the first match. As he hopped out of the cab, he was overwhelmed by the grandeur of the house. It was a two-story square structure with wide verandas on four sides around both the upper and lower floors. There was an ornate portico at the centre front of the upper floor decorated with white wrought iron trim. At the upper level, in front of the portico, a double aspect staircase splayed out to the left and right, then curved elegantly back inward to meet at a central path. A row of trimmed camellia bushes lined the approach. There were few such grand houses in Brisbane, but those that did exist shared a character that could not be mistaken. The style was emerging as typically 'Queenslander' in design.

Hamish tried to tell himself he was attending an afternoon of lawn tennis to support a friend. But he knew he was making that up. Rita didn't need his support. She was confident in any situation and had many, many friends. He tried not to think about the real reason for attending a sport he had no interest in and no affinity for. If Rita invited him to swim with sharks, he would do it, so he could be with her.

Hamish heard laughter emanate from the other side of the camellias and followed the sound. There was an expansive lawn, with a court marked out in chalk and a net swung across it. A group of women chatted at one end while filling plump glasses with punch from an enormous crystal bowl.

Hamish recognised Rita's navy and white stripes as she noticed him and galloped over with a fresh glass of punch.

'Hamish, I'm so glad you came. I was afraid you would get back to that house of yours and stay there. Come and meet my friends.' She placed the glass in one of his hands and led him with the other.

Hamish surveyed the chatting women.

'Are there no men?' he asked.

'Of course not,' said Rita. 'It's a women's match. Men aren't invited.'

'Then why am I here?' he said, nervousness turning to panic.

'You're special,' she said, laughing. 'You can be one of the girls for the afternoon. I want you to meet Collette.'

A tall, athletic-looking woman caught sight of them and withdrew from the group. She took long strides toward them. Her plain flannel skirt was even shorter than Rita's, and her arms were bare. They were slim but muscular and tanned. The woman's face was more handsome than pretty.

'You must be Dr Hart,' she said as she held out her hand. Hamish shuffled back a step. He was used to women waiting to be introduced. His hand trembled when he took hers. 'Collette,' he said, slipping into the informality of the occasion.

'Do you play, Doctor?' Collette asked.

'Good heavens no,' Rita said on his behalf. 'He's never exerted himself in his life.'

Hamish thought the assessment somewhat harsh. Still, he allowed himself to be herded toward a group of seats arranged alongside the court for spectators.

A group of ladies in cheerful gowns that seemed more appropriate to the seaside than the lawn of a grand house joined him.

Rita and Collette played the first match in opposition to one another. It was clear Rita was new to the game and completely outmatched by her opponent. But she wasn't shamefully bad. Her racquet managed to connect with the ball in a few difficult shots in the corner of the court. And she was quite adept at tapping the ball lightly enough that it slipped over the net to fall irritatingly close on the other side. Too many times, the ball fell well out of reach of even Collette's long arms. At the end of the match, the two women fell over one another, hugging and laughing while the audience clapped, whistled and hooted.

Hamish clapped politely, wondering how he found himself an honorary guest among this rowdy bunch of women.

Rita's face shone from exertion and excitement. She removed her little sailor's cap to reveal her hair stuck to her crown in a moist mess. She glanced across at Hamish, and he shouted, 'Well done!' She looked pleased to have him there cheering her on, and he immediately shed any reservations he had been entertaining about being there. He could also see why she was attracted to the tall, accomplished Collette.

Rita and Collette joined Hamish and the other spectators to watch the following matches. During the match next but one from that of Rita and Collette, a woman took an unlikely shot and fell sideways, catching her ankle beneath her and crying out in pain. Rita and Hamish ran onto the court. Rita held the woman still while Hamish released her ankle from beneath her body and examined it. It was already swelling. They wrapped a cold, wet towel around the ankle, and together they assisted her to stand. All the ladies gathered around her to offer recommendations for the treatment of a sprained ankle.

The incident triggered an early afternoon tea. The guests retreated to a closed garden at the back of the house, where a buffet of sandwiches and sweet little cakes was set up. Collette and Rita supported their wounded colleague, one on each side to a chair by the buffet.

Hamish found the cakes delicious and enjoyed the easy banter of the women. All in all, he had to admit to himself it was a pleasant afternoon. He was impressed by the freedom and sheer joy the women experienced when released from the confines of their corsets and bustles. The physical exercise was healthy, but the freedom of personality struck him as the most important change.

He left the afternoon of lawn tennis in an unexpectedly happy frame of mind. The only niggling thought to disturb him was the growing attachment between Rita and Collette. While he understood it, he didn't have to like it.

CHAPTER TEN

Queensland Figaro Saturday 16 August 1884.

Samuel Griffith's new Immigration Bill is perhaps the most barefaced sham that has ever been proposed by a Government treacherous in its political traditions. The cry of 'Queensland for white men' put Sam into power. He made the grandest promises. The hollowness, deceit and humbug of that cry were exposed over and over again, but to no purpose. All the argument in the world would be upset by some brainless blatherer who only had to yell out senselessly, 'No Coolies!' And the working man's head ran away with him. The sugar industry made the North. Now the Queen Street Ministry is determined to ruin that industry by making a reliable source of labour taboo.

Saturday 2 February 1884.

A firm very largely interested in sugar-manufacture in Queensland has placed the whole of its properties in the market and set upon them a price amounting to only half the sum at which they were valued by experts some six months ago. Sam Griffith has caused these properties to depreciate in value to the extent of one-half, within six months, besides the very large sum the firm has extended in improvements during the period mentioned.

HAMISH

Three days after Wallace left for Cloverton, Hamish travelled by coach to Logan to check on him. He would have to rely on the Daniels' hospitality overnight and return on the first coach the next morning though he was confident they would welcome him having doubtless tried Wallace's lamb stew and dumplings.

When Hamish stepped onto the veranda, he was not disappointed in his welcome. Red came out first, yapping and jumping at his legs, followed by Charlotte Daniels, who held out a tiny gloved hand to greet him.

'Welcome to you, Dr Hart,' she said. 'We were hoping you would come today. I can't tell you how indebted I am to you for recommending our cook. The scones are the lightest I've ever had.'

'Have you tried the lamb stew yet?' asked Hamish.

'Last night,' she said. 'Heaven. We adore Wallace. We hope he stays with us forever.'

Hamish felt the first pang of guilt in relation to his plan. He expected Wallace to be back with him in a week or two at most.

As Charlotte moved closer to him, he detected the sweet scent of rose water in her hair. She was wearing a day dress that was low on the shoulder, with a lace collar falling from her neck to the bodice. He could see glimpses of pearl skin beneath the lace. The skirt had a short train that trailed behind her as she walked into the house. It gave the impression she was gliding, her feet not touching the ground.

'Wallace has cooked up a pork roast for lunch,' she said. 'After lunch, you two can talk. He can let you know if he's happy to stay with us,' she smiled. Hamish could not help feeling affected by her beauty. A perfect china doll in the most imperfect of settings.

After lunch, Hamish and Wallace sat in the mess, enjoying a cool breeze. Red followed them and sat on Hamish's feet to acknowledge he missed him.

'How do you like it?' asked Hamish. 'I haven't lost you for good, have I?'

Wallace laughed, and Hamish realised he had missed him.

'They are an insular lot, the family,' Wallace said. 'Keep to themselves. But the staff are full of gossip.'

'That's good news. What have you found out?'

'I've not met Alice Tennyson. She returned to Tennyson House shortly after you left Cloverton. And Charlotte stays in her room much of the day. While she's decorative, she doesn't strike me as a happy woman. She showed me around the kitchen and left me to it. I'm sure she's grateful to have passed on the responsibility of cooking. Daniels is out at first light and returns only for lunch, then is out again immediately. He seems stressed about the harvest. He's working himself too hard. But I've hardly spoken to him.'

'It's been all work for you, then?'

'Fortunately, the workers enjoy a drink in the evenings. They drag a wooden barrel over and set it alight, then everyone sits around it drinking and yarning. Lips are loosest in those circumstances.'

'You join them then?'

Wallace grinned.

'That must be a hardship for you.'

'Nothing I won't do to assist,' said Wallace. 'Anyway, they all hate McDonald. Not one of them is sorry he's dead. In fact, Simpson says he's sorry the Kanaka didn't kill him. Thinks it would have been a fitting end.'

'Do they have any theories?' asked Hamish.

'Not to speak of. They all say Daniels is a fair man, and they can't understand why he put up with McDonald. Simpson said he must've had something over Daniels, but Hotham snapped and told him not to be stupid.'

'Interesting.'

'I did learn that young Alice and Hotham had a budding relationship last year – nothing serious, mind, but promising. Then out of the blue, Daniels announced she was marrying Pete Tennyson. Hotham took it hard for a while. The boys think Daniels and old Tennyson arranged it so they could bring the two holdings together. It'll be a powerful property when they settle it. The combined plantations will dominate South-East Queensland.'

'I'm impressed,' said Hamish. 'Have you any sense of how the mother and daughter get along?'

Wallace shook his head. 'No. As I said, I haven't met Alice, and Charlotte spends most of her time in her room. The boys don't talk about her. I get the impression she has little to do with the operational side of the plantation.'

'You've done well in three days,' said Hamish. 'Within a week, you'll know all their secrets.'

'That I will.' Wallace grinned.

'Something Daniels said the other day bothered me,' said Hamish changing the subject. 'He believes the Immigration reforms are going to make it impossible for plantation owners to survive. He's afraid that if they replace Kanakas with European labour, the workers will band together and strike for decent wages.'

'Aye, they will,' said Wallace. 'And so they should.'

'But Daniels says the industry can't afford to pay higher wages. That they'll not be able to produce the sugar if it comes to that.'

'Maybe we need to rethink how sugar is grown and produced in this country,' said Wallace.

'I don't understand.'

'Wealthy landowners like Daniels hold the property. Their wealth comes as the result of other people's labour, not their own. They become rich on the backs of the labourers who do the work of production. If land were distributed to more people, farmers who contributed their own labour, for example, the profits would be distributed more evenly.'

'It's true that men such as Daniels think it's part of the natural universe that one man's labour ought to be at the disposal of another,' Hamish agreed.

'Exactly. A labourer's wage is the exact amount it costs to sustain his labour and not a penny more,' said Wallace.

Hamish thought for a moment. 'I recall our Premier, Samuel Griffiths, saying that a man's labour is not a commodity but part of himself. It cannot be treated as property or something for sale unless the seller and the purchaser are on equal terms. Of course, it is rarely the case when there is equal freedom of contract between employer and employed. The employer has the wealth, and the weaker party has to accept the terms the stronger party chooses to give in order to ensure his livelihood.'

Wallace nodded. 'The only way the employee can get a measure of freedom is to form a combination with other workers. This gives each of them strength as a group, in the bargaining process.'

'I have some faith in this fellow, Griffiths,' said Hamish. 'He might yet champion a fairer system within Queensland.'

'Don't put too much of your faith in him,' cautioned Wallace. 'He's still one of the ruling elite. He will protect his own when it comes down to it.'

'I can't help thinking the future of this plantation is at the heart of the murder,' said Hamish. 'Did Jock McDonald have an opinion on the coloured labour question, do we know?'

'If he did, it seems to be that the coloured labour ought to be made to work till they drop. He appears to have had no empathy for them as men.'

'That may have been his value to Daniels. He was able to work the coloured labour hard. Daniels may not have had the constitution for it himself.'

CHAPTER ELEVEN

Eastern Districts Chronicle Monday 12 June 1885.

Fire! That terrible, devastating element, which can be either a friend or fiend – one which, in a few short hours may lay waste the possessions of the wealthy, or in time of distress and need may befriend the poor and helpless, we say: how tremendous is its power, either for good or the reverse. This afternoon, between the hours of three and four o'clock, the inhabitants of the town were alarmed by the repeated ringing of the police bell and the volunteer call, plainly telling, by their rounding at such an hour, that something out of the ordinary was amiss. One had not far to look for the cause of the alarm, for situated upon an eminence, overlooking the picturesque valley, stands the residence of one of our most prominent citizens. As the roaring flames sped their way upwards, and the thick, gloomy columns of black smoke curled upward into the heavens, there to mingle with a purer atmosphere, one could plainly see that the terrible work of devastation and waste had begun.

The clanging of the police bell, with its ponderous weight heaving to and fro, the shrill blast of horses' hooves, and the incessant roll of carriages and traps (which had already been got in readiness), the noise of many voices, all combined to make a perfect Babel, and to add alarm and amazement to the circumstance. A number of pedestrians could be seen making their way in the direction of the fire, while others, hurrying to and fro, here and there, in absolute confusion and consternation, was indeed a sight rarely witnessed in our otherwise quiet little country town.

As the fierce flames with their firey tongues licked the adjacent outhouses, it was very doubtful indeed whether the house could be saved from the fury of the flames; smouldering masses of hay were blown by the soft afternoon breeze from off the burning stack, while the heat was something terrific, and defied the efforts of all present to do anything to save the burning mass. One by one, the outhouses caught fire, the crackling wind and burning timber, the smoke from the stack, and the fierce flames combined to render all human efforts unavailable. By this time, two hundred and fifty persons had arrived on the scene, amongst them a number of the men working on the railway line, who, it must be said to their credit, acted with an amount of courage and bravery in rescuing sundry articles from the burning mass. It was utterly impossible to do anything to stay the progress of the flames, water was useless, and human efforts more so. The only thing to do was to stand by and watch property being laid waste, corn consuming, and hay going as chaff before the wind. Of course, in due time, the fire had burnt itself out, and the majority of those who had gone there for the purpose of affording some help or relief had to return home disappointed.

HAMISH

Hamish spent the afternoon sipping tea on the veranda. An oppressive heat hung low over the plantation. Watching the clouds become swollen and grey over Stradbroke Island, Hamish wiped the sweat from his brow. He thought about how muggy it would be in Brisbane. At least at Cloverton, the soft breeze wafted up from the river to cool him.

By four in the afternoon, the sky had deepened to an oppressive olive, and the distant sound of thunder warned of a late summer storm brewing. Hamish watched the men rush to haul the last carts of cane to the mill before the light faded any further. There was a strange stillness in the air, making the voices of the men as they called out to one another sound hollow. Hamish experienced a sense of anticipation. It was difficult for him to sit still, but there was little he could do. Wallace was preparing the evening meal, Daniels was helping Gerard bring the horses in from the far paddocks, and Charlotte was still in her room. Ginny was rushing through the house, closing shutters.

By half-past four, the sky had darkened to a deep purple. A clap of thunder close to the house made Hamish jump. Charlotte came from her room wide-eyed and alarmed, and Daniels pounded up the front steps and into the house.

'The horses are in the stables,' he said. 'The storm sounds close now.'

He motioned to Hamish to follow him into the sitting room. 'Drink?'

Hamish nodded, and he poured whisky from a decanter into crystal glasses.

A streak of light flashed across the window behind Daniels, followed by a clap of thunder so close it rocked the house.

Charlotte came into the sitting room and ignited the gas lights. She settled into a large armchair by the window and stared out at the storm. Lightening that travelled in great sheets from heaven to Earth illuminated the side of her face. Everyone braced themselves for the rain.

Hamish noticed Daniels looked older than he had when he met him only days earlier.

'Will the storm have an impact on the harvest?' asked Hamish.

'The storm won't make much difference,' he said. 'The fact I have too few men is what's holding us up. I'm labouring as well as supervising, but without McDonald and the men I recruited last week, we're not going to get all the cane harvested and milled. I have stockpiles of cane from the smaller holdings waiting to be processed as well as our own. I'll have to return to Brisbane with you tomorrow, Hart. I need to bring in more men.' He glanced toward his wife, but she didn't look away from the window.

Daniels slumped in his chair. 'The harvest is already late this year. It should have been over by the end of December. We're four weeks behind already. The floods in December slowed us down, and we lost half a dozen men while we couldn't work. I sent them north to help at the plantation up there. When they completed that job, they took the opportunity to ship back to the Islands. If the cane we've already harvested isn't milled immediately, it will reduce in value – less juice, poor quality. We'll have a third of our expected yield at best.'

Charlotte didn't move a muscle as he talked. She continued to stare out at the darkening sky.

They sat listening to the explosions of thunder that came more and more frequently, bracing themselves for the deluge that must come. A few fat drops of water splashed hard onto the window beside Charlotte's face, and she turned her eyes inward. She rose and left the room. A few seconds later, she returned to say dinner was being served. Though the storm had put them all on edge, Hamish was hungry and glad the meal had not been delayed.

They took their seats and enjoyed the warm aroma of Wallace's potato and leak soup as Ginny ladled it from a large tureen. Hamish felt his taste buds tingle. A basket of freshly baked bread rolls sat in the centre of the table. 'Ah,' thought Hamish, 'crusty on the outside, fluffy in the centre.' His mouth began to water. A gloomy light had descended on the room from the storm, but the promise of a hearty meal was comforting.

As he was about to take his first mouthful, an almighty crack sounded, and a white light flooded the room. Followed by darkness. Ginny scurried in from the kitchen and ran around the room, relighting the oil lamps. Hamish, Daniels and Charlotte tried to refocus on the meal, but the thunder kept coming. There was another loud crack, and the closeness of it caused Hamish's hand to slip as he lifted the spoon. Liquid spilled onto the tablecloth. Ginny ran over to mop it up.

'Sorry,' Hamish said. Then there was a call from outside.

'Daniels, fire!'

Daniels threw aside his napkin and ran for the front door. Hamish was close behind him. There were men running in every direction. Daniels began shouting orders. Hamish saw a woodpile alongside the mill had caught alight. He looked up at the sky. The few earlier drops of rain had dried up. Surely it would pour down soon.

A line of men had formed between the water tank and the mill. They were passing buckets of sloshing water from man to man.

'It's caught the structure,' yelled Hotham. Daniels joined him at the main entrance to the mill, where a great yellow flame leapt from the mill into the sky. The corner of the mill was gleaming. Red sparks blinked on and off as the fire made its way up toward the roof.

Hamish joined the bucket line. A few minutes later, he saw Daniels carrying a large blue globe. Hotham helped him to heave it high, and they threw it into the fire. The globe exploded, the glass shattered, and the chemicals it held ate the flames. The wood pile went dark and still. But the fire had made its way up the wall where it continued to lick and burn at the old wood. Thunder and lightning added to the confusion while Hamish and the others passed bucket after bucket of water along the human line. Daniels and Hotham placed themselves at the front of the line and poured the water from the buckets onto the fire.

'Don't let it reach the roof,' screamed Daniels. 'If it reaches the roof, the mill will be lost.'

The muscles in Hamish's shoulders burned. The repetitive action, left, bucket, slosh, right – it was burning into his body. He had never moved as quickly for so long. Ash covered his face and hands. When he tried to wipe the sweat from his brow, he only succeeded in wiping it into his eyes. He was struggling to see through the sting when he heard Hotham's voice.

'Where's Stratton?'

Out of the corner of his eye, Hamish saw Daniels stop and look around wildly.

'God, no!' Daniels yelled as he ran toward the back of the mill. Hamish stepped out of his place in the line and ran after him. The boiler room was attached to the mill, separated by half a timber wall. Daniels and Hamish ran through the narrow entrance. The space was thick with smoke. Hamish tried to call out, but smoke filled his throat. He stumbled forward until he could see the shape of a man flat against the ground. Daniels saw him at the same time. Together they gathered him up, all skin and bone, and Hamish held him against his chest. He hauled him out and lay him on the grass. Eddie Hotham appeared behind him. 'Stratton,' cried Hotham.

Hamish pressed his fingers to the man's neck to check for a pulse.

'We need water,' said Hamish.

Daniels ran back to the front of the mill to grab one of the buckets. He soon reappeared alongside Stratton, who was lying face-up on the grass with Hamish kneeling beside him. Daniels poured water on them both. The old man coughed and spluttered. 'He's alive!' cried Hotham.

Hamish's hair hung wet and lank across his face. He looked up at them. 'I could have told you that without the water,' he said, wiping his face with the back of his hand. 'He's suffering from smoke inhalation. Carry him indoors and tell Charlotte to bring him water...to drink,' Hamish added.

Daniels and Hotham carried the old boiler operator toward the house. Hamish heard Daniels mutter, 'I can't afford to lose the bloody sugar boiler attendant as well.'

When Hamish returned to his spot in the line, there was a man he hadn't met before, but there was no time for introductions. He grabbed a bucket and resumed passing it along the line. He noticed Wallace had also joined the line. Soon he saw two more men ride over the hill toward them from the west. He recognized one of them as Vincent from Cedarwood. 'We saw the smoke,' he said as they joined the line, Vincent's one gold tooth catching the light from the fire. Hamish settled back into the rhythm of passing buckets of water along to the next man. As he passed each sloshing bucket to Vincent, he noticed how quickly he moved. Hamish felt sluggish alongside him. He shook off his growing exhaustion and quickened his pace.

Daniels and Hotham were back in a matter of minutes. 'I'm going to get on the roof,' said Hotham looking up. 'If we wet the roof, we may save it.' Daniels organised a fork in the line and diverted some of the buckets of water toward a ladder at the side of the wall. The buckets were passed upward toward Hotham. Hamish could see the flames rising, skipping and dancing up the side of the mill toward the roof. The flames were growing taller with every passing moment, and the buckets of water did little to moisten the timber. It hungrily welcomed the flames.

Hamish saw the timber shift.

'Get down!' Vincent shouted. 'It's going to fall.'

Hotham scrambled down from the roof and stood alongside Daniels, Vincent and the man that Hamish didn't know. The four of them stared upward as a great tower of orange flame engulfed the roof. 'It's going to go,' said Daniels in despair.

At that moment, the heavens opened, and great thundering sheets of water fell from the sky. The rain poured down, stinging the faces of the men who had them turned upward. Ash ran down their faces, arms and legs. All at once, a cheer rang out, and everyone shouted together.

The timber building sizzled and smoked, and finally, the red flames were vanquished. Within minutes the fire was out.

Hamish followed a scraggly line of men, wet to the skin and dripping with soot, up toward the house. They all stopped on the veranda, knowing they were not in any state to enter. Charlotte and Ginny brought out jugs of lemonade. Alice handed Hamish a glass.

'Dr Hart. This is my husband, Peter,' she said. So that is who the stranger was. Hamish shook the man's outstretched hand.

'We came as soon as we saw the smoke,' he said. 'Alice wouldn't stay behind, though I tried to make her do so.'

Hamish smiled at Alice. 'I'm quite sure no one could stop Alice from doing anything she made up her mind to do,' he said.

Gradually, the men who had come from neighbouring farms took their leave. Vincent and his men from Cedarwood were the last to mount their horses and head for home. Hamish, Wallace and the family wandered into the sitting room, still feeling numb from shock.

'We'll stay the night,' Alice told her mother, who had resumed her place in the chair by the window.

'Of course, dear, I wouldn't allow you to travel at this hour.'

Peter Tennyson took the final sip of whiskey from his glass. Reaching tired arms around his wife's shoulders, he said, 'We should retire. It's been a long night.' Alice lent into his body, ready to go with him.

They were all surprised to hear a sob from the settee. Daniels was crouched with his arms curled around his knees and his head hanging almost to his lap. His back shuddered as he sobbed.

Hamish realised he hadn't paid Daniels any attention since he and Hotham found the boiler attendant, Mr Stratton.

'Are you hurt?' Hamish asked. He went to Daniel's side, ready to examine him for injury.

Daniels lifted his head, revealing eyes swollen from ash and tears.

'I'm not injured,' he said, 'but I fear I may be ruined. The death of my manager, the loss of the extra labour and now this...I don't know if we can come back from this. Not when we were already so far behind. We'll lose this year's harvest and slip deeper into the Government's debt.'

'You're exhausted,' said Tennyson. 'The damage to the mill is not that great that you'll not be able to operate. Perhaps a day or two will be lost to repairs, but that's all.'

Daniels took a deep breath and regained his composure. 'I don't know we can be sure the building is safe within that time,' he said. 'But I suppose we won't know until it's light and we can inspect the damage. Forgive me. The events of this last week have overwhelmed me.'

'That's the spirit,' said the younger man. 'The catastrophe you have constructed in your mind will be far worse than the reality when seen in the light of day.'

The advice sounded admirable to Hamish, and he couldn't help thinking the two plantations would probably do well in Pete Tennyson's hands into the future.

'Has Ginny filled the tub?' Daniels asked.

'With warm water, in the kitchen,' said Alice. 'Wash up by the fire and get some sleep, father. Things will seem brighter in the morning.'

Daniels put his hand out to Hamish as he passed him. 'Thank you for your help tonight, Hart,' he said. 'I'm sorry your visit to Cloverton has been so...eventful.'

Hamish took the man's hand and shook it.

Alice and Peter took their leave and retired to Alice's childhood bedroom, leaving Hamish and Charlotte in the sitting room. Hamish thought he, too, should get washed up and retire. 'I'll bid you good-night,' he said to Charlotte, who was staring out the window at the stars.

Charlotte turned toward him and caught his eyes in her pale blue gaze. 'Someone is trying to destroy my husband,' she said.

Hamish was unsure how to respond. He found her vulnerability unnerving.

'The killing of Jock McDonald, the fire tonight, these are part of a calculated campaign to cause our ruin.'

Her eyes were so steady, so blue, Hamish could not look away.

'How so?' he said. 'Do you believe the fire was set deliberately? Isn't it more likely to have been the result of a lightning strike? And why would anyone want to cause your husband's ruin? Why kill Jock McDonald?'

Charlotte turned her head from Hamish and continued to stare through the window.

When she turned away from him, it was almost like experiencing physical pain. She had turned to him for help, and he couldn't help her. Instead, he bombarded her with questions and demonstrated beyond any doubt he was not her knight in shining armour. He was not capable of saving anyone. He wanted to go to her, hold her, feel her cheek against his chest as she sobbed, but a sense of his own inadequacy stopped him from doing so.

'I'm sorry,' he muttered as he took himself to the bedroom assigned to him.

He slept in fits and bursts, the smell of smoke filling his nostrils and the rush of fire ringing in his ears. At first light, he gave up the attempt to sleep and dressed. When he wandered into the kitchen, still rubbing the sting from his eyes, Wallace was baking bread for the family's breakfast. There was a pot of porridge on the stove. The familiar sight of Wallace and the welcoming smells of the kitchen improved his mood.

'Good morning,' said Wallace. 'You're up early. You're not the only one, mind. Daniels is already outside examining the damage to his mill.'

'Charlotte thinks the murder and the fire are deliberate attempts to destroy her husband's business,' said Hamish.

Wallace closed the heavy iron door to the oven.

'Odd way to go about it,' he said.

'I know,' agreed Hamish. 'And who would want to ruin him in any case?'

Wallace poured them both tea and sat opposite Hamish.

'Alright then, who benefits from the ruin of William Daniels?'

Hamish thought. 'Peter Tennyson?' He suggested.

'How would Tennyson benefit? The two holdings are coming together. That gives Tennyson a share in the place. It's in his interest to improve the prospects of Daniel's business.'

'On the face of it,' agreed Hamish. 'What about Vincent?'

'From Cedarwood?' asked Wallace.

'His land will be surrounded by the plantation,' said Hamish.

'It's surrounded now,' said Wallace.

Hamish ignored him. 'He gave the impression it was of no concern to him when Bellamy and I spoke to him, but that may not be the case.'

'Doesn't he bring his cane to Cloverton for processing?' asked Wallace. 'How does burning the mill before his cane is processed benefit him?'

'True,' said Hamish. 'The most important problem with

Charlotte's theory is this – why would anyone with a grudge against Daniels bother killing Jock McDonald? While Daniels insists McDonald was a good worker, he was hardly indispensable. Hotham indicated if it came down to a choice between himself and McDonald, Daniels would choose Hotham. Even Daniels said McDonald was likely to become redundant once the merger took place.

Wallace reached down to collect the scruffy red terrier and lift him onto his knee.

'Setting fire to the mill shed doesn't achieve much either,' he said. 'It seems clear to me the fire was triggered by the lightning. I've thought for a week that storing dry timber so close to the mill was a mistake. Not for the cook to comment, though, is it? My question is this: why does Charlotte Daniels think someone is trying to destroy her husband?'

Red tried his best to scramble onto the table where a tray of bacon sat, waiting to be fried for the family's breakfast. Wallace set him back on the floor and slipped him a strip of the bacon. Red trotted outside with his prize.

CHAPTER TWELVE

The Capricorn Saturday 20 September 1884.

One of the greatest difficulties in the consideration of spiritual phenomena has been the inability of producing such phenomena in public or before anything but a limited number of witnesses. It requires little practical experience in seances to satisfy the investigator that the phenomena are dependent upon conditions, but what those conditions are remains a mystery to him. It seems that certain persons, called Mediums, generate a more intelligent motor in the brain, producing the physical phenomena attributed by Spiritualists to disembodied spirits, by Occultists to spooks and by quasi-scientists as neo-scientific cerebra. General experience shows that rentable people, easily influenced and readily drawn from any dependence on rational thought by suggestible surroundings, are always available and in sufficient numbers to fill a parlour or coffee house.

HAMISH

Hamish was exhausted when he disembarked from the coach in Brisbane. It was already midday, and he hadn't slept well after the fire. His lungs felt as though he had swallowed the fire itself. He was looking forward to reaching his home and slipping into his favourite blue armchair for a nap. There was a cab waiting for the coach, so he climbed in, even though he could have walked home. When he reached his front door, he noticed a letter tucked underneath. The contents of the letter reinvigorated him immediately. The cab had not left. He called to the driver and jumped back on board. 'Lady Bowen Hospital,' he said. Ten minutes later, he had collected Rita, and they had arrived at Petrie Terrace.

All was quiet at the depot. Bellamy was not in his office, though the door was open, and they could see the familiar pile of papers scattered across his desk. Constable Pennyweather was at his own desk with a carriage clock in pieces before him. His face was tensed with concentration as he tried to manipulate a tiny screwdriver into the back of the clock's mechanism. He barely looked up at them with one eye as he nodded for them to go through to the cells. Hamish didn't stop to enquire about why the police constable was trying to fix a clock. It seemed to him that Pennyweather might well be suited to a number of professions, more so than policing.

Kaelo showed no emotion when they entered his cell.

'Good Morning,' Hamish said cheerfully.

Kaelo looked at him without smiling.

Rita sat on the bench close to Kaelo, and he jumped, shuffling a few inches away from her before settling.

'Hamish had news about your father's wife,' she said.

Hamish remained standing and read the letter aloud.

Dr Hart.

We are responding to your enquiry in the Brisbane Courier. An Aboriginal woman, originally of a tribe in the Mackay region and going by the name of Araluen, worked for my husband and myself as a housemaid these past twelve months. We found her to be honest and hardworking and were disappointed when she left us to attend to her son, who was, we believe, being cared for by relatives in Maryborough. The child is apparently about five years of age and has been in an accident, which resulted in his being crippled. We are sorry to say that we do not have the names of the relatives in Maryborough, nor do we have a forwarding address. Nonetheless, we hope this information assists you in your enquiries.

Yours,
Mr and Mrs M.L. Sanderson

'This could be the woman we are seeking,' said Hamish. 'The age of the child fits.'

Kaelo stood up and paced from one side of the cell to the other.

'I should go to them,' he said.

Rita glanced at the open cell door swinging on its hinge.

'You can leave anytime, Kaelo,' said Hamish.

Kaelo's dark eyes glistened in the dim light of the cell.

'Sergeant Bellamy says to stay here until someone is charged with the murder,' he said.

'That would be ideal,' said Hamish, 'But he can't make you stay.'

Rita cut in, 'Hamish, you can't be suggesting Kaelo leave here, where he is safe, and travel to Maryborough on so little information?'

'Where is this place?' asked Kaelo.

'North,' said Rita. 'It would take days by coach or steamer to get there.'

'I will go now,' Kaelo said, leaving through the open cell door for the first time since he had been placed in the watch house.

'Wait,' cried Rita, flashing an annoyed glance at Hamish.

As Kaelo headed for the front entrance of the Police Station, Sergeant Bellamy strode in.

'Woah!' he cried as Kaelo crashed into him. 'What's going on?' He blocked the Islander's path with his body.

Rita and Hamish caught up.

'We found out his father's wife and son are in Maryborough,' Rita said. 'Hamish,' she looked at him with disbelief, 'told him he could go to them.'

'No, I didn't,' said Hamish.

'Yes, you did,' said Rita.

The three of them stared at Hamish.

'Very well, I did, in a manner of speaking,' said Hamish. 'I pointed out he was not being held under any charge...officially....'

Constable Pennyweather entered the foyer and looked back and forth between his boss and the doctors.

'My office,' said Bellamy to Hamish and Rita.

'Escort Kaelo back to the cell,' he said to the Constable. 'And lock the door.'

Hamish and Rita followed Bellamy into his office. Hamish felt like a schoolboy.

'From the beginning,' said Bellamy.

The sergeant looked excessively tired. Hamish began to wonder if there was more to the dark circles under his eyes than the strain of the case. Dehydration perhaps. He made a note to himself to advise the sergeant to drink more.

Rita explained about the letter and Kaelo's reaction. 'Understandable,' she pointed out, 'under the circumstances.'

Bellamy's stern gaze fell on Hamish.

'If he leaves now, while we have no evidence to arrest someone else for the murder, those above me will insist on having him dragged back here in chains. I've had enough trouble getting permission to conduct the investigation. There are plenty who would prefer Kaelo be charged for murder and the case closed.'

'There is no reason in law to restrain him,' Hamish said. 'It's an infringement of his rights.'

Bellamy lent his elbows on the desk and glared at Hamish.

'He has no bloody rights, Hart. He's in the colony as indentured labour, and at present, he is not under contract. By law, he should be sent immediately back to where he came from.'

Hamish stood up to his full height, then leaned over the top of Bellamy.

'He has rights as a human being,' he said.

Rita rolled her eyes. 'For pity's sake, sit down,' she said to Hamish. 'While you two fluff your feathers like roosters, you are both missing the point. Of course, Kaelo has the right to walk out if he chooses. And the likely result of that is, the Polynesian Protector will pick him up and hand him over to a police sergeant more inclined to please his Inspector than Bellamy here. Even if he somehow makes his way to Maryborough, he has no chance of finding this woman on the little information we have. I suggest we explain to Kaelo we will attempt to find an address for the woman and make initial contact from here. In the meantime, it would be safest for him to stay under the protection of Sergeant Bellamy.'

When they had all agreed, they explained the plan to Kaelo, who agreed to wait in the watch house. But they locked the cell door as they left anyway.

'I'm having lunch with Collette,' said Rita as they left the Police Depot. 'Why don't you join us?'

'Won't I be superfluous?' asked Hamish.

Rita hooked her arm in his. 'Of course not,' she said. Leading him down the hill toward Queen Street, they turned onto Edward and continued to the corner of Edward and Charlotte Streets. The Exchange Hotel was a popular meeting place, one of the oldest hotels in Brisbane, a town where no building or institution could be said to be truly old.

Rita stood on her toes to see over the lunchtime crowd. Her face lit up when she saw Collette in a booth toward the back of the room. Hamish's heart skipped a beat.

'Collette!' cried Rita tugging Hamish through the diners.

Hamish noted that the cool, light, flannel costume was one common among women who regularly played tennis.

'Have you been playing?' he asked.

'Yes, all morning,' she said proudly, edging along the bench seat to make room for Rita to sit beside her. Left with no option but to sit opposite, Hamish slid onto the bench.

'I positively smashed Mr Sommers here, didn't I, darling?'

Mr Sommers was also wearing light flannel trousers and was flushed from neck to forehead. Hamish couldn't tell if it was from the alcohol or the after-effects of overexertion.

'Bertie,' he said, raising his glass to Hamish. 'I'm Collette's cousin. She's trying to kill me. I put it down to jealousy. As the eldest male, I stand to inherit the family fortune.'

Hamish laughed.

'Do you play?' asked Bertie.

'Good God, No!' exclaimed Rita.

Collette slapped her playfully on the arm. 'Let him speak for himself,' she said.

'No,' said Hamish. 'I don't play sport.'

'Quite right,' said Bertie. 'Too much exercise over excites the blood. I keep telling Collette, but she's obsessed.'

'I think it's healthy for women to be outdoors and moving about,' said Rita. 'It's wonderfully freeing to be rid of the corsets and heavy gowns.'

'Do your parents approve of your dedication to tennis?' asked

Hamish.

Bertie almost choked on a mouthful of beer. 'Uncle Claude is consumed with anxiety about it,' he said when he had recovered. 'He hates Collette getting about without a corset and running around the tennis court. He complains she comes indoors perspiring in a most unladylike manner and leaves herself susceptible to drought.'

Collette lowered her lashes and laughed.

'When that woman was lamed the other day,' he went on, 'Uncle Claude exploded. Bertie feigned the facial expression and voice of his uncle and said, 'I'm not going to have my daughter laid up with sprained ankles, twisted wrists, strained tendons and colds in the head!'

They all laughed.

'He'll have to get used to it,' said Collette. 'Now that womankind has discovered the joys of outdoor sport, there will be no turning back. I think I'll take up rowing next. Join the men rowing past the Regatta every morning.'

'I'm in,' said Rita, raising her glass.

Hamish groaned.

'You can cheer me on from the shore,' she said, squeezing his hand across the table. Hamish noted Collette had her arm entwined through Rita's.

Hamish leant across the table so Collette could hear him. 'Rita tells me you are a member of the Society for Psychical Research,' he said. 'Are you a believer or a sceptic?'

Collette's lips twitched a little as though she were about to accept a challenge. 'I am neither,' she said. 'I believe all phenomena ought to be subject to open enquiry.'

'It seems open enquiry of late has revealed a series of tricksters,' said Hamish.

'There are two sides to every coin,' responded Collette, 'and I find both interesting.

'Recent events exposing trickery involved with séances in this city have been both entertaining and instructive. On the one hand, they exhibit the credulity of the believer who is seeking to obtain converts, and on the other, they exhibit the lengths to which a non-believer will go to expose at any cost what he considers to be in error.'

'Nonetheless, it must be said,' argued Hamish, 'the evidence falls in favour of trickery rather than the existence of genuine spirit phenomena.'

'I disagree, Doctor. The assumption that late events are an absolute exposure of spiritualism cannot be maintained. Whatever truth or error there is in the phenomena of spiritualism, the truth is not to be tested by proving that certain persons whose enthusiasm runs away with their discretion are too ready to accept trickery as a genuine phenomenon,' said Collette.

'How else is it proved one way or another?' asked Hamish.

'My mentor, William James, defines true beliefs as those that prove useful to the believer,' said Collette. 'When new observations fit comfortably with what one already believes, they can be accepted as true.'

Hamish flicked back his fringe and straightened his back.

'Are you saying that objective truth does not exist?' he cried.

'If by objective truth you mean a truth that does not rely on one marrying parts of their experience with new parts – then no. It does not exist. The value of truth utterly depends upon its use to the person who holds it.'

'This leaves us nowhere,' cried Hamish. His voice was rising.

'James is writing a book on the principles of psychology,' Collette went on without any sign of noticing Hamish's discomfort.

'The principles of psychology or of psychic phenomena?' he quipped.

It was Collette's turn to straighten her back.

'My dear sir,' she said, keeping her tone measured, 'are they not one and the same?'

Rita sipped her drink slowly. Hamish noticed she was careful not to look him in the eye.

Hamish continued, 'Of course, we do have to reckon with the morbid love of the marvellous, which often prepares the ground for delusions. People sit at a table determined that something wonderful is going to happen, and it does.'

'Quite so. People fit what they see with what they already believe, or are prepared to believe, is true. Nonetheless, occasional exposures of credulity do not dispose of the whole question. We must conduct investigations with care and caution.'

Hamish and Collette had been so involved in their debate, they didn't realise the others at the table had stopped chatting to listen to them. They were silent, waiting for Hamish to respond. He felt a tingle sweep up the back of his neck and his ears burned. He knew they had turned red. He smoothed back his hair and tugged at his collar, tight as it was at his neck. He hadn't meant to become embroiled in a debate that had the potential to become an argument with Rita's friend.

Bertie broke the silence, saving Hamish from further discomfort.

'Our Minister approached the subject on Sunday,' he said, putting his glass down and taking on an air of solemnity. 'Father Brian says spirits are liars and deceivers, opposed to all law, destructive to the distinction between right and wrong and devoid of all moral character.' Bertie sat back in his chair and grinned. 'I think I might rather like them.'

Everyone laughed.

Encouraged, Bertie continued. 'He also said spiritism is the enemy of marriage, and of social and domestic happiness and the forerunner of political anarchy. That's when I knew I was hooked!'

Bertie had broken the spell. Hamish could sense there was no way to return to a serious debate at this point. He smiled graciously and joined the laughter.

The following day's consultations went well. Between Mrs Kembler's respiratory difficulties and her gout, she felt the need to consult with Hamish one morning each week. Hamish knew she had recommended his services to the women in her bridge club. He saw two of the club's members, in addition to Mrs Kembler, that morning. Rather than being bored by the chronic illnesses of the middle-classes, as were many of his colleagues, Hamish was interested in them. He saw a role for the family doctor in diagnosing and managing conditions throughout the course of the patient's life. Business was still slow in his new practice, but it was building through recommendations from his patients.

Nonetheless, he reminded himself he could hardly concentrate on building the practice while distracted by a murder enquiry.

Hamish washed his hands and was about to go to the kitchen to prepare lunch when there was a knock at the door. He answered it to a freckled young telegraph messenger who handed him a message.

Alice unwell. Charlotte anxious. Requests your attendance at Cloverton as soon as convenient. Wallace.

Hamish set the telegram on the kitchen bench. He cut a slice of ham from the leg he had purchased the previous afternoon on his way home from the Exchange. He had been expecting to be home for a few days at least, and he was looking forward to eating his way through it.

Alice unwell. He wondered what that meant exactly. Was she seriously unwell? *As soon as convenient.* He looked at his leg of ham. Even tomorrow would not be *convenient.* As for today, the coach would have left already. If he were to travel to Logan this afternoon, he would have to ride. He cut some cheese. Then again, Wallace would not have sent the message if it were not urgent. Wallace was not prone to snap judgements or undue excitement. Hamish ate the ham and cheese he had prepared, then he picked up the telegram again.

'Damn,' he said aloud.

He left the comfort of his house, hailed a cab and directed the driver to take him to Petrie Terrace Police Depot.

As he entered, the sergeant was in the front foyer speaking with his constable.

'There you are, Hart,' he said when he saw Hamish enter. 'I was about to send Pennyweather out looking for you. I've had the Inspector in my office this morning. He's at his wit's end. There was a protest on the street outside the depot earlier. The public are becoming impatient. They're calling for the Kanaka to be tried and hung.'

'Kaelo,' Hamish corrected him.

'Yes. Kaelo. I've no new information to convince the Inspector to wait. The Mayor's become involved and wants to hold a town meeting. He wants to discuss the threat posed by the Polynesian Labourers. The whole thing is political, of course. He's trying to advance the push to stop the immigration of blacks to Queensland. He favours the Premier's proposal for German labour. For all the difference that will make.'

Bellamy seemed to realise he had strayed off the point.

'I can't hold them back much longer, Hart,' he went on. 'I'm afraid if I don't have solid evidence of another killer by the end of the week, this is going to take on a life of its own. They will have the Kanaka hung. They'll use him to make a political statement.'

'Kaelo,' repeated Hamish. He showed the sergeant the telegram from Wallace.

'I think I should go at once,' said Hamish.

'I agree,' said Bellamy. 'Apart from the possibility of a medical emergency, we might gain new information to assist us with this case.'

Hamish shed any reluctance he'd been feeling about travelling immediately to Cloverton.

'I'll need to borrow a horse for the ride,' he said.

'Don't be ridiculous,' said Bellamy. 'I'm not having you ride all that way alone. You'll get lost going through Cedarwood in the dark. I'll send for the trap and driver.'

Hamish was offended that Bellamy thought he would get lost. But in the end, he had to agree that his assessment was accurate. He was appreciative of the offer and said so.

'Just get going,' urged Bellamy. 'We need evidence to tie this murder to someone at Cloverton, or the K... Kaelo will hang.'

CHAPTER THIRTEEN

The Southern Coast Advertiser Wednesday 12 November 1884.

Some time ago, all the population of Brunn in the Austrian States were thrown into commotion by the appearance of the devil, in person. His satanic majesty was, as he is always represented, perfectly black, with two enormous horns, goat's ears, a body covered with hair, horse's legs and cloven feet, but he seemed decidedly out of spirits.

The old men and women of the place fell on their knees and prayed to the saints to protect them against the terrible Prince of Darkness, but the young men had the impiety to laugh and scoff at him.

That evening, a peasant woman was lying in after having been delivered of a child, the devil suddenly leapt through a window, clanking a chain, and demanding that she either give him the child to be carried to the regions below or make over to him 100 florins of silver. The poor woman, greatly terrified, at once produced the money, and the devil pocketed it, after which he went away. The next day the woman told the parish priest of the visit and added that she had collected the 100 florins penny by penny to pay the church for religious services.

'Did you tell anyone you had the money?' Said the Priest.

'Only the midwife,' said she.

'Well, tell the midwife that the devil was mistaken in supposing you only had 100 florins, for that you have 50 florins more, and say you are glad he did not compel you to give them up. The devil will perhaps pay you another visit after that, but I will be there to exorcise him.'

The woman told the midwife what the priest had said. The next night the devil reappeared and demanded 50 florins, but at the same moment, the priest rushed forth and seized him by the neck and charged him with being a thief. The devil, it turned out, was the husband of the midwife.

AMISH

Hamish arrived at Cloverton after dark. He stepped from the trap to feel something soft under his boot. It yelped before he had a chance to put his weight on his leg. 'I'm sorry, mate,' he said, leaning down to scruff the terrier's head. Red skipped about his legs as he strode up the front stairs. 'What's been happening here, Red?'

The dog barked.

Charlotte met Hamish at the door. 'Thank you so much for coming immediately,' she said. 'I've been terrified, and we thought you may not be able to travel until tomorrow.' She turned to William, who had come to stand behind her. 'William, take Dr Hart's driver to the servant's quarters and have Ginny make up a bed for him.' Red scurried between them into the sitting room. He appeared to have made himself at home at Cloverton.

Daniels did as he was told without question.

Hamish followed Charlotte into Alice's room to find her sound asleep. Pete Tennyson looked up in surprise from the armchair by the bed where he was settled with a rug over his knees. Red stood at his feet, looking at Hamish eagerly.

Hamish placed his palm on Alice's forehead. 'She's not feverish,' he said.

'There seems no reason to wake her. Perhaps we can go to the sitting room, and you can tell me what has been happening.

Once they were all seated, Wallace appeared with tea and toast. Charlotte was perched on the edge of the settee, wringing her hands. Red climbed into Hamish's lap.

'I had no idea they sent for you, Doctor,' said Peter Tennyson, taking the cup Wallace handed him. He glared at Charlotte as though he expected an explanation.

'I begged Wallace to send a telegram,' she said. 'I've been anxious all day.'

Tennyson ignored his mother-in-law and spoke to Hamish. 'I brought Alice over to see her mother this morning,' he said. 'She said she was not feeling herself, but there was no sign for concern at that time. A little before lunch, she said she had a backache and went to lay down. She didn't want any lunch when it was offered, then this afternoon...' he hesitated.

'There was a small bleed,' said Charlotte. 'Alice was in terrible pain, and she realised she'd had a bleed. I gave her a powder, and she went to sleep. Oh dear! Is she losing the baby, doctor?'

'Exactly how much blood?' asked Hamish.

Tennyson wriggled uncomfortably.

'Not much,' said Charlotte. 'A half a cup, I suppose.'

'It doesn't mean your daughter is losing the baby,' said Hamish. 'Indeed, it's not uncommon for such a bleed prior to the commencement of labour.'

'But it's too soon,' cried Tennyson.

'I'll examine Alice when she wakes,' Hamish assured them. 'There is no need to become overly anxious at this stage.'

'I'm so grateful to you for coming,' Charlotte repeated.

'As am I,' said Peter Tennyson, 'although I would have liked to be included in the decision to send for you.' He shot a sideways glance at his mother-in-law.

'I suspect tomorrow may have been soon enough, rather than have you gallop through the night, as we've done.'

'I fear tomorrow may be too late,' said Charlotte. 'If the baby comes through the night, without anyone in attendance....' She wrung her hands so vigorously the knuckles turned white.

'Does Alice have a midwife arranged?' asked Hamish.

'She does,' said Charlotte, 'but Maggie is away at present. Alice was not expected to reach her time for some weeks, and there are no other women expecting in the area at this time.'

'I wanted her to have a doctor attend the birth,' Tennyson cut in. 'I was hoping she could travel to Brisbane when her time was near to lie-in at the Lady Bowen Hospital. I believe it has lately become evident that professional support in a specialist clinic such as the Lady Bowen ensures improved outcomes for both mother and child. I've no reason to distrust old Maggie, I'm sure she has attended the delivery of many a bonny bairn in her day, but as we have the money to pay, I was hoping for the best for Alice.'

Hamish wasn't convinced women were any better off at a lying-in hospital than they were with a local midwife. Midwives generally had a lifetime of experience, and women preferred the comfort of their own home. But he didn't say anything. It was largely irrelevant at this point; he thought Alice's confinement was nearing its end.

'Let's not get ahead of ourselves,' said Hamish. 'There may still be time for Alice to travel to Brisbane for the birth if that is her wish.'

'I should get back to her,' said Tennyson as he bowed to Hamish and left the room.

'Do you truly believe there is no cause for concern, Doctor?' asked Charlotte with tears in her eyes.

Hamish bent down to scratch the wiry hair at the back of Red's neck. He chose his words carefully. 'Mrs Daniels...'

'Charlotte,' she interrupted.

Hamish smiled. 'Charlotte... without examining Alice, I cannot be certain of anything. But while she's sleeping, I believe it's best to leave her to rest. Tomorrow we'll know more, I promise you. You should sleep as well. If Alice does go into labour early, she'll need her mother.'

Charlotte was getting ready to ask more questions.

'Good night Mrs Daniels,' said Hamish.

Charlotte held his gaze for a moment. He wondered whether she would take his direction or dismiss it. Either way, the moment was uncomfortable. He breathed easily again when she finally released his gaze and turned to leave the room.

When Charlotte left him, Wallace came in for the empty teacups and gestured to Red to remove himself from the doctor's lap.

'I hope I did the right thing in sending for you,' he said. 'Charlotte was insistent.'

'You did the right thing,' Hamish assured him. 'While there's no immediate urgency, I suspect things may take a turn for the worst in the next day or so. How long have they been married, do you know?'

'Six months,' said Wallace.

'Not a good sign then if she's about to go into labour.'

Wallace motioned for Red to follow him. 'Good night, sir,' he said.

Hamish was so exhausted he fell asleep immediately. It felt like he had only been asleep for minutes when a piercing scream woke him. He leapt from his bed and stumbled into his trousers. He was trying to correct his focus after waking from a deep sleep when Charlotte's white face appeared in the doorway. He had time to register the terror in her countenance before she rushed off toward Alice's room. Hamish followed her, both bursting through the door as Pete Tennyson was pushing out from his side. They collided in confusion.

'What's going on?' cried Charlotte.

Tennyson stepped aside to allow Hamish and Charlotte to see Alice sitting on the edge of the bed.

'There's something wrong with the baby,' she cried.

The sheet was wet, and there was a small patch of watery pink blood.

'What happened?' Hamish asked.

'I woke up and saw blood,' she cried, 'I thought the baby was dead.'

Hamish placed his hand on her shoulder and eased her from the bed onto the armchair.

'Wake Ginny, if she is still asleep, have her come at once. Alice needs to be washed, and we need clean sheets on the bed.' Hamish said to Tennyson.

He watched as Tennyson withdrew, leaving Charlotte still standing in the doorway, Daniels peering over her shoulder.

'What the devil?'

'Alice has had a fright,' said Hamish. 'Please wait in the sitting room while I see that mother and baby are well.'

Charlotte looked hesitant, but they both moved away from the door.

Hamish used his hands to assess the position of the baby. The skin across Alice's abdomen was stretched taught, and Hamish felt a solid kick from within.

'Your baby is fine,' he said. The infant has engaged in the pelvis in readiness for birth. When is your due date?'

'I am unsure of my dates,' she said hesitantly.

'I believe the birth of your child will be quite soon,' said Hamish. 'I can send for my colleague, Dr Rita Cartwright, if you'd like.

She works at Lady Bowen Hospital. She has a great deal more experience in these matters than do I. She could be here within a few hours if she comes by the early steamer.'

'I would appreciate that, Doctor Hart,' Alice was trembling.

Ginny entered the room flustered and carrying a pile of clean sheets. It was evident she had been woken up, but she moved with swift efficiency as she removed the soiled sheets and replaced them. Hamish told Alice to remain in the armchair until he returned to assist her to bed. He excused himself and joined Charlotte, Daniels and Tennyson in the sitting room.

'Both mother and unborn are well. She's not experiencing birthing pains, so I am not too concerned. Still, it may be solicitous to send for my colleague from the Lady Bowen Hospital. It would put all our minds at rest.'

'Thank you, Doctor,' said Charlotte. 'We cannot thank you enough.'

Hamish sent Gerard to wake the telegrapher at first light and send a message to Rita.

It was late morning when Hamish stood on the veranda watching the steamer wind its way along the river. He was fascinated when it edged into the pier and docked. How convenient it must be to have one's own pier, he thought. Then he caught sight of Rita as she disembarked looking fresh and radiant. He walked toward the bank, and her smile filled him with warmth. Red appeared from nowhere and ran in circles around Rita.

'Thank you for coming,' he said.

'I wouldn't have missed a chance to come to Cloverton for the world,' she grinned.

Hamish laughed. 'Come. I'll introduce you to the family.'

William and Charlotte Daniels were taking their seats in readiness for lunch.

Daniels stood immediately when Rita entered with Hamish.

'This is Doctor Rita Cartwright,' he said.

'A female Doctor!' said Daniels. 'I've heard of such a thing in Europe but never here in the colonies.'

Rita held out her hand to him. 'I studied in London,' she said. 'We cannot register to practice medicine in Australia as yet, but I do believe it will not be long.'

Daniels kissed the back of her hand lightly.

Charlotte seemed to brighten at the sight of Rita.

'We are grateful for your attendance on our daughter,' she said.

'How is she?' asked Rita.

'She was sleeping when I checked in on her ten minutes ago,' said Charlotte. 'Come, I'll take you to her room.'

Hamish followed the women. 'Have there been any incidents since her fright during the night?' asked Rita.

'None,' said Hamish. 'Alice slept peacefully. I checked in on her this morning, and she said she was well. I didn't examine her, knowing you were on your way.'

Alice was sitting up in bed flipping through a newspaper. Red was curled up in the armchair, with one eye open to keep watch on her.

'You are awake,' said her mother surprised. 'This is Dr Rita Cartwright. She has come to examine you, dear.'

'Let's get to know one another first,' said Rita. 'No hurry.' She removed the terrier and sat at the edge of the chair.

Charlotte watched over them. 'Thank you, Charlotte,' said Rita. 'Alice and I will be fine.'

The tone was dismissive, but the words were spoken in a voice that sounded like warm sugar. Charlotte left them reluctantly. Red stood firm by the bed.

Within moments Alice and Rita were chatting about the confinement like old friends. Realising he was superfluous to the proceedings, Hamish left them to it.

'Come on, mate,' he said. But the terrier stood his ground. Hamish glared at him for a moment before he relented. 'All right. Stay there then, and keep an eye on proceedings,' he said as he left. He knew his permission was redundant. The dog was not going anywhere.

An hour later, Rita joined him on the veranda. As if he had been watching for her, Wallace appeared with a glass of lemonade.

'Do you know where Tennyson is?' Hamish asked him. 'I've not seen him this morning?'

'He returned home before you were up,' said Wallace. 'He said he had business to attend.'

'I'm surprised he didn't wait for word of Alice's examination,' said Hamish.

Rita tilted her head to one side. 'It's best he didn't wait if he has urgent business,' she said. 'I can detect no problem with the confinement. She is certainly close to her time, though, and that infant is full-term. By the way, your dog is standing guard over her if you are looking for him.'

Rita raised one perfectly arched eyebrow. 'She tells me she and her husband have been married six months.'

'That's correct,' said Hamish.

Rita smiled. 'Not so uncommon,' she said. 'As long as she's married, people will be willing to overlook a discrepancy in the dates.' She took a sip of her drink.

They were contemplating the implications of the early birth when they became aware of a presence.

'I heard your voice,' said Charlotte. 'Is my daughter well?'

Rita jumped at the realisation that Charlotte was behind her.

'Your daughter is fine,' she said. 'She's resting now. I would like her to remain in bed. Another bleed at this stage would be troubling. I'm expecting the baby will be born quite soon.'

Charlotte didn't reply.

Hamish knew Wallace had an excellent sense of what was appropriate conversation in front of someone considered a servant, so he wasn't surprised when he hurried from the room. Hamish also knew that Wallace was invisible to Charlotte unless he was preparing her meals. If he had stayed, she would have been oblivious to his presence. Hamish had his own way of blending into the background. He settled into the wicker chair and remained silent.

'You have a beautiful home, Mrs Daniels,' said Rita.

'Please call me Charlotte,' she smiled.

'And I, Rita,' said Rita smiling back.

First names, that's sound progress, thought Hamish.

'It's an Eden in the bush,' went on Rita, 'the river, the gardens, the backdrop of mountains. A painter could not compose a lovelier picture.'

Charlotte's eyes clouded.

'Perhaps when one lives with such beauty, one becomes too easily accustomed to it. It becomes harder to see the beauty through the monotony of everyday experience,' she said.

'Monotony?' cried Rita. 'But you have had nothing but excitement this past week. Hamish informed me of the death of your manager and the fire. You must be wondering what could happen next?'

Charlotte didn't look up from her hands, clasped firmly in her lap.

'I admit my husband is anxious about the plantation,' she said. 'It does sadden me to see him so. I believe there is someone intent on destroying his business. And my daughter's condition concerns me. But as for my own needs, they are few.'

How strange she is, thought Hamish. He wondered that he had not noticed her detachment earlier.

'You must be looking forward to the new addition to the family. A new baby is a magical event,' said Rita.

'Oh yes,' agreed Charlotte, her eyes lighting up for a fraction of a second. 'I'm looking forward to meeting my first grandchild. Alice will be settled with her new family, and she will be financially secure. My work as a mother will be complete.'

'Is Alice your only child?'

Charlotte's lips pursed, and the light went out in her eyes.

'Yes,' she said. 'She is the only child who lived.'

She paused.

Rita remained silent, waiting.

Hamish held his breath. He was afraid if he breathed, Charlotte would remember he was there and stop talking.

'I had a son,' Charlotte went on. 'He died from fever at six weeks of age. He hardly existed at all. That was before Alice. He would have been twenty-one now.'

'I'm so very sorry,' said Rita. The corner of Charlotte's mouth twisted upward.

'I dream Alice's baby is a boy,' she said. 'I dream it every night.'

Not an entirely healthy dream, thought Hamish, but perhaps understandable.

'Would you have liked to have more children yourself, Charlotte?' asked Rita.

The pretty face turned hard like a crack had appeared and distorted its shape.

'God did not wish it. And I did not want to tempt fate. The loss of my son was too horrible to bear. I contented myself with a healthy daughter and hoped one day she might produce a grandson.'

Hamish felt a prickle of discomfort. It didn't seem healthy that Charlotte was so reliant on her daughter producing a male child.

'What if the baby is a girl?' asked Rita cheerfully. 'Will you be disappointed?'

'Maybe a little. But there will be more children.' Charlotte smiled.

'Do you have brothers and sisters yourself?'

'No,' said Charlotte. 'I am an only child, as was Alice. My father was an important man in London. We had wealth and comfort. I wanted for nothing as a child. My father passed away when I was eighteen. We found out my father had speculated in a mining company in South Africa and lost a large sum of money. The house had to be sold. My mother was humiliated. I decided to sail to Australia to seek my own fortune. There was nothing to keep me in London.'

'How courageous of you to travel so far alone,' cried Rita. 'Your mother must have been consumed with worry for your safety.'

'I doubt it,' said Charlotte. 'We were never close, and she was tending her own wounds at the time.'

'Nonetheless, you fared well. You landed in Queensland and found William,' Rita said with enthusiasm.

Charlotte met her enthusiasm with a lack of emotion.

'I met William,' she agreed. 'He had not long bought this land. It was a cotton plantation in those days. He was enthusiastic about the prospect of the sugar industry. He was right to be. The industry was booming for a decade. He built this house, created the mill.' She stopped short. 'Well,' she said, 'as you know, the industry is failing now. Apparently, the Europeans are producing beet sugar for the market. And the Premier is forcing an end to the coloured labour.'

'Your husband is clever, Charlotte. He will diversify, as he did when he shifted the plantation from cotton to sugar.'

'Oh yes. He is flexible. He is talking about increasing the capacity of the rum distillery. There will never be a time when the market for rum is depleted,' she said.

At that moment, Ginny appeared on the veranda to inform them lunch was ready to serve. They settled at the dining table where William Daniels joined them.

Wallace entered with roast pork on a platter, surrounded by his crusty baked potatoes. The aroma filled the small room, and they all forgot about everything in anticipation of the meal.

'It seems we are more deeply indebted to Doctor Hart each day,' said Charlotte. 'He introduced us to our new cook, Wallace.'

Wallace beamed at Rita, who smiled politely back at him. 'Good day to you, Mr Wallace,' she said.

Wallace nodded, showing no indication he had ever seen the lady before. He placed the platter on the table and returned to the kitchen. Ginny served each of them a plate overflowing with delicious, perfectly baked pork and vegetables.

Full and satisfied from the ample meal, Rita returned to sit with Alice, and Hamish sought out Wallace to see what he had found out about the family.

He met Wallace in the mess. It was the perfect place to ensure they were not overheard because they could see in every direction. No one could lurk behind them, listening to their conversations, and no one could approach without being seen.

'Rita is getting along with mother and daughter,' mused Wallace.

'Yes, she is,' said Hamish. 'I wonder how well they get along with one another.'

'According to the workers, they've never been close,' said Wallace. 'But there was no sign of overt animosity until a few weeks before the wedding. There seems to have been a falling out. Alice became cold toward her mother. Stopped speaking to her, other than when it was essential to planning the wedding.'

'That's interesting,' said Hamish. 'What caused the change? Do you think there might be more to the relationship with Eddie Hotham than you were led to believe?'

Wallace dug a cigarette from his pocket and lit it.

'Where'd you get that?' cried Hamish.

Wallace looked at the thing in his hand. 'Daniels gave it to me,' he said. 'He wants me to know how much he appreciates me coming to work for them at short notice. Says it means the world to Charlotte.'

There was another pang of guilt for Hamish.

'I suppose you'll be telling me you're staying next,' he said, only half-joking.

Wallace grinned.

'Getting back to Alice,' Wallace said, the cigarette perched expertly in the corner of his mouth. 'I do think there may be more to her relationship with Hotham. Eddie Hotham believed so. According to Simpson, he was devastated when the engagement between Alice and Peter Tennyson was announced. Everyone had expected Alice would marry Tennyson, so no one else was taken by surprise. But Eddie Hotham may have had his own ideas because he seems to have been shocked by the announcement. Simpson says it was like he had been blind-sided.'

'So, regardless of how Alice felt, Eddie Hotham may have had designs on Alice,' said Hamish.

'Have you had a chance to talk to Hotham about this?'

'No. I haven't had occasion to get close to Eddie Hotham. He keeps to himself, a bit aloof if you know what I mean. It would seem unnatural for me to strike up a personal conversation with him.'

'I agree,' said Hamish. 'But I could initiate such a conversation.'

At that moment, they saw Ginny running across the grass from the house.

'Doctor,' she called. 'Doctor Hart!'

CHAPTER FOURTEEN

Newcastle Morning Herald Saturday 31 October 1885.

A member of the French Academy of Medicine recently presented to his colleagues two mites of humanity of whom he is legitimately proud; for the fact that the couple of wee infants, each of which could be held up for view in the joined palms of his two hands were alive and strong enough to utter cries, is proof of the success that has attended his efforts to rear prematurely born babies. The tiny specimens of our race which excited the admiration and curiosity of the Academy of Medicine came into the world, one four months, and one four months and a half, it is estimated, before they were due. They weighed at their birth a trifle over a couple of pounds each and had so little vitality that they only just escaped being stillborn. The infants, however, did just breathe, and the spark of life was not allowed to become extinct. They were placed in a humidity crib; their fragile bodies were nourished by artificial means, until, under constant care and attention, they are now, at six weeks old, able to take the breast, and will, it is believed, survive the accident of premature birth.

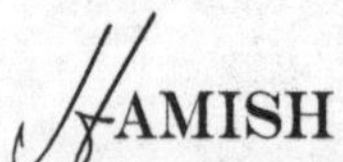

HAMISH

Hamish took the steps to the veranda two at a time. Rita was at the top of the stairs.

'What is it?' he cried, struggling to catch his breath.

'Alice,' said Rita. 'I'm sure her time has come.'

'Good Lord,' said Hamish.

Rita led him along a narrow hallway to Alice's room.

Hamish entered the room to see Alice lying flat on the bed,

panting. Her face was pale and covered in sweat. As Hamish placed his palm on the large mound stretching against the sheet, Alice let out a cry. She arched her back and followed up with a long guttural growl. The skin under Hamish's hand tightened. Then as the contraction passed, he felt her muscles loosen, and her body relax again.

'How frequent are the contractions?' he asked.

'Very frequent,' said Rita. 'I'm going to carry out an internal examination, Alice,' she said. 'Do you mind if Doctor Hart is present?'

'Do what you have to do,' cried Alice.

Rita removed the sheet covering Alice and lifted her gown.

'This is it, Alice,' she said. 'It is time to meet your baby.' Rita poured water from the jug on the washstand over her hands, then dried them and rubbed them together to warm them.

She placed her hands on Alice's abdomen and cupped them around the shape of the baby. 'The head is down,' she said, turning to Hamish. 'This baby is definitely full term and a healthy weight at that.' Hamish breathed a sigh of relief. This had been his assessment as well, but he was anxious he may have been mistaken. He knew of the existence of warm-air incubators for babies born prematurely. But it seemed unlikely there would be such equipment available in Brisbane.

Alice let out an almighty howl and her back arched once more. 'Everything is as it should be,' Rita said. 'It will be over in no time, and you will have your beautiful baby.'

Hamish stood back. 'You have more experience in this than I do,' he said.

Rita moved herself to where she could be of most help to Alice. 'Alice will achieve this particular task with or without either of us,' she said.

Alice took a deep breath as she grappled with another wave of torturous pain. As the pain subsided, tears rolled down her cheeks. 'Did you bring chloroform?' Hamish asked.

Rita looked up at him, a slight indication of frustration in her eyes. 'No,' she said, 'but labour has only begun. I think this is going to be over quickly. I don't think there'll be any need for chloroform.'

Alice cried out again, and her whole body contorted. Her face was crimson.

'You must breathe,' said Rita. 'Hamish, hold her hand and remind her to breathe. I'll let you know when to push, Alice. Don't waste all your energy too soon.'

Hamish held on to Alice's slim fingers while they gripped his own like a vice through every contraction. He soon established a rhythm for her breathing. After forty-five minutes of alternating breathing times with periods of torturous pain and heroic bearing down, Rita cried, 'Push now, Alice, with all your might. Keep on pushing, more Alice, more, don't stop, one more monumental push, Alice....'

Alice looked to Hamish like she would expire from the effort. She squeezed his hand so tightly he felt her fingernails pierce his skin. Still, he willed her to keep going.

At last, Alice fell back against the bed, exhausted. Rita handed a greasy bundle to Hamish. 'It's a boy,' she said to Rita.

Hamish looked the infant over and, finding everything in order, handed him to his mother. She lay with her son face down on her chest, his little arms and legs tucked beneath him for some minutes while Hamish and Rita cleaned up. Hamish was washing his hands in the basin when he heard the door swing open and Charlotte rush in, a torrent of nervous energy. She swooped onto the baby and went to pluck him from his comfortable spot on his mother's chest. Rita caught her by the wrist as she was about to lift the child. She held firmly and spoke with gentle authority. 'They need their rest,' she said, maintaining her grip on Charlotte's wrist. Charlotte resisted momentarily, then allowed herself to be led from the room. She looked back at the child as Rita and Hamish accompanied her out.

They all needed time to relax after the excitement of the birth. Hamish and Rita headed for the kitchen.

'That baby is definitely full term. Eight pounds at least,' said Hamish when they were alone.

'I know,' said Rita, helping herself to the warm scones Wallace had recently taken from the oven.

'There are only two possibilities, either Alice was having a sexual relationship with Peter Tennyson prior to marriage, or....'

'Or Peter Tennyson is not the father,' Rita finished his sentence.

'Oh dear,' said Hamish. 'This child is the heir to the largest sugar plantation in southern Queensland. The last thing the family will welcome is doubt over paternity.'

'Are you going to raise it with them?'

Hamish looked thoughtful.

'Under normal circumstances, I would consider it none of my business,' he said. 'Mother and baby are healthy. But in light of the murders, it might be relevant.' He looked at Rita.

'You won't know unless you ask,' she said.

Everything had gone so smoothly they knew Alice would have been fine without Rita's attendance. But Hamish worried about how eager Charlotte was to take control of the child.

'I think I'll sit with Alice,' said Rita when she finished her tea.

'You can read my mind,' said Hamish.

'Of course, I can read your mind,' laughed Rita. 'I'm surprised you ever doubted it.'

An hour later, Rita joined Hamish in the sitting room. Clouds had gathered over the plantation, and a cool breeze had brought him in from the veranda.

'I've told Charlotte that Alice is sleeping,' she said. 'She can join them as soon as Alice wakes and hold the baby if Alice is in agreement.'

'If Alice sleeps for too long, Charlotte will explode from frustration,' said Hamish. 'She's been pacing the verandas for an hour. Although she seems to have retired to her room now.'

'Alice is worried about her mother's controlling nature,' whispered Rita so she could not be overheard.

'I confess I'm worried as well. She's too attached to the idea of this baby replacing her own child who passed,' said Hamish. 'Surely, it's a fleeting emotion and will pass.'

'I'm not so sure,' said Rita. 'Alice says she didn't want the child born at Cloverton because it will cement the idea he belongs here, in the mind of her mother.'

'Do you think Charlotte is that controlling?'

'It doesn't matter what I think,' said Rita, 'Alice believes she is.'

Late that afternoon, Hamish returned to the bedroom to find Alice and the baby snuggled happily together. Charlotte was in a chair beside the bed, her face beaming. The difference between her countenance now and during her earlier interaction with Rita was astonishing. Her wish had been fulfilled. Here was the boy that would replace her own son.

'Good afternoon,' he said.

They both appeared pleased to see him. Alice had the glow that comes from producing a healthy baby. Charlotte was smiling from ear to ear.

'Is he feeding?' Hamish asked, touching his chubby leg.

'Oh yes, he's very strong,' Charlotte answered on Alice's behalf. Alice smiled.

'You look well enough,' Hamish said. 'Would you like me to check you over anyway?'

Charlotte stood. 'I must go now. I promised to call on our neighbours and relay the good news.' She kissed her daughter and grandson goodbye and left.

Hamish sat in the chair vacated by Charlotte. Everyone seems healthy and content, he thought. He set aside his suspicions of tension between mother and daughter as unfounded. They were all living through a stressful period in their lives. He acknowledged that the birth of a child is an emotional event for a new mother and grandmother.

'I'm quite well,' said Alice. 'It was good of you to offer, but I am in no further need of a doctor.'

'Good,' said Hamish. 'The burden of my profession is that I'm happiest when my patients no longer need me.'

Alice turned her face away.

'He is a fine, healthy boy,' said Hamish. 'Full-term, at that.'

Alice blinked, but she didn't look back at him. Instead, she glanced down at the furry head tucked into the crook of her arm.

'I don't wish to be indelicate...' began Hamish.

'Then don't,' said Alice, her icy stare turning to meet his eyes. The acid tone he recognised from their first meeting had returned.

'I do need to ask one question, Mrs Tennyson. Is your husband the father of this child?'

Alice continued to look into his eyes, but she said nothing. She looked neither embarrassed nor offended. Her face was blank. How long had she practised this lack of expression to produce it so perfectly?

Hamish considered how he might pursue an answer to the question before deciding not to bother. He knew an icy denial that would not be shattered when he saw one.

'Well then,' he said, rising. 'I'll leave the two of you in peace. 'You must rest today.' 'Have the family sent word to your husband? I would've expected him to come galloping up to meet his son before now?'

'Word has been sent. Apparently, my husband is engaged in important business and will attend as soon as he is able.'

Hamish hesitated. 'You have been engaged in important business yourself,' he smiled.

Alice did not return his smile as he left the room.

Hamish and Rita decided to board the steamer returning to Brisbane. It was a beautiful evening, and the journey was a pleasure. Cool breezes came from the sea, and they enjoyed delightful views of the cane and crops along the river frontage. When they left the mouth of the river and turned along the coast, the breeze developed into a chilly wind. Rita wrapped a woollen scarf around her head and neck while Hamish lifted the collar of his coat. They remained side by side, clinging to the railing. Rita inched closer to him and used him as a windbreak.

'Why do you think Peter Tennyson did not come to his wife immediately after the child was born?' Hamish asked. 'Do you think he suspects the child might not be his?'

'Maybe he's simply focused on his work. Many men are. They stay as far from any contact with the messy business of birthing as possible.'

'Yes, but a son and heir?'

'He'll turn up now the awful part is over, and he can brag to his friends about the bonny baby boy.'

'He won't be bragging if the baby is not his own,' said Hamish. 'He must be confronted on the subject, but I'm not having that conversation alone. That's a job for Sergeant Bellamy.'

'I fear Charlotte has an unhealthy obsession with the infant,' said Rita as they gazed at the wetlands along the coastline nearer to Brisbane.

'I do wonder,' said Hamish. 'But surely her eagerness is natural, given the loss of her own son. I think she'll calm down as time goes on. Her only goal is to see her family happily settled.'

'Do you believe so?' Rita raised her eyebrows as she turned to him.

'What do you believe?' he said, a touch of defiance in his voice.

'I believe when her father died, her goal was to come to Queensland to recreate the family of wealth and power she had known as a child.'

'Nothing wrong in that is there?' said Hamish.

'It was a satisfactory arrangement when the plantation was doing well. They were building the home and family she craved. Then her son died, and it was the first time since the death of her father she couldn't have exactly what she wanted.'

'It must have been such an excruciating loss for her. It would be so for any woman.'

'Many women suffer the loss of an infant. I'm not denying the pain of that. But there is something manipulative about Charlotte.'

'Do you think her a calculating woman?' asked Hamish.

'Extremely so,' Rita responded.

'That's a little unfair.'

'Not only calculating, I think she may be slightly unbalanced.'

Hamish looked shocked. 'On the basis of what?'

'Alice says she has been trying to escape her controlling influence all her life.'

'Mothers and daughters,' mused Hamish. 'I like Charlotte. There is a sweetness about her.'

Rita appeared as though she was about to choke. 'There is nothing sweet about her, Hamish, despite appearances. I've listened to your stories about Charlotte for a week, and I'm more concerned than ever now that I've met her.'

They were silent for a few minutes, watching the coastline move by.

'I'm going to talk to Collette about her,' Rita said at last.

'You are what?' exclaimed Hamish. 'You can't discuss police business with Collette.'

'I'm not going to discuss police business. I am going to discuss the mental health of an acquaintance. Collette will offer to speak with her. I know she will'

'No!' Hamish cried. 'Bellamy will have a fit. He's in the middle of a murder investigation. You can't bring your friend in to analyse the family and confuse matters.'

'Charlotte is grieving for her lost son; even after all these years, she needs help. It has nothing to do with your sergeant's murder investigation. I believe she is suffering from melancholia.'

'She may well be. Indeed, I believe you would find if such things were possible to measure, we are all suffering to some extent from melancholia. But you can't muddy the waters of a murder enquiry by introducing someone offering spurious treatments for ill-defined conditions to an already vulnerable family.'

'Spurious treatments? Ill-defined conditions? Do you not believe melancholy to be a serious and definable complaint?' Rita watched Hamish closely while he continued to stare at the shore.

'On the contrary, I believe melancholy to be one of the most prevalent conditions of our time. The prevalence of melancholy, mild or intense, particularly among the educated classes, would be portentous if it could be faithfully measured. I see it every day in my practice. The cultivated don't allow their feelings to show. Still, when they visit the doctor, and the mask is set aside in the consulting room, cheerfulness fades into despair. Many successful and wealthy men and women state they are nigh exhausted from the effort of concealing their melancholy. But it is so serious, and so widespread, it requires scientific enquiry and the development of treatments that can be measured for their effectiveness.'

Rita was silent. This was an unusual circumstance for her. Hamish wondered if he'd been too harsh.

When Rita had formulated a response, she said, 'I don't think we need to wait until science has fully defined the condition before we make some attempt at treating it. We can record successes and failures as we go. Collette is knowledgeable and sensible, and I believe she can be of help to Charlotte.'

Hamish had been enjoying his time alone with Rita as the steamer putted its way toward Brisbane. He didn't like any discord between them.

'Since she has waited this long,' he said, 'Charlotte can wait a little longer for help. Bring your Collette to meet Charlotte by all means after the murder enquiry has been resolved.'

Rita was only trying to help a woman she saw as being in need, after all. But the constant talk of Collette made him irritable.

'Very well,' agreed Rita. 'I'll let Collette know she must wait until after the murderer has been identified before making contact with Charlotte. I had planned to introduce them, and I doubt there will be the opportunity for social introductions before all this is resolved anyway.'

They both took pleasure in seeing the mouth of the Brisbane River open up before them. It meant they were not too far from home. A gust of wind blew Rita's scarf into Hamish's face, and he tried to flick it away. He got his fingers caught in the wool, and as Rita pulled back, the scarf came off completely and was nearly lost over the side of the steamer. Hamish caught it just before the front end hit the water. He rolled it in as though he were reeling in a fishing line and handed it back to Rita triumphantly.

'There's no need to be so proud of yourself,' she quipped, 'since you're the one who tore it from my neck in the first place.'

'It wasn't my favourite anyway,' he said. 'More functional than aesthetic.'

'Unlike the fashionable designs worn by Charlotte Daniels,' Rita replied. 'I'm surprised she can move about with all that fabric pulled back into a bustle. Why do women wear those things? They're grotesque.'

Hamish looked sideways at her. He wondered why the conversation had returned to Charlotte.

'Women are slaves to social convention,' she went on. 'Fashion is an extreme expression of social convention. It represents the need to be seen as part of an elite group.' She smiled at her divided skirt. 'I prefer to be healthy and free to do whatever I like. I can ride my bicycle in these.'

'Charlotte Daniels lives on a rural property in Queensland,' he said. 'She doesn't need to wear high fashion dresses to fit into society. Indeed, her clothes are out of step with the other women in the area. You don't approve of those tight-fitting bodices and long skirts in the Queensland climate?' he asked Rita.

'Of course, I don't. The Rational Dress Society says....'

'What society?'

'The Rational Dress Society. A group of women in London founded the society to object to women's fashion that is restrictive or unhealthy. We have similar groups in Australia. I have been to many public lectures on the subject. I'll take you next time since you are suddenly so interested in Lady's fashion,' she said.

'I'm not that interested.' Hamish couldn't think of anything worse than an afternoon lecture at the Rational Dress Society.

'You don't like Charlotte Daniels, do you?' he said.

'Honestly, Hamish, I think she resembles a plucked and skewered fowl, with a terrifyingly tight band around its centre. The bird-like appearance of all these fashionable women makes me laugh.'

Hamish was shocked at her directness, even though he had pressed her for her opinion.

Rita softened a little. 'At the same time, I pity Charlotte. Fancy being so determined to appear better than your neighbours that you confine yourself to the indoors through clothing that is so inappropriate to the climate and freedom of movement that it prevents you ever leaving the house.'

Hamish was still reeling from the passion of her view of Charlotte Daniels. He had to admit he had allowed himself to develop a soft spot for her. She seemed vulnerable, and it made him feel protective of her. He also found her attractive. While he agreed with Rita on the topic of fashion, Charlotte's overt femininity stirred him. It had to be acknowledged that it contrasted sharply with the independence and no-nonsense of Rita's personality.

CHAPTER FIFTEEN

The Telegraph Saturday 18 July 1885.

As much misapprehension exists with regard to the costume of the Rational Dress Society, and especially respecting the dual skirt, I wish to describe it with what may be even wearisome minuteness. The skirt is by no means the only reform we advocate, but it is the only thing in our programme which is a departure from received notions. In looking at the skirt, it is not at once evident that instead of one garment enwrapping both the lower limbs, there is a petticoat for each leg. So, it is that anyone so clad is especially alive to her two-leggedness by reason of her increased activity of limb. Having the gain promised by the name of the dual skirt depends a good deal on the length of the tunic, upper skirt, or polonaise worn with it. Those who have the full courage of their opinions will perhaps shorten their drapery and the dual skirt also and present an appearance approaching that of a tennis player. The skirts should quite clear the ground. They should reach the insole or thereabouts. Each half of the skirt should be a yard or three-quarters of a yard at the ankle. Our Society recommends that the skirt and the underclothing be fastened to a broad band fitting around the hips, so avoiding pressure of any sort around the waist, or if preferred, hooks or buttons can be sewn on a bodice to correspond with buttonholes on the skirt. If, as I have said in the Health Journal, the weight of skirts is hung from the waist and not supported as reason would dictate by the bony framework of the body, it causes displacement of internal organs. For the top part of the dress, our society favours any loose bodice or jacket but forbids bands, ligatures or any pressure from below the ribs to the top of the hips. In our costume, the weight of clothing is minimised because the dual skirts clothe the body fully and evenly. Fewer garments are needed, and each garment is of a simpler form.

HAMISH

Hamish was about to take his first bite of warm toast when Rita came into view, leaping up the stairs taking two at a time. 'I'm on my way to Lady Bowen,' she said. 'Stopped by for breakfast.'

She was wearing the divided skirt again. She swished the ample yard of fabric around one leg, back and forth. Hamish saw that while the garment looked like one piece when she stood with her legs together, it fell into two separate legs when she moved them about.

'It allows freedom of movement,' she said cheerfully, demonstrating with her legs kicking upward one at a time.

'That it does,' agreed Hamish.

Hamish found himself reluctantly enjoying the way she was energised by this new commitment to exercise. His reluctance was due to his own distaste for physical exertion, he knew. It was difficult to maintain a general rationale against exercise when he could see the evidence before him of increased energy and vibrance.

Rita went straight down to the kitchen and prepared the tea and toast. She was as comfortable in Hamish's home as he was. And Wallace wasn't there to feed them. Hamish caught himself regretting Rita would never share his house with him. But wallowing over his feelings for Rita was a pointless exercise. Rita was who she was, and he loved her exactly as she was. Even if that meant she would never marry him.

'Hamish, I wish you would at least try to like Collette. I'm sure you'd find her interesting if you gave her a chance,' said Rita as she carried the breakfast tray upstairs. Wallace was following along behind her.

'I don't dislike Collette.' After a moment's hesitation, he added, 'but I can't pretend to believe in spiritualism.'

'Collette doesn't blindly follow spiritualism,' Rita pointed out, 'she is open to ideas that go beyond what science can currently explain. She has an intelligent mind. She questions what we think we know to be true.'

'Questioning is healthy, but I fear some people jump too quickly to conclusions that celebrate deviation from what is an accepted truth simply because they are excited by them.'

'We're attending a séance tonight. I'm looking forward to it, I've never experienced one before. Why don't you come along, see for yourself?'

'Rita! You can't be seriously attending a séance?' Hamish laughed. 'I knew séances would come up. This is what I mean. This is sensationalism, not scientific enquiry.'

'You have closed your mind – no serious scientist would close his mind to new possibilities or experiences.'

'Fine,' said Hamish, rolling his eyes. 'I'll attend your séance and do so with an open mind and heart. Is your friend conducting it?'

'No. A medium called Mrs Samuels is conducting the séance. It's to be held at the Harrison's, the same house you visited for the tennis tournament.'

'Quite the place for novel experiences,' commented Hamish.

Rita ignored the quip. 'Mrs Samuels is well known for her talents in communicating with the spirits. Apparently, she conducted a similar séance at Grosvenor Hall during the season in London.

Collette has been asked to observe the event and write an article for the Psychic Society.'

Hamish arrived at the house at the precise time stipulated by Rita, and he found the building no less commanding in the dark. Two tall gaslights marked out the edges of the claw staircases, and Hamish chose one to ascend. He wondered when there would ever be so many guests that two staircases were needed to accommodate them. The house seemed to be in darkness, except for a hall light flickering just inside the front door. Hamish thought for a moment he may have come on the wrong evening, then he heard footsteps on the stair behind him. He turned around to see Sergeant Bellamy lower on the same claw, with a woman who was short, plump, and pleasant looking on his arm.

'Bellamy,' Hamish cried, unable to keep the surprise from his voice.

'Surprised to meet you here as well, Doctor. This is my wife, Agatha.' The woman beamed at him. Hamish noticed her almond-shaped brown eyes, soft and cheerful, her smile white against her olive skin. She exuded warmth immediately, and Hamish enjoyed the feint odour of patchouli that surrounded her.

'A pleasure to meet you, Mrs Bellamy,' he said, taking her gloved hand in his and bowing gallantly, breathing deeply as he did so.

'Dr Hamish Hart,' he said.

Bellamy seemed eager to explain his presence at such an event. 'I was invited by Mrs Harrison, our hostess this evening and the owner of this lovely house,' he said. 'The idea is to have guests present who are known for their objectivity. I wouldn't have accepted, but Agatha was insistent. I didn't want to disappoint her.'

'I imagine you were invited for the same reason, Dr Hart?' commented Agatha.

'Certainly,' agreed Hamish, knowing his only reason for attending was that Rita had asked him to come.

They entered the dimly lit hallway together. The sound of chattering voices and rising excitement could be heard coming from deeper in the house. The woman who had been introduced to Hamish as Mrs Harrison at the tennis afternoon emerged from a room to the left of the hallway, the room evidently the source of the excited chatter.

'Good evening,' she said. 'Welcome to our little experiment, Sergeant... Doctor.'

'My wife Agatha,' said Bellamy. Mrs Harrison held both Agatha's tiny hands in her own formidable ones.

'Come with me, dear,' she said as she shuffled Agatha away from the men and seated her in the room. Hamish and Bellamy followed and were ushered by a man Hamish didn't know to seats nearer the back of the room. All the seats had been arranged to face the same direction, at the culmination of which was a dark cabinet, narrow and tall with a thick curtain pulled back. A chair sat in the centre of the cabinet, facing outward to the audience. The doctors, scientists and the inspector, indeed all the men, were seated to the back of the room while the women were seated closest to the front. Hamish chuckled to see that Rita was seated in the front row with

Collette rather than at the back with the sceptics.

As if she could feel his presence, Rita turned around and nodded to acknowledge Hamish. Her left eyebrow raised in surprise at seeing Bellamy seated beside him.

Hamish guessed there were about twenty-five people in the room. He recognised some of Brisbane's most prominent citizens, including two lawyers and a well-known physician from the Brisbane Hospital. He also recognised the reporter from the Brisbane Courier who had tried to question him outside the Police Depot the morning after Jock McDonald's death. Did these people believe in this nonsense? How many of them came out of curiosity? Or to expose a sham? The evening was shaping up to be more significant than he expected.

'Attention, everyone,' called out Mrs Harrison from the front of the room. Her voice, deep and sharp, captured the room immediately.

When everyone was silent, she welcomed them and explained the evening's proceedings.

'Four ladies from among us will now take Mrs Samuels into another room and assist her to change her costume into a gown selected by us,' she said. She nodded for four ladies from the front row to proceed. Hamish recognized two of them from the tennis afternoon. They led the medium from the room while the guests were left to postulate on the importance of this step among themselves. There was an excited murmur across the room as individuals shared their interpretation of proceedings thus far. Some declared they had read of similar processes followed in London.

When the medium returned, she was fully dressed in black, a plain gown with a high collar and a simple skirt that touched the floor. Her grey hair was pulled tight into a bun at the back of her neck. Hamish was reminded of a stern school mistress he had feared in Melbourne during his adolescence. The four women resumed their seats in the audience. The medium sat upright in the chair within the cabinet, her back straight and stiff. Only her face could be seen clearly. As Hamish stared, his eyes registered what appeared to be the woman's disembodied head. At the same time, his brain reminded him the rest of her was simply camouflaged by her black gown against the black internal walls of the cabinet.

A committee of four men was selected by the hostess. The men proceeded to tie a cord around the medium's neck and waist, securing her to both her chair and the wall of the cabinet behind. One end of the cord was passed to a gentleman in the front row. Mrs Harrison explained this was so the gentleman could detect any movement made by Mrs Samuels within the cabinet. A piece of plaster, two or three inches long, was placed across her mouth to prevent any possibility of her using her voice.

'While the singing of hymns is common prior to many séances, in this case, we ask that you remain silent,' announced Mrs Harrison. 'That way, we will be able to hear any movement that should take place in the cabinet.'

Hamish glanced around the room. He felt no compulsion to break out in song, and he doubted anyone else in the audience did either. He did have to admit the effort being made to validate the integrity of the experience was impressive.

When everyone agreed that Mrs Samuels was tied securely and could not move, the cabinet curtain was lowered, leaving the medium within. Half the gas lights in the room were extinguished, leaving the room in subdued light. Hamish noticed the crowd strain forward, tense and anxious to see what would happen next. It seemed like an age, but it was less than two minutes before a female form, much larger and taller than Mrs Samuels, appeared at the door of the cabinet. She had an unusually pale face and long, flowing black hair. She stared directly at a male guest in the centre of the room. Hamish strained his eyes to make the man's face out in the dark, but he didn't recognize him. The gentleman stood up and cried, 'My sister!'

The figure whispered, 'Brother.'

The words were barely discernible to Hamish. However, guests assured one another throughout the room that they had heard her say it. The figure disappeared as quickly as it had appeared.

Hamish stretched his neck to make out any details in relation to the cabinet. However, he could see nothing; the thick curtains were still drawn.

Following a moment of silence, a vapour emerged from the top of the cabinet. The vapour quickly assumed the face of an aged female, hovering over the cabinet.

'George,' called a thin voice. At least Hamish thought it was George.

'Mother,' cried a man in the audience.

Hamish put his hand to his mouth to shield a smile.

'Mother!' The man stood and addressed the vision directly. 'How did you pass, mother?'

In appropriately spectral tones, the vision answered that her demise had come quickly, a complaint of the heart. 'It was swift, my son. I have no regrets.'

The man confirmed the circumstances of his mother's death to be true, and the vapour vanished. There was an outbreak of gasps in the audience.

'Silence!' cried their host.

Suddenly, there emerged from the cabinet a tiny girl speaking in a childish voice.

'It's Maudie,' cried a woman seated in the third row. She prodded the lady beside her. 'Don't you remember Maudie from the séance at the Thistle-Thwaites?'

'Yes, yes,' said the woman enthusiastically. 'It's the same child, poor lamb.'

The child disappeared as quickly as the others had done.

Next, a young man was reduced to an audible sob as an apparition of his deceased sweetheart appeared and told him to give the engagement ring to Dottie. Hamish was lost to his curiosity, and he struggled to see the woman's features in the smoke. The young man declared he was certain the apparition was his fiancé.

After a few more manifestations, the remaining gaslights were switched off, and the room descended into total darkness. A hush of anticipation fell. Two illuminated forms, weird and beautiful, flashed into view and moved across the room, almost over the heads of the guests. Their movements created no noise at all, glittering shadows gliding through the darkness. One of the shadows appeared to drop a luminous white rose, the petals separating as they fell to the floor.

The audience let out a combined gasp.

Hamish rolled his eyes. He was no stranger to spiritual experiences. When on Stradbroke Island, he experienced sensations he could not explain. There was the small, hairy man who seemed to follow him through the bush, and the eagle that swooped low over his head several times, his large yellow eye glaring directly into his soul as though it were judging him. These visions caused the hair on the back of his neck to stand upright. But he experienced no similar sensations here. This was illusion and trickery. Entertainment at best, exploitation at worst.

The lights were switched on, and the audience applauded. When the curtain on the cabinet was lifted, Mrs Samuels was found as she had been left, securely bound to her chair and the cabinet wall, the plaster firmly across her lips. The gentleman who held the end of the cord throughout said he had not detected the slightest movement. The medium looked exhausted. The four women who had assisted her in changing her costume had to support her from the room. Hamish was at a loss to understand why the medium was spent. She had done nothing more than sit in the cabinet with her eyes closed the whole time.

Hamish and Bellamy filed out with the other guests to a reception room at the other side of the hallway, where refreshments were laid out. The excitement among the guests was palpable as they crowded around Mrs Samuels and Mrs Harrison. Hamish took a plate and loaded it with bread and butter, and stood in a corner waiting to catch sight of Rita.

Sergeant Bellamy joined him.

'What do you make of that?' asked Hamish.

'It's hardly necessary to say the show created a profound effect of awe on the guests,' Bellamy said.

'They did look taken in,' agreed Hamish.

Just then, Rita and Collette emerged. Rita looked sheepish.

'How did you find the séance?' Collette asked Hamish.

'There was certainly a great deal of showmanship,' he replied.

'You were not impressed?'

'I was indeed impressed,' Hamish assured her. 'A great deal of skill and effort has gone into producing the effects witnessed tonight.'

'You're not left wondering about possibilities beyond our understanding, then?'

'Quite the opposite. I'm left wondering at the ingenious use of dim lighting, vapour, an illusionist's cabinet, skilled actors probably rescued from the street, and the incredible properties of phosphorescent oils.'

Rita looked away from Hamish. He knew she would not want Collette to see her smiling. He felt validated, and he suspected Collette would feel betrayed if she caught the look on Rita's face.

Agatha joined them with a plate full of muffins and a face flushed with excitement. 'Was that the most astonishing display you have ever seen? I shall be talking about it for weeks. To have witnessed such an event!'

After the séance, Sergeant Bellamy travelled in a cab with Hamish as far as his home. 'My wife is still excited by the séance,' Bellamy said. 'While I don't wish to dampen her spirits, I couldn't bear to hear one more rendition of tonight's events. She will ride home with neighbours later. That way, they can share their enthusiasm for the evening's entertainment.'

'I completely understand,' said Hamish. 'I appreciate the opportunity to compare notes on the investigation.'

He relayed his recent visit to Cloverton, the event of the birth and the question around paternity. 'In short, we cannot be sure Peter Tennyson is the father,' said Hamish.

'I'm going to need to ask that question myself,' said Bellamy. 'If someone was poisoning Jock McDonald, there is at least a reasonable chance the birth of this baby is linked to the murder.'

'It may be no more complicated than a young woman and her betrothed being intimate prior to wedlock,' suggested Hamish.

'It might at that,' agreed the Sergeant. 'But alternatively, it may be that the new heir of one of the most valuable parcels of land in Queensland is not who he seems.'

Hamish shifted uncomfortably. The cab was cramped. He could feel Bellamy's breath on his neck when he spoke. 'Why kill Jock McDonald, though?' He said almost to himself.

'Perhaps he was the father?' offered the sergeant.

'Jock? No,' said Hamish. 'Alice detested the man.'

'Plenty of reasons to hate him, I would have thought. Perhaps he forced himself on her? He sounds like he could have been the type.'

'She could be overcompensating, I suppose,' suggested Hamish. 'If she did have feelings for him but doesn't want anyone to know. Either way, I'm convinced Alice is not going to tell us, and I'm not sure we can find out any other way.'

'We have to ask Peter Tennyson,' said Bellamy.

Hamish's left eyebrow shot up. He pushed back the hair that had fallen over his face.

'He won't welcome that,' he said.

Bellamy lent back against the leather upholstery of the cab. 'People rarely welcome the kinds of questions that come with a murder enquiry,' he said.

Hamish tried to think through the possibilities. 'If Tennyson tells the truth, we'll know whether the baby is likely to be his or not,' he said slowly. 'We'll only have his word to go by. On the other hand, if what he says indicates the baby is not likely to be his own, we won't be any closer to identifying the father.'

'Let's say it was Jock,' said Bellamy. 'Who would our suspects be?'

Hamish thought about it. 'The obvious choices would be Pete Tennyson or Alice's father, William Daniels.'

'My thoughts exactly.'

'We need to know whether either of them spent sufficient time with McDonald in the days prior to his death to have been slipping arsenic into his food or drink.'

'I imagine Daniels would have had the best access. He'd be speaking with him daily. Mrs Daniels has already said they drank together in the evenings. Wallace could probably find out whether Tennyson was around more often than usual. By the way, how is Wallace going down there at the plantation? It seems a bit rough; you're sending him off like that.'

'He's happy to do it,' said Hamish.

'He's an interesting character,' said the sergeant. 'I know you picked him up from Dunwich last year, but what is his background, exactly? He strikes me as an intelligent man who refuses to live up to his potential.'

'Very perceptive, Bellamy. Wallace is extraordinarily intelligent;

he just hides it well.' Hamish smiled. 'He was a ship's cook for most of his life prior to his employment at the asylum at Dunwich. His step-father sent him away to work on the ships at thirteen.'

'He seems to have an ingrained distrust of authority,' said Bellamy.

'Yes, partly due to being sent away by his mother and step-father, I suppose. He had a somewhat conflicted relationship with the ship's captain when he was a boy.'

'Conflicted?' asked Bellamy.

Hamish hesitated. 'The Captain took him on as a... well a companion of sorts. On the one hand, he took advantage of the boy, but on the other hand, he was kind to him, schooled him in literature and the arts. You'll find Wesley Wallace the most cultured ship's cook you've met,' laughed Hamish.

Sergeant Bellamy yawned. 'It's been a long day, beginning with the Inspector and his demands that we move this case along and ending with a séance of all things. I'm convinced the murder of Jock McDonald is tied in with this family at Cloverton. I'll not sleep properly until we find out how and why.'

'And who,' added Hamish.

'Yes, who is the most important. But we have little time. I can't hold off the Inspector much longer.'

'It hasn't been a week since the incident at the Albert,' said Hamish.

'The Inspector won't let it go two weeks, my friend. You mark my words. The South Sea Islander will hang if we don't find out who is responsible in the next few days.'

'Kaelo,' said Hamish.

The sergeant shot him an unapologetic glance.

The cab came to a stuttering halt outside Hamish's house.

'I need to interview Peter Tennyson tomorrow,' announced the sergeant. 'Will you come?'

Hamish hesitated while he went over a rationale each way in his mind. He would prefer to be getting on with his practice, but he didn't have any appointments scheduled. He could visit some of the wealthy families he was courting for business. He had an open invitation to join the Wrights for lunch. He climbed out of the cab and looked back at the Sergeant.

'Yes,' he said, 'see you in the morning.'

The cab rattled off down Wickham Terrace while Hamish stared up at the light in his sitting-room window. Had he left a gaslight on? That would've been dangerous, and unlike him. Was he that distracted? He raced up the stairs, half expecting to find an intruder rummaging through his possessions. Instead, he found Rita perched on the blue armchair, her legs swung carelessly over one of the velvet arms. He took a second look at her boots, unsure whether he was more uncomfortable that he could see them under the short skirt or that they were slung across his favourite chair.

'I let myself in,' Rita announced.

'I see that,' said Hamish.

'You should have seen your face during that séance,' she laughed. 'I couldn't believe you actually came, but the look on your face was precious!'

Hamish removed his coat and threw it on one end of the settee. He sat on the other end and eyed Rita carefully. 'I'm glad I was entertaining,' he said. 'Why are you here? It's late.'

Rita swung her legs off the arm of his chair and sat forward. 'I stopped by on my way home to talk to you,' she said. 'I saw you leave in a cab with Bellamy, but I thought you would be home before I arrived.'

'I think the driver may have taken the longest route possible. We were talking and not paying attention.'

'Tell me about the meeting with Bellamy,' Rita said.

'He thinks McDonald might have been the father of the baby,' said Hamish.

Rita laughed out loud.

'What?' said Hamish.

'From everything you have told me, McDonald sounds like an awful man. Why would a girl like Alice, with a high opinion of her own worth, allow herself to be compromised by a man like him?'

'Bellamy suggested he may have forced himself on her,' said Hamish.

Rita laughed again, almost falling off the chair as she did so.

Hamish realised just how tired he was.

'Oh Hamish,' she said, 'Does Alice strike you as the kind of girl to be bullied? She's terrifying.'

Hamish let a small snort pass his lips. 'Yes,' he agreed. 'She is terrifying. Poor Bellamy is terrified.'

'No,' said Rita, 'whoever fathered that child did so with Alice as a willing partner.'

'Do you think the father is her husband?' asked Hamish.

'Wouldn't be uncommon,' said Rita. 'That could mean the birth has nothing to do with the murder,' said Hamish.

'A possibility.'

'We're travelling back to Cloverton tomorrow. Until we find out who fathered the child, I simply can't let go of the feeling that the paternity of that child may be a key element of the case.'

Rita's face took on a seriousness that alarmed Hamish. 'I'm sorry I made you come to the séance,' she said. 'I didn't do it to make fun of you. I knew how you would react, and I admit you are right to be sceptical. I found it all a bit much myself. It's only that Collette is dedicated to either validating or refuting these phenomena. She has this passion to know.'

'Nothing to apologise for,' said Hamish quietly, 'I was curious. I didn't think you were making fun of me, not until just now anyway,' he smiled. 'I'm tired. I'm meeting Bellamy at six in the morning.'

'Good night, Hamish,' said Rita as she swept down the stairs and climbed onto her bicycle. Hamish recognised a wave of concern rising. Should a lady be riding a bicycle at this time of night? He thought not, as a rule, but Rita didn't fit within the rules.

Hamish went downstairs to lock the door; he wanted no more unexpected visitors that night. He noticed a pile of letters on the hall stand by the door. Rita must have picked them up off the floor and placed them there when she let herself in. Shuffling through them, he found a couple of notices from companies with whom he had done business for medical supplies and a letter from his mother. He put them aside to read later. There was also an envelope with a small, clean script. He didn't recognize the handwriting. He opened the seal and unfolded the note within.

Dear Dr Hart,

I am writing to you about your recent advertisement in the Maryborough Chronicle. I am praying you are as kind a gentleman as I imagine you to be and that you are seeking this Aboriginal woman, Araluen, with the intent of easing her burden. I believe the woman to whom you refer in your newspaper enquiry is working as a cleaner at the hospital where I am also employed, as a nurse. At least she was recently working there. I wanted to ask her permission before contacting you, so I made enquiries of the other cleaning staff. I heard that she has been absent from work of late because her son, who is about five years of age and suffering from paralysis for some twelve months, had taken a turn for the worse, and she is unable to leave the child's side. I was presumptuous enough to seek the woman out at her home. I hope you understand this was done purely out of concern. I was shocked to find her living with the child in the most miserable circumstances, in a ramshackle hut built from corrugated iron on the outskirts of town. Is it any wonder the child is ill? The other families living in the area have been removed to a reserve for their wellbeing. The woman you seek avoided being forced to join them as she claims to be of South Sea Islander descent. She has documented evidence of marriage to a South Sea Islander. Nonetheless, I am confident from my enquiries that she is, in fact, Aboriginal and comes from the Mackay region. She is quite alone in her plight, and I fear there is little hope for the improvement of her situation.

I implore you, good Doctor, if it is within your power to improve this woman's prospects and those of her child, please do so as soon as possible. I have included my return address, as it will not be possible for you to reach this woman through the regular post. I am happy to relay correspondence on your behalf.

Regards, Arrabella Woods.

Hamish placed the letter back on the hall stand with the others. He and Rita would have to talk to Kaelo as soon as possible. But he was leaving for Logan first thing in the morning. The exhaustion of a few minutes earlier was replaced with anticipation. He felt certain they had found Kaelo's father's wife. It seemed to Hamish that the boy had not been in an accident but had suffered infant paralysis. He was aware that parents commonly lied about the cause of their children's disability due to the stigma associated with the condition. He would have to see the boy and examine him to be sure. Would Kaelo have enough of his father's money to bring Araluen and the child to Brisbane? If he did not, Hamish decided he would pay for the trip himself. There was no question in his mind about meeting the cost. Still, he did wonder if his assistance might be resented as uninvited interference.

Hamish climbed the stairs to his bedroom and found himself lying awake, despite the lateness of the hour, thinking about how he would organise the trip from Maryborough to Brisbane for Araluen and her son. Where would they stay when they arrived? It seemed from the letter that Araluen had little support in Maryborough. She could not be worse off in Brisbane. Would she want to come? He would need to communicate through this nurse who wrote to him. Should he travel to Maryborough himself? Good Lord, would Kaelo want her brought to Brisbane? Hamish stopped himself there. These questions were not his to answer. His responsibility was to share the information in the letter with Kaelo and take instructions from there. He hoped he would prove sensitive enough to walk the line between supporting Kaelo in his quest and taking over control of the man's life. He forced himself clear his mind to allow sleep to enter.

CHAPTER SIXTEEN

The Daily Telegraph Saturday 4 August 1886.

A man, a native of Donegal, employed at the Pyramid Plantation as an engine driver, met with a fatal accident yesterday when he caught one of his legs up to the knee between the rollers of the mill. He was brought into the hospital that night, and though the leg was amputated, he died this morning. It is believed he has a wife in Brisbane.

HAMISH

The morning light was already intense at six o'clock when Hamish met Bellamy outside the Police Depot. The sergeant had arranged a buggy as they would be travelling to both Tennyson and Cloverton. Neither of them were looking forward to the discussion with Peter Tennyson about the paternity of his wife's child. They didn't expect him to respond well to being asked if he was the father. He would be cornered into either admitting infidelity prior to marriage, thereby casting a shadow over the virtue of his wife, or admitting she had been unfaithful during their engagement, casting her in an even darker light and wounding his own pride in the process.

'There ought to be a formality to the interview this morning,' Bellamy said. 'I will ask the questions. I would have you take notes. We need the exact words spoken. Often people give away more than they hope to, with their choice of wording.'

'I absolutely agree, Sergeant. You take the lead.' Hamish could think of nothing worse than having to ask this particular question. He was hoping to disappear into a corner of the room and pretend he was not there.

When they rode up toward Tennyson House, they saw it was grand in comparison to the house at Cloverton. It wasn't larger, but it had a more formal air. It lacked the wide verandas; instead, a stone staircase led to a solid door framed by an ornate stained-glass surround. A telegram had been sent ahead, so they were reasonably sure Peter Tennyson would be at the house waiting for them. Their expectations were proven well-founded when he met them at the front door. He led them into a study that would have been at home in any of the grand houses of Europe. There were leather chairs with brass studding, a large desk of English Oak with a leather inset and leather-bound books lined three walls. The remaining wall was adorned with an imposing oil by John Constable. This house did not have the country Queensland charm of Cloverton. Everything about it was European, and it seemed ludicrously out of place in its formality in the Queensland bush.

After the initial introductions were complete and they were settled into the soft leather chairs, Hamish and Bellamy congratulated Mr Tennyson on his new son.

'On that topic,' Bellamy braced the subject, 'we are in the unfortunate position of having to ask some sensitive questions of you.'

Tennyson remained standing and drew in the sweet smoke from his pipe.

'You are aware, I am sure, that Mr McDonald was poisoned, and we are investigating his murder?' said Bellamy.

'Yes, I am aware.'

'Although this is sensitive, we need to ask, Mr Tennyson. You do understand?'

'Ask what? Get on with it, whatever it is.'

'You and Alice have been married six months, I believe,' the sergeant said.

'We have,' said Tennyson.

'The baby is full-term,' said Hamish, unable to keep his mouth shut when it came down to it.

There was no sign of recognition on Tennyson's face.

'The Doctor means to say the baby was conceived at least two months before your wedding,' said Bellamy, flashing Hamish a warning look.

The blood visibly rushed to Tennyson's face. He gave the appearance he hadn't given the discrepancy a moment's thought.

'You are mistaken, Doctor,' he muttered.

'There is no doubt,' said Hamish.

Tennyson's eyes searched the room as though he were looking for something to reassure him. He paced from behind the desk to the closed door and then turned and came back again. He glanced up at Hamish, a look of confusion across his eyes. When at last he regained his focus, he stood tall and spoke with certainty and anger in his voice.

'How dare you,' he said. 'How dare you enter my house and make such disgusting insinuations against myself and my wife. I must ask you to leave immediately.'

Bellamy stood up. 'I'm afraid the questions are necessary Tennyson, regardless of how distasteful you find them. We need to know whether you and Alice had relations prior to the wedding? If you did not, you cannot possibly be the biological father of the baby born the night before last.'

Tennyson's face had become so red he looked like he might have a cardiac event. 'Please remain calm, Mr Tennyson. We don't mean to cause you or Alice harm or embarrassment. If you simply answer the question, we will say no more to anyone.'

'Get out!' raged Pete Tennyson. He was loud enough that the butler opened the door to see if everything was all right. 'See these men out,' he growled through gritted teeth.

Hamish and Bellamy followed the butler out of the room and out of the house. He shepherded them until they were on the front porch, the door closing convincingly behind them.

'What do you think of that?' asked Bellamy.

'I think that might have been a no,' said Hamish. 'No. We didn't have relations, so who the bloody hell is the father of that child everyone presumes to be mine.'

Bellamy nodded. 'A bit of a bloody mess, isn't it?'

Hamish and Bellamy travelled on to Cloverton after their meeting with Peter Tennyson. They were both silent as they thought about the discussion Tennyson would be having with his wife.

They strode up the grand stairs to the house at Cloverton and rang the bell. Ginny let them in and told them they would have to wait as Mr Daniels was at the mill. They asked her to let Wallace know they were there.

A few minutes later, Wallace joined them with tea and his famous scones. Hamish caught Wallace up with the news of their interview with Tennyson emphasizing the offended response. Wallace sucked air through his teeth. He was about to comment when he was struck silent by the sight of Charlotte at the door. Charlotte had halted in the doorway seeing Hamish and Bellamy in her sitting room.

'I'm exhausted, gentlemen,' she said quickly. 'I hope you will excuse me if I take tea in my room.' She asked Wallace to bring her a tray and turned to leave.

'If we could have just a moment,' interrupted Bellamy. 'We need to ask a somewhat sensitive question.'

Charlotte stopped and clasped her hand to her chest.

'I think I know what your question is, Sergeant,' she said quietly, turning back toward him. 'And I have no intention of answering it.' She looked at Wallace. 'Bring the tea,' she said brusquely, then she glided from the room.

Hamish and Bellamy stared after her.

At that point, Ginny entered, and Wallace delegated the setting of a tray for Mrs Daniels.

'Talk to Hotham,' he said to Hamish and Bellamy.

'Do you think he knows who the father is?' asked Hamish.

'I know he's the only decent man here.'

'You said he and Alice were close prior to her engagement?' asked Bellamy.

'That's the word here. But there has been no talk of indiscretion.'

'But Hotham must have entertained the idea of marriage if he was so upset when Alice agreed to marry Tennyson,' said Bellamy.

'That you would have to ask him,' said Wallace.

'I can't believe Jock McDonald could have been the father,' said Hamish. 'That's the only option that would make sense in light of the murder.'

'No one here has spoken of an interest between Alice and McDonald, nor of any incident of aggression. If McDonald was involved, Alice has remained quiet about it,' said Wallace.

'Someone fathered the child,' said Hamish. 'Alice is the only person who could know who with any certainty.'

'Do you think Charlotte knows anything about it?'

'She knows the baby was conceived out of wedlock. I'm convinced of it.'

'The trouble is, our list of suspects for the murder includes everyone at Cloverton,' said Hamish.

'If Jock McDonald is not the father of the baby, it could mean the murder has nothing to do with the pregnancy,' said Wallace. 'Remember everyone hated McDonald, except perhaps Daniels.'

Bellamy shook his head slowly. 'I don't know,' he said. 'In my experience where there is a secret, there is a motive.'

'What about the upcoming merger of the two plantations? Is there a way in which Jock McDonald could have been an impediment to that going ahead?' said Bellamy.

'I can't see it,' said Hamish. 'Daniels said himself he would have sent him to work in one of the other businesses.'

'There's a lot at stake,' said Bellamy. 'It will be a large concern once the merger is complete.'

'The word around here is the peak has passed for the sugar industry. Costs outweigh market prices. If the government puts a stop to the Kanaka labour, it will finish the industry, according to Daniels,' said Hamish.

Wallace looked up from his teacup. 'There is the land, though, isn't there?'

He had the attention of the other two men. 'The railway will be open in less than six weeks, the line between South Brisbane and Logan. These pioneer planters will find an increased value on their land, such that they won't need to worry about the price of sugar. When connected by railway to Brisbane, the distance is shortened sufficiently to class these lands as almost suburban. The fertile soil, the river frontages, the picturesque views will tempt plenty of men of means to make this district their home, I would have thought.'

'He's right,' said Bellamy. 'The value of this land is not in the sugar. In the long run, it is in progress.'

'And the new baby is part of the next generation, the generation to profit from this progress,' said Hamish.

Hamish was startled when he heard the clock strike the hour. 'Three o'clock,' he said, 'We'll need to leave now if we hope to be in Brisbane before dark. The buggy is much slower than the horses across the land between here and Cedarwood.'

Bellamy looked at the clock as though it could tell him what to do next.

'I'll send the buggy back,' he said. 'I'm not leaving until we speak with Eddie Hotham.'

'I'll tell the driver,' said Hamish.

'We'll need to impose on Daniel's hospitality again,' continued the sergeant.

Wallace returned to his kitchen to prepare the evening meal.

Hamish and Bellamy walked across to the mill. They stood watching as the cane was trucked upward to the top of the chute and poured down to be crushed under the rollers. It was dark inside the mill. They could see shapes, but not individuals. The constant hammering of the thrashers made it impossible to hear anything else. Hamish tried to understand how the process worked. He could see the labourers filling the carts with the harvested cane, and he could see it travel up toward the chute. Beyond that, everything was dark. He couldn't see Daniels or Hotham from where he stood. He became mesmerised by the rhythmic rattle of the carts, the swoosh of the chute and the rumble of the rollers.

Suddenly, there was a crashing thud. The rollers stopped and the cane rushed down the chute and landed in a chaotic pile on top of the stuck rollers. The carts clattered to a standstill. Daniels came rushing from the darkness within the shed.

'What's happened?' he shouted. Stratton came out from the boiling room.

Two South Sea Islander men who had been winching the carts up to the top of the chute stood staring into the pan with the rollers.

Hamish reached the rollers at the same time as Daniels. The cane was piled high in the pan. Sticking out from the mass of cut cane was a human hand clenched as though desperately trying to claw itself free.

'There's someone caught in there,' murmured Hamish.

'Get him out,' cried Daniels.

The men climbed into the pan and began clearing away the new cane that had fallen on top of the rollers. With each armful of cane, they removed they uncovered more of Eddie Hotham's twisted body. Finally, his face was clear, and they saw his eyes open in a frozen look of horror. Bellamy stared on as Hamish climbed into the cane to check if he was alive. Though it seemed obvious he was not, everyone appeared to hold their breath while Hamish checked for a pulse. There was an audible collective groan when Hamish shook his head.

The rollers had come down on top of Hotham before jamming. Hamish climbed out and returned to Bellamy while Daniels helped the South Sea Islanders extricate the body from the machine. Stratton carefully worked the gears to lift the rollers while Daniels pulled away the corpse. The labourers dragged the body onto the grass beyond the mill.

Bellamy followed them while Hamish stayed a moment staring into the roller tray. As he walked out onto the grass, he missed his stride when he saw Charlotte standing calmly by Bellamy's side.

'What are you doing here?' cried Hamish.

'I heard the crash of the machines,' she said. 'I came to see what had gone wrong.'

Ginny was running from the house, her eyes as wide as saucers.

'Take her inside,' Hamish said to Ginny, eager to get both women away as quickly as possible.

'My husband...,' cried Charlotte.

'Your husband is fine,' said Hamish, 'you can see it is so.' He placed his hand on her back and gently pushed her toward Ginny. He watched as they clung to one another all the way back to the house. He saw Wallace coming toward him from the house at the same time.

The mangled body of Eddie Hotham was carried by the labourers through the back of the house and into the washroom, being the coolest place to keep it until the undertakers could come.

Later, Bellamy, Hamish and Daniels stood in the library drinking whiskey.

'How could such an accident happen?' asked Hamish.

'I don't know,' said Daniels. Hotham was my most experienced man. He knew these machines completely. He could cajole them into working when they stopped. He could pull them apart and put them back together again. I can hardly believe he would put himself in a situation that would allow this to happen.'

'Are you sure it was an accident?' asked Bellamy.

Hamish looked alert.

'What are you talking about?' asked Daniels.

'I'm asking if you think this was an accident?' repeated Bellamy.

'Of course, it was an accident. What else could it have been?'

Bellamy didn't respond.

Daniel's eyes grew wide. 'What? Another murder?' he cried.

Still, Bellamy said nothing.

'How? Why?' cried Daniels, now looking to Hamish for answers.

Suddenly exhausted, Daniels flopped into a chair. He placed his face in his hands. 'I'm ruined,' he muttered.

CHAPTER SEVENTEEN

Glen Innes Examiner Tuesday 22 September 1885.

An English adventurer named Boydell, residing in Vienna, endeavoured to levy blackmail to the extent of 300 pounds on Mr Gladstone, by threatening to disclose a private scandal in which the late Premier would appear to considerable disadvantage. Mr Gladstone handed the matter over to the London Police, and through the Austrian Ambassador, Boydell was arrested and committed. Ten or fifteen years would be a just sentence for such infamy.

Dinner that evening was a sombre affair. Daniels, Charlotte, Bellamy and Hamish sat at the table and picked at the meal Wallace had prepared. Ginny served them, then stood by, waiting in case they needed anything. No one spoke. After the meal, Charlotte said good night and was returning to her room when the sound of a carriage outside surprised them all. Within seconds, a flushed and tear-stained Alice burst through the door. Pete Tennyson stumbled up the stairs after her. Alice threw herself at her mother, sobbing.

'I'm sorry,' said Tennyson, 'I tried to stop her.'

Daniels shook his head and handed his son-in-law a whiskey.

Charlotte led her daughter into the room. 'I want to see him,' Alice cried while her mother repeated, 'No dear.' Alice struggled to free herself from her mother's arms, 'I want to see him,' she shouted, yanking her arm away from her mother's grip.

Charlotte stared into her daughter's face. 'No,' she said.

Alice cried in despair. Daniels had, until this point, been

allowing the women to sort themselves out, but he now stepped in.

He took Alice's hand and brought her close to him.

'I need to see him,' Alice sobbed into her father's chest. Daniels took her hand and walked with her to the washroom.

Charlotte gave an exasperated sigh and headed for her room.

Pete Tennyson was left standing in the sitting room with Hamish and Bellamy. They all felt awkward.

Bellamy was the first to speak. 'We were planning to interview Mr Hotham,' he said. 'That will no longer be possible, obviously.'

Tennyson took a mouthful of whiskey.

'Could Hotham have been the father of Alice's baby?' asked Bellamy.

Tennyson swallowed. 'I don't know,' he said.

Bellamy and Hamish allowed him time to collect his thoughts.

'Alice... I was prepared to wait, but Alice was insistent. I suppose I didn't need much persuading. I would have sworn on the Bible I was the only one. But now I don't know.'

Daniels returned with Alice hanging like a limp rag from his arm. She was as white as a sheet.

'I think you should both stay here tonight,' he said. He transferred the weight of his daughter to her husband's arm, and they retired to Alice's old bedroom.

Bellamy turned to Hamish and spoke in a low voice. 'I want you to examine the body tonight,' he said. 'I have a strong feeling about this. There have been too many incidents related to this household in the last week. First McDonald, then the fire, and now Hotham. This was no accident. You mark my words.'

Hamish nodded. He had to agree something was amiss. He also sensed it all revolved around Alice's confinement, but he couldn't quite see how it all came together.

'Daylight is important to such an examination,' Hamish said. 'I won't be able to carry out the necropsy until morning.'

'In that case, I'll stay in the washroom tonight,' said Bellamy. 'I don't want to risk anyone going near that body before it's properly examined.'

Hamish was taken aback. 'Do you think that necessary?' he asked.

'Absolutely,' said Bellamy.

At first light, Hamish made his way back to the washroom. Bellamy was slumped over an armchair he must have dragged out to the back of the house. He had a government issue blanket thrown over him. Hamish couldn't help admiring the man's persistence in determining the truth. Most people would have cheerfully allowed the South Sea Islander to hang. They wouldn't be prying into the private lives of wealthy and powerful colonials. Hamish stood over the body of the Engineer. It struck him that if he and Bellamy had not pursued this investigation, Hotham might still be alive. But that, even if it were true, did not justify allowing an innocent man to hang.

The body on the table was damaged so severely it was difficult for Hamish to follow a systematic process. He did the best he could, wishing Rita was there to take notes, ask questions and give suggestions. How had it come about that he was performing these necropsy examinations one after the other? His intention was to work as a family physician.

Hamish held the man's head in his hands. Thankfully his head was the least damaged part of him, having missed the ravages of the rollers. His face was intact, but Hamish's fingers slipped into a strange contusion at the back of his head. He bent over for a closer look and saw a gaping slash to the man's skull. He had been hit from behind with a heavy blade, like a tomahawk. The wound was in no way consistent with the damage done to the rest of the body by the rollers. Hamish looked up to see Bellamy standing beside him, staring at the same wound he had seen.

'He was hit in the back of the head, then pushed down the chute,' Bellamy whispered.

'It looks that way,' said Hamish. 'He could have fallen into the chute after the blow.'

'Another murder.'

'I'm afraid so, Bellamy.'

They heard movement in the main part of the house. 'It sounds like the family are stirring,' said Bellamy. 'We'll have to tell them.'

Hamish washed his hands thoroughly, and they joined the family in the dining room.

Charlotte looked pretty, her hair carefully arranged and wearing a crisp, clean gown of the palest blue.

Her daughter's face was swollen and flushed from crying, her hair dishevelled, and she was wearing the same dress she had worn the day before. She looked as though she slept in it. Pete Tennyson looked pale and solemn. He had the dark circles under his eyes of a man who had not slept at all. Daniels was tucking into a large plate of scrambled eggs, but he looked anxious and distracted.

'I have examined Mr Hotham's body,' said Hamish. 'He was hit in the back of the head with an axe, or something similar, before being pushed, or falling, into the rollers.'

Daniels stood up, knocking his chair over as he did so. 'What are you talking about?' he said. 'It was an accident.'

'I'm afraid not,' said Bellamy. 'It was murder.'

They all stared at their plates claiming to be no longer hungry. Alice pushed her chair back and ran from the room, her husband running after her. Charlotte stayed where she was, her head bowed over her plate.

Daniels threw his hands in the air, then retrieved his chair to its rightful place. Instead of sitting, he strode from the room, and Hamish heard him stomp down the front steps.

Hamish and Bellamy followed a few minutes later and walked across the garden to the mill.

'I want to see how it was done,' said Bellamy.

They climbed a steel ladder onto the walkway and progressed to the top of the chute. It was dark with the machinery towering over them and the shadow from the centrifuge.

A wave of nausea rose in his stomach. As he peered into the dark chute, he was reminded of the moment he fell into an abandoned mine shaft at the age of seven. His parents had joined the rush for gold at Ballarat, and he spent his early years searching the goldfields for coloured stones. He'd spent hours in the dark at the bottom of the mineshaft before he was discovered. The experience left him with a lifelong fear of heights and dark spaces. Without him being aware, his hand went to the scar on his cheek, and his fingers ran along the raised skin there.

Hamish stepped gingerly into the shadow, and Bellamy inched in front of him to peer into the chute. Hamish brought his fist down lightly onto Bellamy's head.

'Easily accomplished,' Hamish said.

Bellamy's lips stretched into a thin line.

'Too easy,' he said.

He glanced down at Hamish's feet. 'And here we have it,' he said, picking up a short-handled axe with blood and hair stuck to the blade's edge.

'I want to know where everyone was when Hotham went down the chute,' said Bellamy. 'To hell with the harvest, I want them all interviewed.'

Bellamy seemed to catch sight of someone at the door of the mill.

'Simpson!' he called out. 'Simpson!' A figure disappeared around the outside of the mill.

Bellamy ran after him. Hamish heard him directing Simpson to get all the European workers together. 'You don't think it was one of the South Sea Islanders?' Simpson asked.

'I do not,' said Bellamy.

Hamish was walking back to the house when he noticed Wallace coming toward him, Red skipping at his feet. Wallace motioned toward the mess area, and Hamish followed him.

'I need to tell you something,' said Wallace.

'Have you heard about Hotham?' asked Hamish when they were seated. 'It was murder.'

'I know,' said Wallace. Everyone knows.

Hamish looked surprised.

'Ginny,' said Wallace simply.

Hamish nodded, and a small smile crept onto his face despite his solemn mood.

'Simpson spoke to me this morning about something McDonald told him the week before he died. He said he was coming into some money. Big money. And it would be enough to settle him elsewhere when the merger happened. Said he was planning to go up north.'

'How would McDonald come into big money?' asked Hamish.

Wallace lifted the scruffy terrier onto his lap and scratched the back of his head. Red maneuvered his head, so Wallace was scratching in just the right spot behind his ears.

'Perhaps he knew something?'

'Blackmail?' asked Hamish. Energy surged through his body. 'I think you are right,' he said.

Hamish burst into the house looking for Bellamy. Pete Tennyson met him at the door and led him into the sitting room. Bellamy was in the library conducting interviews to ascertain where everyone was at the time of Hotham's death. The door to the library was closed, and Tennyson closed the French doors leading into the dining room. No one could disturb them unless they entered through the front door.

Tennyson paced from one end of the room to the other, his hands jittering at his sides while Hamish waited for him to speak. He'd had enough experience of nervous patients to know they would get what they wanted to say off their chests as soon as they were ready to do so, and not a moment earlier.

Finally, he turned to Hamish, 'Is there any way you can tell, medically, that the baby is mine?'

Hamish met the earnest look in his eye. 'No,' he said.

'Surely there is something,' cried Tennyson. 'I can give you dates.' He thrust a piece of notepaper at Hamish.

Hamish glanced at the dates scribbled on the paper. He made some quick calculations in his head. 'I can tell you that the baby may be your son,' said Hamish.

'May be? But not certainly?'

'No,' repeated Hamish.

Tennyson began pacing again. 'Doctor, I love Alice with all my heart, and I want the child desperately,' he said.

Hamish smoothed the hair back from his face. 'You should consider the child your own,' he said. 'There is every chance it is your child. Everyone is willing to accept him as yours, so if you wish it, make it so.'

Tears began to fall down the man's face.

'I believe my rival for Alice's heart may have been Hotham,' he said. 'Although my wife continues to deny any relationship with him.'

'What makes you think so?' asked Hamish.

'It is a feeling. Nothing more. She is distraught since his death.'

Hamish sat with his long legs tucked under his chair, his elbows resting on his knees. He heard the despair in the man's voice and wondered if he could've been the one to kill Hotham. Somehow it didn't feel likely. Why would he have this conversation confessing his belief that Hotham was his wife's lover if he'd killed him?

'I'm going to accept the baby as my own and stand by Alice,' said Tennyson as if it were an announcement that would surprise Hamish. 'I don't care what people say.'

'I'm not sure people are saying anything,' said Hamish. 'Outside this family, there is no question.'

Tennyson continued as if Hamish had not spoken. 'Alice will get over this shock, and I will make her happy.'

He sounded genuine.

'I'm convinced of it,' said Hamish. Tennyson's anguish was his own. He did not speak of Hotham or Alice with any malice. Hamish couldn't imagine him hitting Hotham over the head. But he knew Bellamy would not be so sure. Bellamy would rely on the facts. If there had been an affair between Alice and the engineer, it would be much easier for everyone to pretend it had not happened with Hotham out of the way.

Hamish was sharing a pot of tea with Wallace and Daniels when Bellamy finally emerged from the library. 'The workers are accounted for at the time of the murder,' he said.

'They elaborate one another's accounts. Simpson and yourself,' he nodded to Daniels, 'were in the boiler room with Stratton; Gerard was in the stables with two of the Kanakas, and the rest of the labourers were together in the field loading cane. It seems the only person overseeing the chute at the time was Hotham.'

'Did any of the men see anyone else on the property?' asked Hamish. 'Like someone from Cedarwood or Tennyson?'

'No,' said Bellamy. 'No one was seen.'

'Are you planning to travel back to Brisbane today?' asked Daniels. 'The coach has already passed.'

Bellamy was suddenly alert. 'Yes. I need to be home this evening,' he said.

'I can lend you and the doctor horses,' said Daniels. 'I'll have to come to Brisbane myself tomorrow. I need to advertise for a new engineer, and recruit labour. Simpson and I will travel by coach and pick up the horses from the police stable. We'll ride back. The labour can travel by coach.'

'Thank you,' said Bellamy. 'We appreciate your kindness.'

Daniels left the room, and Hamish, Wallace and Bellamy were left to share the morning's events.

Bellamy listened while Hamish recounted the conversations with both Wallace and Tennyson.

'Where are we?' he said.

'It seems most likely Alice and Hotham were having an affair,' began Hamish. 'Then, probably for financial reasons, she agreed to marry Tennyson, and the affair ended. The marriage went ahead, and Alice hoped when the baby was born no comment would be made in relation to timing.'

'Why was McDonald killed?' asked Bellamy.

Wallace chimed in. 'Perhaps McDonald knew about the affair and was threatening to tell Tennyson.'

Hamish said, 'I think it's likely. But why not kill McDonald before the wedding when the marriage could still be prevented?'

Wallace looked thoughtful. 'I don't think this is as much about the marriage as it is about the paternity of the child.'

'That's right,' said Bellamy. 'There is a great deal of money at stake. It is a fortune that carries on to the next generation.'

Hamish said, 'do you think blackmail was involved?'

'If McDonald expected to come into money, it would suggest he was blackmailing someone over this.'

'That could only be Daniels, surely.'

'Or the women,' suggested Wallace.

Bellamy and Hamish looked at him. 'You think McDonald was blackmailing Charlotte or Alice?'

'I think that in any event, Daniels would have to know about it. Neither woman would have access to a large sum of money without Daniels support.'

'Or that of Tennyson,' added Hamish.

'We haven't yet interviewed Daniels in a formal way,' said the Sergeant. 'I think it might be time.'

'I'll catch him before he goes back to the mill,' said Hamish.

Daniels returned to the sitting room reluctantly. 'I have to supervise the crusher,' he said, 'now that Hotham is gone. I can't give you much time.'

'That's all right,' said the Sergeant. 'We won't keep you long.' He made a gesture with his hand toward the library.

'Is this a formal interview?'

'Yes, sir. If you don't mind.'

Bellamy and Hamish let Daniels enter the room, they followed, and Hamish closed the door behind them.

'Tell us about your daughter and her husband,' began Bellamy. 'How did they meet, for example?'

'Good Lord, what does that have to do with anything?' cried Daniels.

'Possibly nothing,' said Bellamy.

Daniels shifted uncomfortably. 'They've known each other since they were children,' he said. 'They've always been close. The families have long had an expectation.'

'An arranged marriage?' asked Bellamy.

'Certainly not! It has always seemed the natural course for events to take, that's all.'

'It would have come as a shock to everyone when Alice fell for your engineer, then?'

'What? No. What are you suggesting, Bellamy?'

The Sergeant didn't answer. He waited patiently for Daniels to realise there was no point in denying it.

'Yes,' he said, at last, letting out a deep breath. 'It was a shock. But fortunately, we managed to persuade her it was a passing fancy, nothing more.'

'We?' said Hamish.

'Her mother and I.'

'Was she easily persuaded?' asked Bellamy.

Daniels didn't respond quickly. Hamish thought he might be trying to decide whether to tell the truth or not.

'Not so easily,' he said quietly. 'The girl had strong feelings for him. But she saw sense.'

'She saw sense? What sense is that?' asked Bellamy.

'Hotham was a good man. Don't misunderstand me. He would have been a good match... for...well, for someone else. But Alice is young. She doesn't know what is best for her. She's grown up getting everything handed to her. I blame her mother. She was spoiled after, well, the loss, you know.'

'Are you referring to the death of your infant son?' asked Bellamy, rather harshly Hamish thought.

'Yes. After that.'

Bellamy put his hand to his forehead as though he had a headache.

'Are you saying, Mr Daniels, that Alice wanted to marry Hotham, but you and your wife found the match unsuitable, so you persuaded her against it?'

'Yes,' said Daniels. 'Mostly, my wife found him unsuitable. You see, she has long regretted marrying me, though we married for love, I think, at the time.'

'Note this down, will you, Doctor,' said Bellamy.

Hamish scrambled to retrieve his notebook and pencil from his coat pocket. He was shocked to notice the colt was still there.

'What makes you think so?' asked Bellamy.

'She has admitted as much. I knew she was discontented, here in the country, without the distractions of Sydney or Melbourne. But I didn't realise how deeply she resented how her life had turned out until the relationship between Alice and Eddie Hotham came up. I told my wife she was over-reacting at first, but she wouldn't listen. She said if we didn't intervene, Alice would destroy her life as she had done and regret it the rest of her life. I was devastated to learn how badly she felt about our marriage.'

'Did Alice share an intimate relationship with Mr Hotham?' asked Bellamy.

Hamish sat with his pencil poised, alert for the response.

Daniels took several deep breaths.

It seemed to Hamish Bellamy had extraordinary patience as they waited for Daniels to answer. Hamish was straining at the bit to know how he would respond.

'She told me she was in love with him,' he said.

'But were they intimate?' pressed Bellamy.

Daniels looked away. 'Good Lord man,' he cried. 'How can you ask that of her father?'

'Nonetheless,' said Bellamy.

Hamish hid behind his fringe, which had fallen over his eyes, but he was still eager to hear the answer.

'Yes,' said Daniels. 'Alice was intimate with Eddie Hotham.'

'Were you and your wife aware she was with child?'

Daniels' head shot up again, and he opened his mouth as if to protest.

'Yes,' he said. 'She told us she was with child, and the father was Hotham.'

'What happened next?' Bellamy asked kindly.

'My wife and I didn't know what to do. I knew Hotham would marry her. He is...was...a decent man. He did have feelings for her, I'm sure of it. But my wife was so passionately against it. She had her mind set on the match with Tennyson. We all did. I don't know if Tennyson suspected he had a rival in Hotham, but he turned up at the house out of the blue and asked for Alice's hand. It was two days after she told us of her condition. Charlotte... we...thought the offer heaven sent. If they married quickly, no one need know about the affair.'

'Alice seems to me the kind of woman who knows her own mind,' said Bellamy. 'How did you convince her to give up her true love?'

'It wasn't true love, Sergeant. Like I said, she's young. We're not monsters. We have only ever had Alice's interests in mind.'

'And the fortune accumulated through the merging of two families,' said Bellamy.

'Damn you,' said Daniels. 'That is for Alice's sake as well. Alice would have been miserable in a life without money.'

'Hotham made a decent wage,' said Hamish.

Daniels looked his way for the first time. 'Not the kind of money that creates wealth, Doctor. The opportunity exists in this great colony to build wealth. Do you think a family such as ours would have acquired wealth and power in England? We would have been swallowed by the mediocrity of the middle-class, at best. Alice will build a vast estate. Or, in a decade or so, when we are old, they can divide the land and sell it for a King's fortune. Her son can grow up to be a member of parliament.'

It occurred to Hamish that one of the other great things about the colony was that any middle-class man could aspire to parliament if he chose. He didn't need to have a fortune behind him. Still, he took the point.

'Don't you think Alice deserved the right to make her own choice?' asked Bellamy.

'She chose, Sergeant. Make no mistake. Alice does nothing she doesn't want to do. She chose to end the relationship with Hotham and accept Tennyson's hand. We put forward an argument, but she chose.'

Hamish stopped taking notes. He could not reconcile the image of Alice distraught over Hotham's body with one of a woman who made the cold-hearted decision to reject him for the hope of money and power. Perhaps she realised too late what she had given up.

Daniels slumped forward in the chair. Every line in his face marked out the fatigue and distress.

'I don't understand what this has to do with the murder of Jock McDonald or of Hotham if it was murder. The drama had passed. Alice was married to Tennyson, and the child was accepted as his own. If Tennyson had any doubts, he didn't express them to me. Why kill either of them?'

'Secrets breed violence in my experience,' said Bellamy.

'What do you think happened?' asked Daniels.

'I have several theories to check,' said Bellamy.

Hamish was just as keen to hear these theories as he imagined Daniels would be.

'One possibility is that McDonald knew about the affair and was blackmailing you. You might want him removed to avoid the scandal.'

Bellamy held up his hand to stop the sergeant. 'No,' he said.

Bellamy went on. 'Perhaps McDonald was threatening to reveal the paternity of the child. He told the workers he was about to come into a great deal of money.'

The surprise evident on Daniel's face indicated this was new information to him.

'Hotham may have suspected the child was his own. He might have attempted to blackmail you.'

'Now wait a minute,' protested Daniels. 'Hotham was a good man. He had integrity. He would never stoop....'

'Of course, there is always the possibility that Hotham wanted to be a father to his own child, once it was born.'

Daniels was sweating now. He was visibly on edge, every muscle tensed. Hamish observed that even the small wrinkles around his eyes were clamped.

'Then there is Peter Tennyson,' said Bellamy. 'He has every motive for wanting McDonald silenced and Hotham dead. Perhaps it was him McDonald was blackmailing. To kill Hotham seems almost natural if he found out he was the father of his wife's child.'

Daniel's face reflected deepening confusion.

'There is always Alice,' began Bellamy again.

'Now that's too much!' cried Daniels.

'Why?' asked Bellamy. 'You said yourself she is a strong woman. Her child's inheritance is secure now, is it not?'

Hamish thought Daniels looked like he was about to vomit.

'I think we should leave the interview there, for now,' Hamish suggested. 'Mr Daniels looks unwell.'

Bellamy hesitated, but he conceded. 'Very well, Daniels,' he said. 'I understand this has taken an incredible toll. We will leave you to digest our conversation and speak again. Doctor Hart, are you ready to return to Brisbane?'

Hamish stood up, and they both left Daniels in the library, broken.

'Do you think he's a killer?' asked Hamish when they were walking to the stables.

'No, I don't,' said Bellamy.

'Me either,' said Hamish.

Gerard was waiting with the horses, saddled and ready when they reached the stables. One horse was a full hand taller than the other and a mottled grey. The smaller horse was reddish-brown.

'How goes your day, Gerard?' said Hamish.

'As good as can be expected,' the man answered, slapping the grey affectionately on the rump. 'In the midst of tragedy.'

'Are you greatly affected by the recent deaths?' asked Hamish.

'It's a terrible thing. Never a better bloke walked this God-forsaken country than Eddie Hotham. I was not surprised to hear Jock McDonald met a violent end, but Eddie Hotham? That's another matter entirely.'

'Was there no one who thought ill of Mr Hotham?' asked Hamish. 'Certainly, Peter Tennyson can't have liked him?'

Gerard loosened the straps of the smaller horses' saddle.

'I keeps meself to meself,' said Gerard. 'But I'll tell yer this for free. Regardless of the pain it caused himself, Eddie Hotham would never have done anything to hurt Alice. You mind how you go now. Some parts of the road are churned up by the work on the new railway.'

Hamish climbed onto his horse and glanced back toward the house. He saw a trap had stopped at the end of the driveway near the stairs. A tall, slim woman climbed down. Hamish thought the figure reminded him of Collette, but he dismissed the thought immediately. It would be one of Charlotte's friends coming to check on her.

CHAPTER EIGHTEEN

The Albury Banner and Wodonga Express Friday 26 January 1886.

In blue-gum steam, we have a most perfect disinfectant, as in no case, after the first 24 hours, was the breath unpleasant, and the swelling in the neck subsided. Towards night the patients generally became feverish and restless, unable to sleep, and it was wonderful to watch the soothing effect of the steam. A bucket was generally placed in the room containing blue-gum water, and a red-hot poker placed in it, which at once filled the room with steam, and very shortly, one child after another would fall asleep. As a rule, most of the little patients suffered very little, laughing and playing in bed. I found that the fresh air had to be excluded, as on opening the windows, even in this mild climate, the breathing quickly became difficult. The blue-gum steam purified the atmosphere of the room. The unaffected children were every evening congregated around the bucket of blue-gum water, and every room fumigated with it, and all the drains flushed with the refuse water. Twenty-four cases were treated as above, with the death of one infant, aged eight months. There were six other children ill in the same family, and not one case of paralysis occurred amongst them, although two were treated with sulphur by their parents, and both were badly affected. I think I can claim for the above treatment: (1) Great simplicity; (2) It follows nature's way of getting rid of the membrane through suppuration; (3) That it prevents paralysis; (4) That it cures the severest cases.

HAMISH

Hamish slept soundly after the ride from Logan to Brisbane. Riding always tired him. He was up early the following morning to collect Rita and go on to the Police Depot. He couldn't wait to share the news they had of Araluen with Kaelo. Rita climbed into the cab, and Hamish shared the contents of the letter from Maryborough while they travelled the short distance to Petrie Terrace.

Sergeant Bellamy was not yet in his office, but Constable Pennyweather was available to take them to Kaelo's cell. When they joined him in the small space, Kaelo again looked embarrassed at having Rita enter such a place.

'We have word of Araluen,' said Hamish immediately. He removed the letter from inside his coat and read it aloud.

When he finished, Kaelo took the letter and stared at it.

'It sounds possible the child didn't have an accident after all,' Hamish said. It sounds like he suffered from infant paralysis. I can't say for sure unless I examine him. The best course of action is to bring Araluen and the boy back here to Brisbane where he can be properly assessed and treated.'

'Is there a cure for this disease?' asked Kaelo.

Hamish removed his hand and looked at Rita.

'Kaelo, do you have sufficient funds to bring Araluen to Brisbane?' she asked.

'My father instructed me to give his money to his wife. This was his dying wish.'

'Hamish and I will pay the travel expenses,' she said without hesitation. 'That way, you can pass on whatever you have to Araluen. But you must stay here until we find out who poisoned Jock McDonald. You must trust us. We'll act on your behalf and arrange for Araluen to come to Brisbane with her son if she is willing.'

'Is this what you want?' Hamish asked.

'Can you cure the child's disease?' Kaelo repeated his question.

Hamish hung his head. 'No. There is no cure. But with treatment, the boy may improve. I would like to treat him. I would like to try, Kaelo.'

They left Kaelo sitting on his bunk with tears in his eyes. They might have been tears of sadness, frustration or relief. Hamish couldn't tell.

'What if she doesn't want to come?' He said to Rita as they were leaving the building.

'We'll make her the offer and see what happens,' said Rita.

Hamish wrote to Araluen, sending the letter to the nurse to pass on. He told her about Kaelo, and he promised to treat Joseph if she could bring him to Brisbane.

Hamish saw her first. A small Aboriginal woman dressed in shabby European clothing cradling a boy that looked no more than four years old, his thin limbs dangling from her arms. Surely the boy had to be closer to six, according to Kaelo's story.

Rita strode over to her and put out her hand. 'Araluen?' she asked.

The woman nodded.

'We are pleased to meet you. Have you had a difficult journey?' Araluen shook her head and looked toward Hamish.

'This is Doctor Hamish Hart,' said Rita. 'I'm Rita Cartwright.'

Hamish wondered why Rita had not introduced herself as Doctor Cartwright. Araluen looked bewildered, and the boy showed no sign of interest in either of them.

'Can I help you?' asked Hamish, putting his hands out to take the boy, but the child withdrew from his touch and snuggled further into his mother's neck, hiding his face.

'He's no trouble,' said Araluen.

'We've organised somewhere for you to stay,' said Rita. 'I have a home that is shared by women escaping their husbands. There are plenty of children there for your son to play with. What's your son's name?'

'Joseph,' said Araluen.

'Come on then, Joseph,' said Rita. 'It's not far.'

'Are you sure I can't carry Joseph?' asked Hamish, taking the bag Araluen was carrying.

Araluen didn't answer. She followed Rita, who had already started walking toward the northern end of Ann Street, where they could find a cab to take them to the house

Joseph looked at Hamish over his mother's shoulder, clearly ready to reject any attempt Hamish made to move toward him. Hamish observed the boy closely. His limbs were small for his age, his arms and legs long and thin, one leg was at least six inches shorter than the other. The short leg was wasted, although it was difficult to see the extent of muscle wastage with the child bundled up in his mother's arms.

The ride to Rita's house was silent. Araluen kept her eyes down, and Joseph remained burrowed into his mother's neck. When they arrived, they were shown their room and the bag containing their few items of clothing was unpacked. Rita suggested they have tea in the kitchen, and Araluen followed silently, still cradling the boy. There were a couple of women at home. One of them was washing dishes in a metal tub. She turned to examine the new woman and her child, then turned back to her work without making a sound.

Araluen's face became stiff. 'These white women, they won't want us here,' she said loudly enough for the woman to hear.

'The women here have been through so much. They have no energy spare to judge others,' said Rita.

Araluen sat down, but she kept a suspicious eye on the woman while sipping the tea Rita handed her. Hamish wondered if she believed what Rita was saying. He wasn't sure he believed it himself.

Joseph, finally leaving his mother's arms, perched himself on a kitchen chair beside his mother and didn't take his eyes off Hamish for a moment.

'We have been told Joseph was in an accident,' said Hamish. 'Is that so?'

Araluen stared into her tea. 'There was no accident. He tried to step out of bed one morning and fell to the floor. He's not walked since.'

'Was Joseph feverish?' asked Hamish.

'Joseph was in my cousin's care when he became ill. She sent for me, but by the time I reached them, he had been with fever for three days.'

'Trouble breathing?'

'Yes.'

'I believe Joseph has suffered from infant paralysis. It's caused by a virus. The effects can be much worse.'

'Worse than him crippled?' cried Araluen.

Hamish spoke kindly. 'There are treatments that improve the muscles,' he said. 'Iron callipers may even make it possible for

Joseph to walk.'

'I don't believe such stories,' said Araluen. 'Not for us. There's no money to pay for medical treatments or clever devices. I don't know how Joseph will even make his own living if anything happens to me. I'm all he has.'

'That's not true,' said Hamish. 'He has a step-brother called Kaelo. Kaelo is very keen to help you both on behalf of his father.'

'What can he do? This Polynesian son of my husband.'

'In the first instance, he has money for you. His father instructed him to find you and give you his money.'

'Why should the man go out of his way to give us his father's money? Why doesn't he keep it for himself?'

'Quite,' said Hamish. 'He could have kept it for himself. But Kaelo has great integrity. All the more reason for Joseph and yourself to consider accepting him as family.'

Araluen stared into her tea. 'What's he want from us? Can't you bring me the money?'

'Possibly,' said Hamish, 'but Kaelo is eager to meet his half-brother. He has brothers at home, and he's devoted to family.'

'We're not his family,' said Araluen. 'He should go back home to his own people.'

Rita thought it wise to shift the conversation to less confronting territory.

'I believe your own family are from Mackay,' she said. Araluen continued to stare into her mug of tea. 'When my husband left, I moved to Brisbane. I needed to find work. A friend introduced me to a European lady who needed a housekeeper. She had a homestead out west, cattle country. She said she couldn't take Joseph, so I left him with my cousin in Maryborough.'

Araluen glanced up, appearing to momentarily search for any sign of judgement in the faces of the European doctor and his female companion.

'My cousin married a white man,' she said, looking back into her tea. 'She was always pale-skinned that one. They have a house, a proper house, and plenty of little ones. It was good for Joseph to stay there.'

'I'm sure Joseph was well cared for in your cousin's home,' said Rita.

'When Joseph didn't get better, my cousin said she couldn't look after her own children and a crippled boy. So, I left my job out west and moved to Maryborough. I worked in the hospital for a while. I could buy food and whatnot. But Joseph didn't improve, and I couldn't stand leaving him alone on the bed every day. I started missing shifts. That's when the nurse found me and told me a doctor in Brisbane wanted to treat Joseph.'

Hamish and Rita were silent while they absorbed the story. When they didn't respond immediately, Araluen appeared to panic. 'That's the only reason I came. I came here because you promised to treat Joseph.'

Hamish's brow wrinkled at her raised voice.

'Of course,' he said.

'And so, I shall. I have patients until one o'clock, then I'll come back and collect you both. I'll examine Joseph thoroughly, and we can talk about a treatment plan for him.'

'I hope the Islander has enough money to pay you,' said Araluen.

'I don't expect payment. I'm interested in the new treatments for Joseph's condition. I'll write about his progress and publish the paper for colleagues to read and learn.'

Araluen looked confused, but she didn't object. Hamish thought she would be prepared to do anything that might lead to an improvement in her son's condition.

'Kaelo is being held in gaol, and he doesn't want you to see him there. He wants to meet you as a free man. The Police know he didn't commit any crime, and their investigation will soon close, so you have a little time before you need to decide whether you want to meet him. In the meantime, Rita has said you are welcome to stay here. You will want for nothing. It should not be longer than a week.'

When Hamish and Rita returned to his house in Wickham Terrace, there was a note from Wallace waiting for them.

Hamish unfolded the note and read the salient points to Rita.

'He says Daniels is at breaking point,' read Hamish. 'Apparently, Charlotte won't leave her room. He has had word from Tennyson that Alice has also locked herself in her room and refuses to eat. Tennyson can't come to Cloverton to help because he is too busy caring for his wife.'

Rita tipped her face to one side. 'He seems to be genuinely devoted to her.'

'Oh, this is interesting,' said Hamish. 'Vincent, the manager from Cedarwood, has gone to Cloverton to help. I suppose he has little choice; his cane is waiting to be processed at the mill, after all. Did I tell you that Vincent has an Aboriginal wife? I met her the day Bellamy and I rode through on our way to Cloverton for the first time.'

'Who has an Aboriginal wife?' asked Rita.

'Vincent, the manager at Cedarwood.'

'Hmm,' said Rita. 'I wonder if she needs any help.'

A light shone in Hamish's eyes. 'She might at that!' he cried.

Rita left for Lady Bowen while Hamish consulted with his morning patients. He wondered if he might need someone to manage appointments for him, as he was hopelessly disorganised what with travelling to and from Cloverton. Mrs Bundle turned up to have her infected toe seen to when he had been expecting Mrs Childers with her migraine. He was able to shift focus quickly, and the patients were unaware of his mistake, but it made him feel flustered and poorly prepared. In the end, he was relieved when the last patient scheduled for the morning left his rooms, and he could sit with a hot cup of tea. He had only enjoyed a sip when he heard the cab he had sent to collect Araluen and Joseph from the women's shelter rumble to a stop in front of the house.

Hamish lifted Joseph onto the examination table while his mother hovered protectively by his side. Joseph watched him suspiciously, but he didn't pull away from him. Hamish smiled and tussled his hair while Joseph carefully monitored his every move without looking once directly into Hamish's eyes.

'Describe the illness that preceded the paralysis,' Hamish said.

Araluen looked confused.

'What happened when Joseph fell ill before his leg stopped working?'

'I've told all I know,' said Araluen.

'Tell me again. Describe whatever details you can remember.'

'I wasn't there when he became ill. I told you. I should've been, but I wasn't.'

'This is not your fault,' said Hamish. 'I believe Joseph has had a virus that led to his condition. Tell me anything you remember of what your sister told you about Joseph.'

'She said the illness took on the look of a cold. He had a crusty nose and a cough for a few days, and he didn't want to play with the others. She said he was just whining about her feet. She reckoned she wasn't too worried because all the children went through those times. When his fever grew worse, she sent for me.'

'Did Joseph see a doctor?'

'Who can pay for a doctor?'

Hamish felt the blood rush to his face. His own fees placed his services out of the reach of children such as Joseph under normal circumstances. The shame of this had not eluded him.

'When I got to him, he was burning up. I slept in the same bed with him, and his body was so hot I couldn't get a wink for three nights. He was sleeping most of the time, and he wouldn't eat or drink. I tried to force him to have a sip of soup from time to time. On the third morning, he felt cool to the touch. He asked for porridge, so I made him a bowl. After he ate the porridge, he tried to get out of bed. I was happy because I thought he was getting well. Until he tried to stand, and his legs crumpled beneath him. He fell on the floor, and I had to bundle him back onto the bed. Over the next week, he gradually grew stronger, but not that leg.' Araluen pointed to the affected limb. 'That one didn't get better.'

Hamish held the boy's left leg in his hands. It was withered and at least three inches shorter than the right leg. He compared the strength in each of his legs and found the withered leg could exert no pressure against his hand.

'I am convinced Joseph is suffering from infantile paralysis,'

Hamish said.

Araluen's face changed from passive to defensive. 'My cousin has a clean house,' she declared. 'Joseph was well fed.'

'I don't doubt it,' he said. 'Many people assume this condition is linked to a lack of hygiene and neglect in children. I assure you, I do not. This condition is the result of contagion. It passes from one person to another affecting each individual differently. Even the children of wealthy families contract it.'

Araluen looked like she didn't believe him.

'There is no cure, I'm afraid,' he went on. 'However, there are some treatments available that may contribute to improved strength in the damaged leg.'

'The doctor at the hospital in Maryborough said nothing could be done,' said Araluen.

'Did the doctor at the Maryborough Hospital examine Joseph?'

'No.'

'Then he can't possibly pass judgement. I think it is worth trying.'

'What is?'

Hamish held the boy's withered leg in his hand while he pondered an appropriate plan.

'I'd like to try a combination of therapeutic massage and use of electrical treatments,' he said.

Araluen looked terrified. 'You're not using electricity on the boy,' she cried. 'The Minister at the Lutheran Church in Maryborough called it the devil's work. He said men of science are trying to replace God with their tricks and illusions.'

'You were allowed to attend services at the Lutheran Church?'

Araluen looked at her feet. 'We could sit outside and listen. There were three of us, black women who follow Jesus. They placed a bench against the wall for us.'

Hamish shook his head and returned his focus to Joseph's leg.

'Electricity is not the work of the devil,' he said. 'If anything, it's God's work that men of science now have access to another powerful tool they can use to ease suffering.'

Hamish's eyes glowed, and he spoke rapidly as he went on.

'Electrical energy travels through the body carrying messages from the brain to the muscles in much the same way as it travels through telegraph wires taking messages all over the world.

The theory is when there is a breakdown in messaging, as indicated by Joseph's crippled leg, it might be restored by electric therapeutics.'

Araluen watched his hands on her boy's withered leg.

'I know you mean well, doctor, but I can't believe my boy's leg will be mended by running electricity through him.' She gingerly placed her hand on the leg.

Hamish realised he had frightened her with his enthusiasm.

'There is also therapeutic massage,' he said, hoping to build trust by offering a less frightening treatment. 'That involves gentle massage applied to the leg with olive oil or stimulating lotions.'

'I've rubbed his leg with dugong oil every day since he fell ill,' Araluen responded.

Hamish couldn't imagine how dugong oil would be any less effective than his own rubbing oils. But he did think some expertise in anatomy might inform the efficacy of the massage itself. Perhaps he could teach Araluen how to carry out a more specifically therapeutic massage. What he wanted to do was try the electrical treatments for himself. He was in two minds about the theory. On the one hand, he didn't believe electrotherapeutics was the panacea for all ills some medical men claimed, but he didn't agree with the Lutheran Minister who said it was the work of the devil either. Electricity didn't equate with the vital force of life for Hamish, but it did represent great potential in the arsenal of tools available to medicine. If a galvanic battery, in the form of a belt around the leg, for example, could stimulate muscular movement when the brain could not, this seemed like a rational treatment prospect.

Still, if Araluen could not be convinced of either the safety or the efficacy of the treatment, it was an academic argument rather than a practical treatment plan. Hamish decided to adhere to a few simple steps he felt Araluen would take on rather than push her away, arguing the case for electrical treatment.

'Go on using the dugong oil for massaging the leg,' he said. 'I'll demonstrate how to rub the leg to improve blood flow and stimulate the muscles.' Araluen watched his demonstration closely and copied his movements perfectly. Hamish handed her a bottle of Richardson's Emulsion of Cod Liver Oil and a bottle of Parrish's Food to restore iron levels. He read the instructions on the bottles aloud to her.

'Do you understand?' he asked.

Araluen took the bottles and nodded.

'Keep up the daily massages as I showed you and give Joseph the medicine,' he said. You can use the dugong oil as an alternative if you wish. We'll talk about the electric belt again in a week.'

Araluen and Joseph left in the cab.

'I'm hoping to convince Araluen of the positive potential for electricity in the treatment of Joseph,' said Hamish when Rita asked him how the consultation went.

'She is afraid of the use of electricity. A Lutheran Minister told her it was the work of the devil.'

'No wonder she is fearful,' replied Rita. She was curled up in the blue velvet armchair, rather like a cat. He handed her a small cup of hot tea and resisted the urge to say, 'don't spill it.'

'Electricity is a well-established source of entertainment in the coffee houses and music halls,' said Rita. 'My favourite demonstration is the Venus Electrifica. They put an attractive woman on an insulated stool and have her hold a chain attached to an electrical battery. The machine sends a charge through the woman, and they challenge a gentleman from the audience to kiss her. When he comes close, sparks fly between their lips. Audiences love it.'

'It's hardly the same thing as using electricity as a medicinal tool.'

'No. But it establishes it in the public perception as a spectacle rather than serious science. More to the point for the Lutheran Minister, if we accept the body is a machine that can be energised through electricity, does that mean there is no need for God?'

'Of course not,' cried Hamish. 'Life is a culmination of elements. Electricity has nothing to do with the soul. I do believe it may stimulate dormant muscles, however. It's at least worth trying.'

'It may turn out to be no more use than Collette's psychic

phenomena,' said Rita playfully.

'Hamish bristled, but he allowed himself to relax. 'It may at that,' he said. 'In any event, I'll need to gain Araluen's trust before I can try it.'

◇◇◇◇◇

That evening, Hamish, Rita and Bellamy had dinner at Hamish's home. Hamish prepared a simple meal of fresh fish. He was no match for Wallace, but he had been cooking his own meals for a long time. The conversation turned to the investigation.

'I think we can be sure of this much,' said Bellamy. 'Eddie Hotham was the father of Alice's baby.'

'And everyone at Cloverton knew about the affair, even though they led Wallace to believe there was nothing in it,' added Hamish.

'They all liked Hotham and they all hated McDonald,' said Bellamy.

'At least one person didn't like Hotham,' pointed out Hamish.

'In my experience, people do not necessarily dislike the people they murder,' said Bellamy. 'Indeed, sometimes they love them.'

'I suppose that's true in a crime of passion.'

'Let's look at each murder separately,' said Bellamy. 'Starting with Jock McDonald, who stood to gain by killing him?'

Hamish thought about it. 'If he was blackmailing someone as we suspect, that person is the most likely to have killed him.'

'Let's follow that theory. Who could have been blackmailing McDonald?'

'Daniels,' said Hamish. 'Or Tennyson.'

'Or Tennyson's father,' suggested Bellamy. 'He was presumably as keen as any of them for the merger.'

Hamish said, 'No one unusual was seen at Cloverton in the week preceding the death of McDonald. Tennyson's father would have had to come to Cloverton several times that week to have been gradually poisoning him. Someone would have commented on it.'

'There is also Alice,' said Bellamy.

'Are you saying Alice killed her own lover?' asked Hamish.

'I'm only suggesting it as a possibility.'

'I can't see it,' said Hamish. 'She was distraught when she found out he'd been killed. Still, I admit you are right. It may have been one of the three you mention who poisoned McDonald.'

Rita was enjoying the meal while listening carefully.

'Let's move on to Hotham then. Who stood to gain from his death?' said Bellamy.

'The same three,' said Hamish. 'Assuming this is about the affair between Alice and Tennyson and the heir to the family fortune.'

'What I don't understand,' said Bellamy, 'Is why Hotham was killed when he was. If he hadn't said anything about the affair prior to the marriage, why expect he was a threat months later?'

'Maybe he had a change of heart when the child was born.'

'That is possible,' conceded Bellamy. 'Regardless, I think we are left with the same three suspects. The killer is likely to have been Daniels, Tennyson or Alice.'

'Or Charlotte,' said Rita, breaking another of the fresh bread rolls.

Both men looked at her.

'Why are you staring at me?' she said. 'Charlotte has the same motive as the other three. She didn't want Alice to marry Hotham, and she wanted the merger to go through.'

'But Charlotte?' said Hamish.

Bellamy continued to stare.

'Oh, for heaven's sake, Hamish, you have been fooled by those big blue eyes. Charlotte Daniels has the same capacity for ruthlessness as any other woman. She shared morning tea with Eddie Hotham most mornings.'

'What?' cried Hamish and Bellamy together.

'How do you know?' asked Hamish.

'Charlotte told me. It sounded to me like they were close. Apparently, he told her of his relationship with Alice before Alice revealed it. He also told her of Alice being with child.'

Hamish and Bellamy continued to gape at Rita.

'The fact remains, she had at least as strong a motive as the others.'

'How did she poison McDonald?' asked Hamish.

Rita held a spoon of raspberry pudding to her lips and looked thoughtful. 'Well, according to Ginny, the teas for both Hotham and McDonald were made separately. Ginny delivered McDonald's tea to him in the mill, and Hotham joined Charlotte in the kitchen for his. The others all met in the mess and made their own.'

'But Charlotte didn't tell me that,' cried Hamish. 'She said they all took tea in the mess.'

'She would, wouldn't she, if she were responsible for the murder?'

'I suppose she could have poisoned the tea,' said Hamish. 'It wouldn't have been impossible for her to hit Hotham over the head and tip him down the chute either. I confess I am having trouble visualising her doing so in her finely embroidered gown and perfectly coifed hair.'

Rita rolled her eyes and removed the dirty plates from the table.

The next morning Bellamy, Hamish and Rita planned to return to Cloverton by steamer. 'This time, we will stay until the matter is resolved,' said Bellamy. 'I have grown tired of these trips back and forth.'

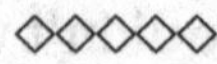

AELO

Kaelo opened his eyes to see two white faces sneering down at him. A sudden rush of panic sent his fists forward. One of the men lurched back from the impact. He fell back against two more men who cursed as they righted themselves and their injured friend. The man who took the force of Kaelo's fist held his nose with one hand and took a gun from his jacket with the other. The second man grabbed Kaelo's left arm in time to save himself from a similar blow to his face.

'Hold the devil still,' shouted the man with the broken nose. Two men gripped Kaelo by the shoulders while another two grasped his legs. Kaelo thrust his body about and tried to kick his legs, but the men's grip was too tight. They dragged him from his bunk, and he felt his back crack as he hit the floor. Yet another two men rolled him onto his side, forced his hands behind his back, and tied his wrists together.

When his arms were immobilized, one man tucked himself under each of Kaelo's shoulders and lifted him to his feet. With the help of the others, they forced him forward and out of the cell. The man with the broken nose held the gun at Kaelo's head and looked as though he couldn't wait to shoot him.

Constable Pennyweather, who had been outside to relieve himself, reappeared within sight of the cell. Before he could register the scene before him, one of the men grabbed him by the arm and threw him into the cell. 'In there with yer youngin',' the man cried as he slammed the bars closed and locked him in.

Every muscle in Kaelo's body tensed. He tried to stand firm, but the six men forced him forward. What did they want from him? Where were they taking him?

When the sunlight hit his eyes for the first time in nearly two weeks, he squinted. It was difficult to gain his focus, but he could see many more men and some women gathered outside the police depot. He heard them shouting, their voices angry, snarling. It took him a few seconds to realise their angry words were directed at him. They crowded around him as the six men at the centre pushed him forward. He could see the sea of colour rolling alongside him, and he heard cries of 'hang him', punctuating the general rumble of the crowd. His muscles ached from the tension of being pushed and pulled against his will. Was this to be his end?

He struggled forward with minimum resistance realizing he could not overcome them all. The man with the gun placed it back in his jacket, a sense of smug confidence lightening his face. He appeared buoyed and validated by the mob.

◇◇◇◇◇

HAMISH

The next morning, not long past dawn, Hamish was roused by the sound of people running past the downstairs window and voices shouting. He wondered what was behind the urgency at this time of the morning. Reluctantly, Hamish pulled himself up out of bed and found his shirt and trousers. He hopped to the window with one leg of his pants still caught on his foot. Peering out from between the lace curtains he counted at least a dozen men gathered in the empty yard beside the old windmill. What the devil was going on?

He finished dressing, keeping an eye on the crowd building opposite his house. More men and a scattering of women rushed up the hill from the town and joined those already gathered. They were agitated. There was an air of anticipation in the crowd. Hamish's awareness was heightened, but he was more curious than concerned until his gaze drifted upwards into the fig beside the mill. Swinging from a branch about twelve feet from the ground was a rope. It was thick and black from this distance, and it hung almost to the ground. The end was tied into a noose.

A wave of nausea caught Hamish off-guard, and he stumbled backward, falling onto his bed. Disjointed thoughts rushed through his mind. They're going to hang someone. But who? At that moment, piqued with confusion and an underlying nausea that suggested he knew what was happening but couldn't articulate it, even to himself, he registered a frantic bashing at his front door. He recognised Bellamy's voice shouting his name.

Hamish tore down the staircase, still in his stockinged feet, and pulled the door open. The sergeant grabbed him by his collar, yanking him through. Hamish resisted. 'My boots,' he cried and stumbled back inside to get them. 'Hurry,' cried Bellamy, 'there isn't much time,' and he rushed back across the road to the crowd. Hamish secured his boots, grabbed his coat from the hall stand and ran after him. From the windmill side of the street, he could see down the hill toward town. A crowd was hurrying up the hill in a pack. They hung together closely chanting. There was someone at the centre being forcibly jostled along. It's Kaelo!

Sergeant Bellamy, Constable Pennyweather and several other policemen stood alert in front of the tree. The mob waiting there moved a little, less sure of themselves with the police presence. But those forcing Kaelo up the hill showed no such hesitance. Their chanting became louder and more determined as they grew closer to their goal. When they reached the yard and were no more than ten feet from the tree, the sergeant and his men, they stopped. Hamish could see now that six men were at the centre of the group gripping Kaelo tightly. He hung limp, worn out from the hopelessness of the struggle against the angry mob.

'Get out of the way, Sergeant!' called one of the men. 'You've not been able to do yer job, so we'll do it for yer. Call your men back.'

Sergeant Bellamy lifted his rifle and fired a shot into the air. The mob on the hill scattered but waited close by to see what would happen next. The men didn't release their grip on Kaelo.

'There'll be no vigilante lynching today,' cried Bellamy loud and clear. 'The Islander will be tried in a court of law if he's charged with any crime at all.'

'The coloureds have been rampaging through our streets, threatening our lives and taking our livelihoods long enough,' cried another man. 'We've had enough. We're making an example of this one.'

The crowd cheered. 'He murdered a white manager. We're none of us safe if he isn't hung for it.'

Bellamy stood his ground. 'The Islander didn't kill Jock McDonald,' he shouted.

'Then who did?' cried someone from the crowd.

Bellamy hesitated for a fraction of a second, but it was long enough to release the pressure, ready to explode.

'He killed him right enough,' shouted someone, and the crowd began all shouting at once. They pushed forward, forcing Kaelo along with them.

Sergeant Bellamy raised his rifle as a warning.

'What are you going to do? Shoot us all?

Bellamy shouted at his men to stand firm.

'If I have to,' he cried.

The line of the policemen between the mob and the tree looked nervous to Hamish. But thus far, they had followed Bellamy's instructions and stood firm. Kaelo was close enough that Hamish could see his eyes. He looked terrified, and Hamish felt terrified for him. Hamish glanced at the noose swinging from the tree, only feet from Kaelo and the mob.

Bellamy let off a shot above the heads of the crowd. Most moved back, away from Kaelo, but the six men tightened their grip on him. For the first time, the odds seem to favour Bellamy and the line of policemen behind him. But Hamish knew the mob was right. The sergeant couldn't shoot them. There would be a riot. It was Bellamy's job to protect the people. Still, the people wouldn't accept the shooting of six white men to save an Islander accused of murder as protection.

Hamish slipped his hand into his coat pocket and felt the cold metal of the colt there. Bellamy couldn't shoot them, but he could. Theoretically. Hamish felt his heart pound in his chest as he maneuvered himself closer to the six men and Kaelo. Everyone was focused on the stand-off between the men and the police sergeant. No one paid any attention to him. He glanced back over his shoulder as he emerged from the crowd, and he noticed Rita. Her face was white with fear. She looked for a moment as though she would run to him, but she remained still, her eyes giving him the encouragement he needed to move forward.

He slipped silently to within twelve inches of the group of six and held his gun directly at the temple of the closest of the men. It was also the man who had pointed his gun at Kaelo, but the gun was now inconveniently tucked in his jacket.

'I will shoot,' Hamish said steadily. 'Make no mistake.'

The six men looked at him in shock. Kaelo looked no less shocked than his captors.

'Let him go,' said Hamish. 'The law will take it from here.'

The six men glared at Hamish, evaluating his commitment. They slowly let go of Kaelo and took a step back. Hamish's legs wobbled, and his hands trembled. He noticed his mouth was dryer than it had ever been. His shoulders slumped as he realised he wasn't sure he could have pulled the trigger.

The tension broken; everything happened at once. Sergeant Bellamy ran forward and took hold of Kaelo, along with Constable Pennyweather. He barked at the other policemen to take the noose down. The six men were shouting threats at Bellamy and Hamish, but they were backing down the hill as they did so. Hamish kept the gun in sight to be sure they didn't change their minds. Within minutes of the whole fiasco coming to a head, a cab pulled up with Inspector Scratchley seated comfortably within. Bellamy spoke to him through the cab window. Hamish saw the Inspector glance his way with a dark expression before turning his attention back to Bellamy.

Hamish felt Rita's hand slip into his, and he allowed the tension in his body to dissipate. He lowered the hand holding the gun and placed back it inside his coat pocket. The crowd had dispersed.

'Tea?' asked Rita.

'Certainly,' said Hamish as they crossed the road to his house. Bellamy must have convinced the Inspector there was nothing more to be done at the scene because the cab pulled away, and Sergeant Bellamy joined Hamish and Rita. The police cab had arrived, and four of Bellamy's men accompanied Kaelo back to the watch house.

'What happened?' asked Hamish when they all had their tea.

'Pennyweather had just taken Kaelo his breakfast,' began the sergeant, 'when six vigilantes came barging into the watch house. The cell wasn't locked because Pennyweather knew Kaelo wasn't going anywhere, but it didn't occur to him that Kaelo needed protection from the people outside. They bundled Kaelo out of the cell and locked Pennyweather in it. Apparently, Kaelo put up a fight, but there was too many of them. That's where I found the constable when I arrived, locked in Kaelo's cell. Thank God I came when I did. Twenty minutes later....'

'Indeed,' said Hamish.

'What did the Inspector say?' asked Rita.

'He said we better bloody well find someone to charge for McDonald's murder in the next forty-eight hours, or he would charge the Kanaka himself.'

'I'm worried about how Kaelo will settle after this morning,' said Hamish.

'I imagine he'll be terrified,' said Rita.

'More than that, I think he might try to see Araluen to carry out his father's wish before he's killed.'

'What are you suggesting?' asked Rita.

'I want to bring Araluen and Joseph to him,' said Hamish. 'Today.'

Bellamy stood up, alarmed. 'We have to get to Cloverton. I told you what the Inspector said. It's more important than ever that we find an end to this.'

'I know,' said Hamish. 'But the urgency for Kaelo will be to complete his promise. He'll no longer feel safe at the station. I fear he'll flee and try to reach Araluen himself. The Daniels and the Tennyson's will still be at Cloverton tomorrow.'

Hamish stood up to indicate his mind was set. 'I'm going to collect Araluen and Joseph,' he said.

'I'll come,' cried Rita.

Bellamy took a deep breath and threw his arms in the air.

'You could always go to Cloverton today, by yourself,' said Rita.

Bellamy stared her down while he considered it.

'We leave first thing in the morning,' he said. He stamped downstairs and left the house, careful to leave the impression he was displeased.

Hamish and Rita caught a cab to the house where Araluen was staying.

An hour later, they arrived at Kaelo's cell with Araluen and Joseph in tow. Hamish went in first. Kaelo was staring out the cell window.

'We've brought Araluen,' Hamish said.

Kaelo did not turn around.

'I told you I don't want to meet her here,' he said.

'I realise that, but I was afraid you would leave to find her if I didn't bring her to you,' said Hamish.

Kaelo turned and looked him in the eye. 'I was planning to leave. I was waiting for my chance. When the sergeant goes away for lunch, the young policeman is alone.'

'It's important you stay, just two more days, I promise. We are almost at a solution. We will have named the killer, and you can leave without any suspicion on your head.' Hamish regretted the promise even as he made it. He had no evidence to suggest the killer would be identified in the next forty-eight hours. He had only the threat from the Inspector and his own wishful thinking.

'Will you meet Araluen and Joseph?' he said. 'Talk, listen, and when this issue of the murder is resolved, you can decide whether you want to be a family or not.'

Unable to contain his curiosity any longer, Joseph shuffled forward until he was standing beside Hamish. Kaelo noticed him there, and a tear slipped down his cheek. Hamish took the boy's hand in his own. 'This is Joseph,' he said. 'Your brother.'

Joseph stood on his good leg, his other leg hanging limp.

Kaelo stretched out his long arms and gathered the boy into his chest. Joseph tried to wrap his skinny legs around the large man, but he couldn't. He clung to him.

Araluen moved forward and stood before the big Islander and her frail son.

'You look like your father,' she said.

Hamish knew at once they would be family.

Rita motioned to Hamish they should leave, and he followed her. On the way out, they ran into Bellamy, who had been watching from a distance. 'I'll see her and the boy home when they are ready,' he said.

'Thank you,' said Hamish.

'Tomorrow,' said Bellamy.

CHAPTER NINETEEN

The Brisbane Courier Friday 23 January 1885.

The first section of the Logan branch railway is now approaching completion, and if necessary, could be used for public traffic in a few week's time. The section, however, stops on the southern bank of the Logan River, not at any particular centre of population, and it is not likely to be opened until communication can be given to Beenleigh, which will probably be at the beginning of March. The route taken by the line is a very uninteresting one, and the scenery that will be presented to the eye of the passenger by rail will not be nearly as pleasant as that along the main road to Beenleigh. The engineers, however, have succeeded in finding a remarkably easy track, much easier than anyone journeying along either the Lower or Upper Logan road would imagine possible.

The line leaves from the South Brisbane branch where there is already a station, then follows generally a south–easterly direction. Just after leaving south Brisbane, it crosses a running stream named Moolabin Creek over which the rails are carried by a wooden bridge. Some 50 or 60 chains further on the line crosses Ipswich Road by a level crossing near the Rocky Waterholes township. It follows Ipswich Road for a short distance, when it tends easterly, crosses the Rocky Waterholes Creek by a bridge and reaches the Rocky Waterholes Station. Here the usual station buildings have been erected, consisting of a small goods shed, platform and booking office and cottage.

Two approaches have been made to this station, one from the Ipswich Road and the other from the opposite direction. The line continues throughout the whole length of the section along easy country with a few curves here and there to avoid the hills. At two miles from the junction, the Salisbury Station, for the accommodation of the settlers in the neighbourhood of North Cooper's Plains, is situated. From the Salisbury Station, the line takes a tolerably straight course to the Sunnybank

Station, five miles from the junction, crossing Stable Swamp Creek. Here all the usual station buildings have been provided for the accommodation of settlers of Brown's Plains. In close proximity to this station are the houses of two or three settlers, but throughout the length of the section, there is remarkably little settlement in the immediate vicinity of the line. From Sunnybank, the railway takes a bend eastward and then, trending again to the south and crossing Bulimba Creek by a bridge, strikes the cross-road about a mile and a half beyond Sunnybank. At this point, a platform has been erected at Runcorn. From the Runcorn platform, the line follows the road for about a mile and three-quarters passing Mr William's nursery, which overlooks the railway. The line continues with much the same kind of formation and through thickly timbered country until it reaches Kingston. Approaching Kingston, the country becomes a little more hilly on each side of the line, and there are some picturesque building sites in the neighbourhood. Mr Kingston, after whom the place is named, has a homestead and a vineyard on the pretty elevation close by. From Kingston, the railway takes a pretty straight course, being carried over Scrubby Creek by a bridge and reaching Loganlea at 14 and a half miles from the junction.

*H*AMISH

Hamish decided he enjoyed the steamer above all other options for travel between Brisbane and Logan, the only disadvantage being the early morning departure. Still, he thought it a shame the opening of the railway was still some weeks away. The railway would reduce the time taken in the journey significantly.

When they arrived at Cloverton, Charlotte was seated, staring through the bay window. She didn't look up when they entered the house. There were two armchairs in the window, so Rita went to Charlotte and settled in the chair beside her. Wallace had seen them arrive and made tea before he led Bellamy and Hamish onto the far end of the veranda, the part that skirted the kitchen. They hoped to have a degree of privacy there, as no one frequented the kitchen but Wallace and Ginny as a rule.

Rita joined them on the veranda ten minutes later. 'I'm sorry,' she said, 'I think I've made a terrible mistake.' Rita was shaking, not a sight Hamish was used to seeing.

'What is it?' he asked.

Bellamy looked alert.

'Apparently, Collette has been here,' said Rita.

'Collette?' cried Hamish.

'Who the hell is Collette?' cried Bellamy, responsive to the nervousness in Rita's voice and the trepidation of Hamish.

'Collette is a... friend,' said Rita. 'She works with women who are suffering from melancholy. I told her about Charlotte grieving for her deceased baby.'

Bellamy's eyebrows shot up.

'But I swear,' she quickly added, looking directly at Hamish, 'I told her not to visit Charlotte until this business with the murder was resolved.'

Hamish took a deep breath. 'Go on,' he said.

'It seems she arrived just as you left the other day,' Rita said.

'She's been here for two days?' Hamish cried.

'Apparently,' said Rita. 'But that's not the worst part.'

Hamish brushed the hair back from his face.

'What's the worst part?'

Bellamy looked to be still in shock that private aspects of his murder enquiry had become a topic of discussion among Brisbane socialites.

'Collette tried to assist Charlotte to make contact with Eddie Hotham in the hope he could identify his killer.'

Bellamy leapt up from his chair. 'She did what?!'

'Sit down,' said Hamish. 'Collette was at the séance the other night. She believes in this nonsense.'

'That's still not the worst part,' said Rita.

They both glared at her.

'Charlotte says she saw Eddie as clearly as she could see me. She said he looked at her with such hatred and contempt in his eyes. She wanted to die. In fact, Charlotte is convinced Eddie Hotham told her she must kill herself.'

'Where is Collette now?' Hamish said in a deeply calm voice.

'She left for Brisbane on the coach just before we arrived this morning. I'm so sorry, Hamish.' Rita's eyes glistened. Hamish realised he had never seen Rita cry.

'I despise you.'

They heard a raised voice in the kitchen and fell silent. They stared at one another, alert to the voice on the other side of the timber wall.

It was Alice.

Charlotte mumbled something, but they couldn't make out what she was saying.

When Alice spoke, the words were clear.

'You are weak. I've been determined all my life not to be like you. Father wouldn't have had to struggle and work so hard to build up this place if you'd been there beside him instead of sulking away in the house. This place was never good enough for you - father was never good enough for you.'

'I have made difficult decisions,' they heard Charlotte say quietly, 'but they've all been for you.'

'Do you mean to make me responsible for staying here and enduring a life you find so objectionable?'

There was a pause, then the quieter voice said, 'No, Alice. I didn't mean that. I have never thought that.'

'What have you ever given up for the sake of someone else?' screamed Alice.

They heard sobbing. Probably Charlotte, Alice sounded too angry to cry.

'You were in love with Eddie Hotham yourself. I knew you were confiding in him, but it didn't occur to me that you thought... that you would allow yourself to think he would... My God, you thought Eddie was in love with you,' said Alice.

Loud sobbing.

'He was sorry for you, Mother. He was in love with me!'

They heard Charlotte sniffing back the last of her tears.

'I know,' said Charlotte. 'He told me.'

'You couldn't stand me being happy, so you brought father on side and convinced me to marry Peter. Did you think he would love you when I was married to another man?'

Charlotte ignored her last comment. 'No, Alice. We didn't convince you of anything. We put forward an argument, and you, as you always do, made the practical decision.'

They heard Alice slump into a chair. 'It matters little now. He's lost to both of us.'

The three of them on the veranda were frozen to the spot. They were fearful of running into one of the women if they returned to the house. They continued to sit where they were until they saw Alice storm down the front stairs. A few minutes later, she rode past them, squeezing her horse's grey flank with her legs like her life depended upon getting away from the place.

When they ventured indoors, Charlotte was nowhere to be seen.

'We need to check on her,' said Hamish, 'see if she is in her room, discreetly,' he said to Rita.

Hamish found Charlotte on the veranda facing the river. She was holding the railing with one hand and staring across the water toward the northern bank. He leant his forearms on the railing beside her.

She had never looked more fragile to him than she did at that moment. He feared she would break if he spoke a word.

Charlotte finally turned her face toward him. 'You are a kind man,' she said, 'and a sensitive doctor.'

Hamish's eyes widened. He was not aware he had shown any particular kindness, and he had not treated Charlotte professionally. He made himself focus on his reason for seeking her out, though her blue eyes confused him.

'You must be feeling battle-weary,' he said, 'with the events of the past week.'

'It all seems unreal,' she responded. 'I feel I am spiralling ever downward and have no place to land.'

Hamish wondered whether he ought to let her know they had heard the outburst from Alice. He decided against it.

'Rita tells me her friend Collette came to visit. I do hope she didn't add to your distress,' he said instead.

Charlotte closed her eyes and swallowed hard. 'Collette did no more than place a mirror before my eyes,' she said, turning back to the river. A few moments later, she faced Hamish again. 'I sense you find me attractive, Hamish.'

His face reddened visibly, but he couldn't find his voice.

'I'm afraid that what I saw in that mirror would not sit well with the view you have of me.'

Hamish placed his hand over hers. Without the gloves, he felt the warm life in her fingers.

'Collette had no right to come uninvited, Charlotte. I'm sorry if she frightened you. The images you saw are not real. It's dangerous to play these games with someone who is grieving.'

Charlotte put a perfect finger to his lips to silence him. 'I know what I saw, Hamish. It was no fault of Collette's. I saw hatred. I always knew Eddie didn't love me. Is it so hateful for a woman of my age to entertain a fantasy of youth?'

'No, Charlotte. It isn't hateful,' Hamish assured her.

'Someone is trying to destroy my husband, Hamish. I swear to the truth of it.'

Hamish squeezed her soft hand. 'I promise I will discover the truth,' said Hamish.

Charlotte turned back to the river and spoke in a whisper. 'I believe you will.' A few moments later, she turned silently and returned to the house.

Hamish stayed on the veranda alone until his heart had stopped pounding. Why did this woman stir such an emotional response in him?

Charlotte retired to her room, and no one saw her again until dinner time. When she emerged, she sat in her usual spot in the armchair by the bay window. She didn't acknowledge Hamish, Bellamy and Rita, who were already in the sitting room waiting to be called for dinner. Rita went over to Charlotte. Hamish sensed Rita could no longer wait for Charlotte to talk to them of her own accord. Placing her hand gently on her shoulder, she said, 'We need to talk to you about Jock.'

Tears streamed down Charlotte's smooth cheeks. Hamish and Bellamy settled on the settee and pretended not to be there.

Rita drew a stool over to Charlotte and sat at her knee.

'Was Jock McDonald blackmailing you?' she asked. 'Did he know about Alice and Eddie?' Charlotte's eyes were vacant, and she continued to look through the window into the distance.

'What about Eddie?' Rita said. 'We know you and Eddie were close.'

Charlotte turned her face to Rita for a moment, and Hamish noted recognition in her eyes. She looked away again, and the tears continued to flow.

'Charlotte, we need to ask you directly. Do you know anything about what happened to Jock and Eddie?'

Charlotte curled over and cradled her face in her hands. She sobbed loudly. Rita made a gesture of helplessness toward Hamish and Bellamy.

Charlotte rose and ran from the room, still sobbing.

Seconds later, Daniels arrived from Brisbane. He stopped as if in shock when he saw Hamish, Rita and Bellamy back in his sitting room. He glanced at them, then rushed into his wife's room where the sobs were audible. Five minutes later, he returned. 'What have you said to my wife?' he demanded furiously. 'I can't quieten her.'

'Sit down, Mr Daniels,' said Bellamy.

Daniels fell into an armchair. 'God,' he said. 'I don't know what's going on. I couldn't secure labourers; only two returned with me. I have nowhere near enough labour to take the cane to production. I'll be lucky to crush the stockpile from the surrounding farms. I've sent for Pete Tennyson to help supervise, although God knows he has his own problems. I don't know how I'll meet the Government lease requirements.' He looked up at Hamish. 'And what the devil have you done to my wife?'

Before Hamish could answer, Peter Tennyson entered from the veranda. Hamish thought he looked worse than Daniels. 'Alice won't leave her bed,' he said as he slumped into the other armchair.

'Good God, her as well,' said Daniels.

'She won't eat. She is weeping constantly. I don't know what to do. I've engaged a wet nurse for the baby. Alice doesn't have the energy for it.'

Daniels looked into his son-in-law's eyes. 'What has happened to us?' he asked.

Bellamy made himself heard for the first time. 'I believe it is time to get to the bottom of this mess,' he said, 'for everyone's sake.' The two men stared at him.

Hamish wondered if they were so involved in their own problems, they had forgotten that two men had been murdered.

'Would you like me to share what I think has happened here at Cloverton?' asked Bellamy.

They continued to stare blankly at him.

'I think Alice and Hotham were in love, and Alice became pregnant. This posed a threat to both of you.' He directed his attention to Daniels, 'If Alice married Hotham, the merger of the two plantations would have been more difficult, perhaps even unlikely.' Bellamy shifted his attention to Tennyson. 'I believe you genuinely love Alice, Mr Tennyson, but if she married Hotham, that would put an end to your hopes.'

'I do love Alice. I have always loved her.'

'I also think Jock McDonald knew about the affair and that Alice was with child. I believe he was blackmailing one of you, and that is why he was killed.'

Daniels stood up. 'McDonald didn't know, surely?'

'Not that I'm aware,' said Tennyson.

'Did everyone know about the bloody affair?' cried Daniels.

'Sit down, Mr Daniels,' said Bellamy. 'It seems just about everyone did know about the affair. Except for Mr Tennyson, here. But Jock McDonald was the only one mean or enterprising enough to tell him.'

'McDonald wasn't blackmailing me,' said Daniels. He looked at Tennyson.

'He didn't approach me,' Tennyson said into his hands.

'Very well,' said Bellamy. 'Then I must conclude it was Alice being blackmailed.'

'No!' cried Tennyson.

Daniels looked around the room as though he was lost. He was clearly trying to get his head around the idea his own daughter had killed two men.

'Why would Alice kill Eddie?' he said.

'I assume because he wanted to be engaged with the child in some way,' said Bellamy.

At that moment, Alice crashed through the door, breathless. 'Mother is by the river,' she cried. 'I saw her as I rode in. She's in her nightgown.'

Peter Tennyson rose to hold his wife. 'Peter, I'm afraid. Please come with me. We'll bring her into the house.'

As she spoke, they were distracted by the sound of Red on the stairs. He was running up and down the bottom four stairs exuding a shrill bark.

Wallace came from the kitchen. 'What's wrong with Red?' he cried. Then he saw the fear in Alice's face.

Hamish caught his eye. 'Wallace and I will go,' he said. 'We'll coax her back.'

Hamish and Wallace ran down the stairs, and Red shot ahead of them. His short legs propelled him forward remarkably quickly. Every hundred yards, he stopped and looked back to make sure they were still following him. Hamish and Wallace kept pace as they headed toward the river. They scanned the bank but could see nothing. Charlotte could not have returned to the house without passing them. The knot in Hamish's stomach tightened. He saw something unusual on the surface of the river, and he felt the energy shift in Wallace; he'd seen it too. Spurred on by a growing panic, they ran the rest of the distance to the river as though there were wings at their feet. Red reached the bank before them and barked wildly at the river. When they arrived at his side, they saw a white gown billowing upward from the surface of the water. They saw black hair floating outward, and their minds finally understood what their eyes were seeing. Charlotte was floating face down on the surface of the river. Without breaking their pace, they splashed into the water, and running became swimming. It took a few long strokes to reach Charlotte and turn her, so her face was upward. Hamish slipped his arm around her neck and cupped her chin in his hand. He swam until his feet could reach the muddy bottom, and then he and Wallace carried the limp figure to the riverbank. Alice, Peter, Daniels, Rita and Bellamy had followed them from the house. They stood waiting, breathless. Red was quiet at last.

Alice threw herself across her mother as Hamish and Wallace laid her on the grass. She held her pale face and called her name. Charlotte did not respond.

'Doctor, do something,' cried Alice.

Hamish was already wiping the wet hair from her neck so he could feel her pulse.

The group watched on, waiting for him to speak.

'It's too late,' he said.

'Do something!' Alice screamed. She lurched at Hamish and pushed him with the full force of her anger and grief. Hamish caught her arms as they thrashed wildly against his chest. He gathered her to him, and she cried.

The others stood stunned. At their feet lay Charlotte, her blue eyes closed, her beautiful hair limp and wet about her shoulders. They couldn't comprehend the reality of what they were seeing.

'I should have ridden directly to her,' cried Alice.

'If I'd gone to her as soon as I saw her by the river....'

Hamish was still holding Alice pressed to his chest. Rita placed her hand on her shoulder. Hamish suspected she wanted to say, don't blame yourself, but it would make no difference.

Peter Tennyson carefully shifted his wife from Hamish's chest to his own and supported her so she could walk. Daniels and Bellamy lifted Charlotte, and they walked slowly back to the house. Wallace carried his terrier in his arms. He found comfort in the warmth of his body and the beat of his heart. Hamish sloshed along beside him, his boots full of water from the Logan River.

When the sad group came up the steps to the veranda, Ginny was standing there, her face white as a sheet. She held a piece of paper.

Daniels lay his wife on their bed, oblivious to the water dripping onto the cover. Ginny followed him silently, holding out the paper, but he ignored her. He gently cleared the hair from his wife's face and straightened her gown, seemingly unaware of Ginny's presence. Hence, she handed the letter to Hamish instead. Hamish took it from her and left Daniels alone with his wife returning to the sitting room where the others were waiting. They sat in silence, apart from the quiet sobbing of Alice into her husband's chest. It was half an hour before Daniels appeared at the door to the sitting room, his eyes swollen and his cheeks wet.

Hamish nodded to Daniels to sit, and he read the note aloud:

I'm so sorry, my dear Alice. I have ruined everything. That beast McDonald deserved to die, and I'm glad I gave him the poison. I am so deeply sorry about Eddie. He told me he would spend the rest of his life mourning the fact that he had lost his son, my dear. I know the pain of losing a son, and it is a pain that cannot be borne. Sooner or later, he would have spoken the truth. I know it. Better to end the pain.

Your loving mother, Charlotte.

Alice sat silently, tears staining her face while her father read out the words. He choked back his own tears, looking as though the horror would swallow him. Everyone was silent for some time before Hamish and Wallace remembered they were wet through. Ginny found them some old work clothes belonging to Daniels, and they put them on. But Hamish couldn't shake the sensation of being wet. His limbs were heavy when he moved them, and he struggled to breathe. It was as though something was slowly suffocating him.

Hamish thought about how such a sudden and shocking event changed the experience of time. Everyone seemed to move in slow motion that afternoon and evening. They didn't talk to one another, and they didn't eat. It would have been difficult for any one of them to say how they managed to get through that terrible night with Charlotte laid out on the marital bed. Daniels didn't appear to sleep at all. Hamish could see, from his bedroom window, his silhouette standing on the veranda, looking out toward the river throughout the night.

The next morning the undertaker came and took Charlotte away. It was a strange thing, but everyone felt able to breathe again. Hamish felt his energy returning. Even Alice looked calm at breakfast.

'Sergeant Bellamy has gone to the telegraph office to send a message to the police depot,' she said. 'He will instruct them to inform the Islander that the matter has been settled.'

Hamish nodded.

Rita joined him and Alice at the dining table, and they welcomed the silver tray of bacon brought in by Ginny.

'My husband has returned to Tennyson House,' Alice went on. 'I'll have our son brought here today. I've decided to stay at Cloverton until father is able to function again.'

'I'm sure your father will appreciate the support,' said Rita. She hesitated before adding, 'the story will be printed in the papers over the next couple of days. Will you be able to cope with that?'

Alice shrugged. 'I'm not as concerned about what people think as was my mother. The story will interest them for a short while, then they will forget. My son is too young to be affected.'

Rita smiled her reassurance.

'This is a new age, Dr Cartwight,' Alice said. 'The railway will change everything in this corridor between Brisbane and the Gold Coast. I regret having to say it, but I feel I can finally look forward to the future. Do you think badly of me?'

Rita shook her head. 'The sadness of another can be so deep and so heavy that it weighs down a whole household,' she said. 'We understand.'

Hamish wasn't sure he did fully understand. But even with full understanding, he couldn't judge this woman who wanted to get on with her life. He had to admit that even though the end to the mystery wasn't one he could be happy about, he was glad it was resolved. He, too, felt lighter and was looking forward to the future.

CHAPTER TWENTY

Australian Town and Country Saturday 15 November 1884.

The Queensland South Sea Island labour trade, which is sometimes designated by other complimentary names, according to the spectacles through which it is viewed, appears to be in its last legs. It is dying hard, though its constitution has been evidently breaking down of late, and this through several causes, some of the chief of which are inherent in itself. No doubt more stringent regulation, Imperial and Colonial, now imposed, and the rigid manner in which they are carried out are of the nature of the last straw on the camel's back, though the simile is hardly a good one, seeing that the camel is the most patient of animals, which the labour trade certainly is not. But dissolution has been hastened by internal disorder, the consequence of a reckless disregard of laws natural and social. Or to adopt a more homely simile, the traffickers in South Sea Island Labour have killed the goose that laid the golden eggs. Those engaged in the trade declare that under its present harassing conditions, it is impossible to carry on the recruitment business profitably. We quite believe it. That the trade is no longer remunerative is evident from the few kanakas that have been taken to Queensland ports of late. But, as we have said, these regulations and their strict enforcement are but the result of the conduct of the skippers obtaining recruits by fair means or foul. Even with the present regulations, stringent though they are, we believe it would be possible to obtain a fair supply of South Sea Islander labour were it not for the distrust engendered in the minds of Islanders by the manner of recruiting in the past. Everything goes to make it evident that the trade will not stand daylight investigation, and the very fact it languishes now that the Government agents do their duty more thoroughly is proof enough that when it flourished, it was because neither the rights nor the feelings of the Islanders were consulted.

Of the cheapness at which the recruiters hold Kanaka life, there has been too much evidence. Of the demoralising effects of the trade upon those who reap but a small collateral advantage, there is abundant proof in the many Government agents who have come to grief in the discharge of their duties.

'How goes it?' called Hamish as he dismounted at Cedarwood. Rita was still astride the grey mare. She swung her leg across the dappled grey and jumped expertly from the horse, smoothing down her divided skirt as she did so.

Vincent put down the bundle of hay he was carrying to greet his visitors. His suntanned face lit up with a wide grin showing off that gleaming gold tooth. 'I'm well,' he said. 'Nasty business at Cloverton. So sad. But I'm sure Daniels will never recover from it.'

Hamish was sombre in his response.

'You're right, I fear,' he said.

Vincent was looking at Rita with curiosity.

'I'm sorry,' Hamish remembered Vincent had not yet met Rita. 'This is Dr Cartwright, a colleague of mine.'

'An honour to meet you,' said Vincent holding out his hand to take Rita's in his. She removed one kid glove to shake his hand properly.

'Come inside, join us for a drink. I'm sure Ruby can scrape up something to eat.'

'Please don't go to any trouble,' began Rita.

'What can we do for you both?' asked Vincent as he ushered them upstairs.

Ruby met them in the doorway. She wore a floral apron over a well-worn dress of plain brown cotton.

'I'm Rita Cartwright,' said Rita holding out her degloved hand. 'I'm delighted to meet you.'

Ruby took Rita's hand in hers. When she smiled, joy flooded her face. Her brown eyes, darker than any Rita had seen before, danced.

'Come in, come in,' she said, moving aside to herd them down a narrow hallway and into the kitchen. There was a camphor laurel table with a bowl of flour at one end.

'I was about to make damper,' Ruby said. 'If you don't mind me getting on, we can all have a cuppa.'

'Not at all,' said Rita. 'I would love to help make damper.'

'Here then, you get that jug of water by the stove and bring it over here,' said Ruby.

Rita fetched the white enamel jug with the chipped blue trim.

While the women busied themselves kneading dough, Vincent repeated his question to Hamish.

'We appreciate your visit, Doctor, but what is it we can do for you?'

'It's rather a long story,' began Hamish. He explained Kaelo's predicament, that he had been accused of Jock McDonald's murder, and how he was now exonerated, given the recent unfolding of events at Cloverton.

Hamish recounted the story of Kaelo's father and his wife, Araluen, and the circumstances of her son, Joseph.

Ruby stopped kneading to listen when Hamish described the plight of Araluen. She watched her husband carefully.

Rita placed the rounds of kneaded dough on a floured tray and pushed them deep inside the woodstove. She held her breath, waiting to hear the response from Vincent.

The tension in the small kitchen built as Ruby also waited.

Finally, tiny wrinkles appeared at the corner of Vincent's eyes, and he smiled. He put his hand to his chin and ran his fingers over the stubble there.

'Well,' he said at last, 'Ruby could do with some help around here, Lord knows. I wonder if Araluen and Joseph would like to work here? What do you think, Ruby?'

Ruby's face beamed for a single moment, then she feigned indifference.

'The woman will have to work. I'm not giving no charity.'

'Of course,' said Hamish, 'I hear she is a hard worker, and I know she would not accept charity.'

Ruby nodded.

'I hope to attend Joseph as a patient, trial some new techniques for strengthening the muscles after infantile paralysis. We may even get him walking again, at least with callipers.'

Hamish looked to Rita for her reaction to his idea. She did not look the least surprised. 'His capacity will certainly improve with treatment,' she said.

'What about Kaelo?' asked Vincent. 'Does he have a contract?'

'It is my understanding he had an agreement with Daniels prior to the incident,' said Hamish. 'But everything seems up in the air at Cloverton at the moment. It seems likely Tennyson will take over management of both plantations.'

'Kaelo is welcome to work here,' said Vincent. 'I don't want to take labour away from Tennyson if he needs it, but if he's unsure, I could do with the help here.'

'I'll pass on the offer,' grinned Hamish.

Rita and Ruby served the warm damper with great pats of fresh butter and golden syrup made from Cedarwood's own sugar cane.

Hamish and Rita rode on to Cloverton buoyant. They knew Kaelo, Araluen, and Joseph would be happy at Cedarwood.

'You realise Kaelo will be sent home when his contract expires,' said Hamish.

'If he is, he will go home satisfied he carried out his father's wishes and did the right thing by his half-brother.'

Hamish glanced over at Rita. She glowed with delight in the knowledge that Kaelo and his family would be settled. He thought about how much he appreciated her friendship, her intelligence, her confidence. Then he recalled how protective he'd felt about Charlotte. He never felt Rita needed his protection. There was nothing vulnerable about her. He wondered if he was in love with Rita, even though he knew she would never love him in quite the same way. But if that were so, why had he been stirred by Charlotte? The two women could not be more different. For the first time, he wondered what sort of woman he might love if he were not in love with Rita.

They both stopped their horses as they came over the last rise before Cloverton. They saw the patchwork of cane and bare land, the trees and the garden hugging the feet of the house and the silver river beyond. 'It is difficult to imagine so much angst brewing in such a flawless setting,' mused Hamish.

They rode on.

Gerard ran out to take their horses as soon as they arrived. He seemed to convey an energy they had never seen before.

When they climbed the impressive wide staircase for what they imagined would be the last time, they experienced a pang of sadness. Cloverton had worked its way under their skin.

Alice came to the door in a functional dress without frills or adornments. She looked confidant and handsome.

'Come in,' she said. 'We've been expecting you.'

Wallace was standing in the middle of the entry hall wearing his best shirt and carrying a well-worn carpet bag.

'We'll be sorry to lose Wallace,' Alice said. 'Not only is he a wonderful cook, but he has also been a great comfort to me over the last few weeks. I appreciate you allowed him to stay until we found a replacement.'

Rita laughed.

'I didn't allow him to stay,' said Hamish. 'I couldn't convince him to leave you.'

Alice kissed Wallace on the cheek, sending the blood rushing to his face and making his eyes sparkle.

'Come to the dining room,' Alice said, leading them. 'Our new cook is not a patch on Wallace, but she prepares a passable beef hot pot.'

When they were all seated, Wallace included, Ginny ladled large servings of beef and gravy from a porcelain bowl at the centre of the table.

'Have you had word from your father?' asked Hamish taking a large spoon of gravy.

'I have,' said Alice. 'Father has found employment managing a plantation in Mackay. We would have dearly loved him to stay here, but he said he wouldn't have been able to settle. I understand that.' Alice's face lost its glow for an instant. 'He loved her, you know, even after....' She shook herself from the moment's sadness. 'More bread?' she asked, handing a basket carrying the aroma of freshly baked yeast across the table.

'How are you getting along for labour?' Hamish asked Peter Tennyson.

'We still have forty kanakas working across both properties,' he said. 'But I don't have the same opinion of the need to use coloured labour as William had. The world is changing, and we need to change with it.'

Hamish and Rita looked at him with curiosity.

'I'm shifting the focus of the business to the distillery,' he said. 'I'll be needing educated men to run the machinery, and I'll employ local labour, as the current contracts expire. There is a great deal more profit in rum than there is in processing sugar. I'll be paying a decent wage for a decent day's work.'

At the mention of a distillery, Wallace almost looked inclined to reverse his decision to leave.

'Do you have a manager to assist you with your new venture?' asked Rita.

'That I do,' said Tennyson smiling at his wife.

'The cleverest in the business,' said Alice.

'Congratulations,' cried Rita, 'You finally have the appreciation you deserve.'

'And the opportunity,' said Alice beaming.

They all lifted their glasses to drink to the new business and prosperity.

KAELO

Kaelo rubbed down the coat of the grey mare. It was the tallest horse he had ever seen. He had not seen any horses prior to landing on the shore of Queensland. He couldn't believe how the sight of them had terrified him at first. His greatest love now was the warm, salty smell of that grey coat. He took in the warmth of the life flowing beneath his fingers, the strength of the muscles. He was learning to ride, but he still found it difficult to accept that such a powerful animal would bow to his will.

'Let him run in the back paddock when you're done,' cried Vincent.

Kaelo smiled. Vincent was a good man. He had agreed to take Araluen on as a cleaner, but she was more like a companion to Ruby. The two women chatted constantly and were known to combine against Vincent when it suited them. He handed over the money his father had entrusted to him, but Araluen showed little interest in it. Vincent offered to help her set up an account at the bank, but

Araluen preferred to stash it in a tin chest under her bed. No one knew how much money was there because Kaelo had never counted it, and Araluen wouldn't let anyone else count it either. There it sat, locked in the chest. Araluen said she might use it to send Joseph to school if Dr Hart could get him walking again. Dr Rita suggested they make Joseph an iron bed on wheels to push Joseph around. If they could manage that, Kaelo would wheel him to the schoolhouse each day and pick him up again in the afternoon. Just because Joseph couldn't walk, it didn't mean he couldn't learn. Kaelo had to remind himself that even Aboriginal children with healthy bodies didn't usually get to go to school. Vincent and Ruby made everything seem possible. After all, Vincent gave him, a man who hadn't seen a horse twelve months earlier, a job looking after his horses.

Kaelo led the grey toward the back paddock. Looking out across the plantation, his chest swelled with pride at the expanse of green cane swaying in the breeze. Almost immediately, he felt a pang of guilt. Could he so easily love this new place and forgo the beauty of his home. He missed his younger brothers. He missed being present to watch them grow into men. His contract, first signed by William Daniels and later taken on by Vincent, was for a three-year term. Would his brothers know him after three years? He would be a different person after three years in Queensland. He felt like a different person already, after everything he had been through. His brothers would be different people too. It suddenly hit him that the world is a vast place. How could his family on Ferguson Island still exist while he lived so far away? When he was on the Island, it had seemed like the whole universe. Now he could understand that this was not so. People were living in Britain and Europe and all over the world, travelling back and forth in ships, fighting wars, building empires. The world had become big. It's not that he didn't know these things before; he just didn't feel them.

He made the world big when he stepped onto that ship. As much as he might long for it, he knew at that moment that he would never be able to return to smallness.

◇◇◇◇◇

AUTHORS NOTE

Between 1863 and 1904, an estimated 62,500 Islanders were brought to Australia to provide cheap labour for the cotton and sugar industries in Queensland. They came from over eighty Pacific Islands, including Vanuatu, the Solomon Islands, New Caledonia and Papua New Guinea. The Islanders were referred to as Kanakas, a Hawaiian term for 'man' and they were collectively labelled Polynesian, although many were Melanesian.

When the first Islanders were shipped to Queensland in the early 1860s, there were no laws to protect them from exploitation. They were forcibly abducted, lied to and tricked onto European ships and then treated as slaves. By the end of that decade, laws had been introduced to regulate the trafficking of 'coloured labour', and an indenture system was established. The Islanders were signed onto three-year contracts. Most had little idea of what they were signing as they were forced to place their thumbprint on the documents. Officially, they were to be paid meagre wages, about one-third of what a white labourer would expect, but in practice, many were not paid at all.

By 1884, the Queensland Premier, Sir Samuel Griffiths, had enacted Immigration Regulations, further controlling the traffic of Island labour. There was high unemployment among unskilled workers in Australia, and the working classes objected to the Islanders being brought in to take jobs that they could do. New regulations around recruitment and shipping meant the cost of bringing Islanders to Queensland to work was becoming prohibitive. Griffith struck deals with European countries, mostly Germany, to bring in indentured labour to replace the 'coloureds' as they called the Islanders at the time. This was the precursor to the White Australia Policy that evolved in the first decade of the twentieth century.

By far, the most controversial aspect of the trade during Hamish's time was the unscrupulous methods of recruitment. It was a lucrative trade, and regulations had been poorly monitored for decades. Ship Captains and crews were not beyond kidnapping, fraud and murder to fill their ship's hulls with human cargo. Some commonly shared stories of the day included luring men on board ship with the promise of guns and ammunition, then setting sail with the men held captive and rounding up males as young as twelve on the Islands and forcing them on board at gunpoint.

Once on board, the men had numbers tied around their necks, and they were registered on the ship's log. Most of them, in the first decade, had no idea what was happening to them. However, it must be said that as time went on, the ships kept coming, and some labourers returned to Australia voluntarily. Some also followed previous generations, as was the case with Kaelo.

The Islanders travelled in crowded, filthy conditions in the hulls of ships, often in chains. Their health had usually diminished by the time they reached the plantations, and it often deteriorated further with the heavy labour required of them in addition to poor housing conditions and limited food supply. The death rate of the Islanders working on the plantations was high. They were often buried where they fell, and no one was notified of the loss.

The Islander labourers were supposed to be paid a set wage, meagre though it was, and this money was to be handed over to them under the witness of the Polynesian Protector. The men were encouraged to release the money to the Protector for 'safe-keeping'. The idea was they would collect their money at the end of their contract and take it home with them. Many men died or ran away from intolerable conditions prior to the completion of their contracts. Their money was then held by the Government under the 'Curator of Estates' or 'The Missing Kanakas Fund.' Often no one was notified of the loss.

By Hamish's time in the 1880s, the Queensland public had become alert to the problems inherent in the traffic of Islanders for labour. There was a divide in sentiment between the plantation owners who believed they needed the cheap labour to sustain their businesses and the white working-class Australians who needed employment. At the same time, workers were beginning to feel their strength when they formed collectives and bargained for fairer wages and conditions.

The regulations established by Samuel Griffith ensured that Island labourers could not be employed in domestic service or skilled positions. Medium size plantations commonly had forty to sixty Island labourers to do the heavy work of clearing land, planting, cutting and carting, with half a dozen European employees to run the machinery and fill management roles. 'Time-expired' Islanders were expected to be on the next ship home at the end of their contracts. Often ships returning to the Pacific would drop the cargo of Islanders randomly at whatever Island they landed on. Labourers were not necessarily returned to their own homes at the end of their contracts.

It was against the law for hoteliers and publicans to serve alcohol to Islanders. Nonetheless, plenty did, and newspaper reports of drunk and disorderly Islanders in Queensland towns were plentiful. People who were struggling to find jobs at decent wages took every opportunity to object to the Islanders. The language used in describing their behaviour was emotive and divisive. For example, they were described as presenting a 'source of grave danger to life and property' and of 'drunken brawls and rampages through the town wielding tomahawks and rifles.'

By 1885 the sugar industry in Queensland had passed its peak. There was a surplus of sugar available from plantations closer to the markets in Britain and Europe than Australia. Unemployment and poverty in Europe was at such a height that farmers there were growing beets for sugar production as an alternative to cane. Profit margins were shrinking for Australian cane growers who needed modern machinery to process their cane at increased quantities for economy of scale, but at the same time were not able to sell the processed sugar at a premium. Added to these challenges, an increase in labour costs was making small holdings no longer viable.

Finally, regulations around recruitment and transport of Islanders were being enforced. Several ships in the mid-1880s were captured, and their Captains were prosecuted for not meeting the new requirements. Many ships travelling to the Pacific were returning empty, unable to recruit now the use of force was no longer available to them. By 1904 the practice had stopped. The fact remains Australia was involved in the trade of black slaves for decades after the practise was abolished in Britain, Europe and America.

Shawline Publishing Group Pty Ltd
www.shawlinepublishing.com.au